SIX IN THE WHEEL

MIKE SARTAIN, THE REVENGER

Six in the Wheel

A WESTERN DUO

Frank Leslie

FIVE STAR
A part of Gale, a Cengage Company

GALE
A Cengage Company

Farmington Hills, Mich • San Francisco • New York • Waterville, Maine
Meriden, Conn • Mason, Ohio • Chicago

LIBRARY OF CONGRESS CATALOGING-IN-PUBLICATION DATA

Names: Leslie, Frank, 1963– author. | Leslie, Frank, 1963– Bittersweet war. | Leslie, Frank, 1963– Gold dust woman.
Title: Six in the wheel / Frank Leslie.
Other titles: The bittersweet war. | Gold dust woman.
Description: First edition. | Waterville, Maine : Five Star Publishing, a part of Cengage Learning, Inc., [2018] | Series: Mike Sartain, The Revenger
Identifiers: LCCN 2018000903 (print) | LCCN 2018004927 (ebook) | ISBN 9781432843038 (ebook) | ISBN 9781432843021 (ebook) | ISBN 9781432843007 (hardcover)
Subjects: | BISAC: FICTION / Action & Adventure. | FICTION / Westerns. | GSAFD: Western stories.
Classification: LCC PS3552.R3236 (ebook) | LCC PS3552.R3236 A6 2018b (print) | DDC 813/.54—dc23
LC record available at https://lccn.loc.gov/2018000903

First Edition. First Printing: July 2018
Find us on Facebook–https://www.facebook.com/FiveStarCengage
Visit our website–http://www.gale.cengage.com/fivestar/
Contact Five Star™ Publishing at FiveStar@cengage.com

Printed in Mexico
1 2 3 4 5 6 7 22 21 20 19 18

TABLE OF CONTENTS

* * * * *

THE BITTERSWEET WAR

* * * * *

CHAPTER ONE

One of the five men around the campfire in the Davis Mountains of west Texas froze as he was about to pour coffee into the tin cup he held in his gloved right hand.

He stared suspiciously into the heavy darkness around the pulsating light of the dancing flames. "Hey—what was that?"

"What was what?" asked the man to his right—Dean Harvey Dade. Dade blew on his own steaming cup of belly wash. "I ain't heard nothin'. Besides, Killigrew's out there with that big seventy-caliber of his."

"If he woulda heard anything," said Richard Green, a rangy outlaw from Oklahoma whose face had been badly scarred from a run-in with a mountain lion when he was only thirteen years old, "we woulda heard that Sharps, and there'd be no mistakin' the sound, neither."

Green snorted and chuckled through his broken teeth, lifting a bottle of whiskey to his scarred lips.

The first man who had spoken, Kansas Charlie Sale, said grudgingly, " 'Spose you boys is right. I reckon I'm a mite on the fidgety side. Especially since that jehu in Dobbs said the Revenger's been seen in the Bend of late."

"Yeah, Dwight—we oughta head straight down to Mexico, forget about your plan of holin' up here for two weeks amongst all these rocks and cactus to let our trail cool. Let's just cross the border and be done with it."

This came from Rock Arnold, a former Confederate soldier

9

from Georgia, who'd lost a hand at Cold Harbor and now sported a nasty-looking steel claw in place of it. He'd been speaking to Dwight Mills, who considered himself the leader of the West Texas Hellions, the name he himself had dreamed up for his mixed bag of stagecoach and train robbers.

Mills was reclining against his saddle, under the stone lip of the escarpment in whose midst they'd bivouacked. Mills's Stetson was pulled down over his close-set eyes. "I done told you why we was here, boys. Since we killed them marshals in Abilene, posses are likely scourin' the country, cuttin' off all trails leadin' to Mexico. We gotta stay up here till the excitement has died down. Then we can head to Mexico, dig up the gold we buried on the other side of the border, and we can all diddle as many *senoritas* as we want before we're screamin' from the Cupid's itch. Now, kindly shut up. I'm tired. It takes a lot of thinkin' to do all the thinkin' for six corked-head fools on a daily basis."

"Goddammit, there it was again!" Kansas Charlie Sale dropped his cup in the fire, causing steam to wash up from the spilled, sputtering coffee, and gained his feet. Backing away from the fire's glow, he slipped his Frontier Colt .44 from the holster lying flat against the front of his right thigh and clicked the hammer back. "Goddammit—I know I heard it that time. Somethin's movin' around out there, boys!"

Mills poked his hat brim up off his forehead, sat up with a sigh, and stared down the rocky, night-cloaked hill sloping away beyond the fire, opposite the barren stone scarp that flanked the camp. The others stared in the same direction, everybody quiet, listening.

"Pshaw," said Dean Harvey Dade, grinning. "Kansas Charlie's just got the fantods on account of he raped that purty young wife of the Red Mesa relay station manager . . . *after* he gut-shot the woman's husband so's the poor man could roll around screamin' . . . an' *watchin'*."

"What do you think, Charlie?" Mills asked, reclining once more against his saddle. "You think the man's ghost is gonna come gunnin' fer ya?" He grinned as he tipped his hat back down over his forehead and laced his hands on his belly.

"You know I don't believe in no ghosts." Kansas Charlie Sale stood back against the jutting stone escarpment, at the edge of the pulsating firelight, holding his cocked Colt straight out in front of him, probing the heavy darkness with his eyes. "I just know I heard somethin'—that's all." He raised his voice and called into the dark: "Hey, Killigrew—that you out there?"

Green laughed mockingly, rubbing the lip of his bottle against his grimy shirt. "Ah, he's got the Revenger on his mind. He done believed what that old coach driver told him about Mike Sartain bein' in the Bend, an' he—"

His voice was choked off suddenly, replaced by a dull thud and a splattering sound.

"What the . . . ?" said Rock Arnold, sitting on a rock to Green's right and back a ways, making a face as he spread his arms and looked down at his shirt. It was splattered with something dark and warm, and the dark and warm substance was speckled with what looked like porridge.

But of course it was not porridge, but bone shards that had come from Richard Green's blown-apart head, and Rock Arnold realized that very fact at the same time the heavy thunder of a big-caliber rifle resounded like the report of a mountain howitzer over and around the boulder-strewn slope.

Green's head—or what was left of it—was still bobbling around, nearly hollow at this point—on the Oklahoman's shoulders when Dean Harvey Dade's startled yell was rendered stillborn by another large, fast-traveling, 500-grain chunk of lead shattering his front teeth and grinding through his mouth and skull before exiting the back of his head and plunking into the right thigh of Kansas Charlie Sale, who still stood with his back to the escarpment.

Kansas Charlie yowled at the fist-like punch and scalding burn of the bullet, inadvertently firing his pistol into the ground halfway between himself and the fire, and dropping to both knees. He yowled again as he rolled onto his left hip and, tossing away the Colt, clutched his bloody thigh with his right hand.

"I told ya, you stupid bastards!" he screamed against the ripping echo of the heavy rifle's cannon-like blast.

Somehow, Rock Arnold got it into his head that Killigrew was firing the shots with his formidable Sharps rifle, which he'd used during his time as a sharpshooter during the War Between the States. Arnold stood with his bloody shirt basted against his chest, shouting, "Killigrew, what the hell do you think you're doin', you crazy son of a *bitch*?"

Mills scrambled up from his saddle, yelling, "Get away from the fire!"

Another bullet sang out of the darkness to miss Mills by a cat's whisker and slam into the coffee pot, sending coffee hissing onto the coals and steam rising like that from a locomotive's pressure-release valves. Yet another bullet screeched from the black night to blow Rock Arnold's head apart as the claw-handed outlaw scrabbled for the pistol stuck behind the waistband of his pants.

At the same time, the outlaw leader, Mills, ran into the shadows to the right of the fire.

Lying on his side at the base of the escarpment, Kansas Charlie saw Mills's silhouette crouch and extend his pistol. Orange flames stabbed from the barrel of Mills's Schofield as the outlaw leader sent three quick bullets hurtling down the slope, though Kansas Charlie had no idea who or what his target was.

Kansas Charlie himself had seen nothing of the shooter, not even the flashes of the big-caliber rifle the bastard was using to take the gang down most wickedly and efficiently.

Mills turned and ran off along the shoulder of the slope. The darkness had just swallowed him from Kansas Charlie's view when a fierce-sounding *ka-thunk!* rose from the outlaw leader's direction.

Mills gave a high-pitched, ripping scream. Kansas Charlie heard the man fall as again the big gun's pounding echo rolled out over the boulder-strewn slope and likely had the coyotes heading for their dens with their tails between their legs.

"*Ohhhh!*" Mills wailed. "You baaast*ard!*" He sobbed, choked another sob back down his throat. "Whoever you are—you're gonna diiie, you bastard! You're gonna die *slowww!*"

A bullet screamed through the darkness, landing somewhere with a resolute *plunk!*

Mills wailed again. He sobbed girlishly and shouted, "Ohhhhh, you're gonna die slow, amigooooo!"

Kansas Charlie could hear Mills's spurs chink and his boots rake the ground as he rolled in agony.

Kansas Charlie's heart was turning somersaults in his chest, and his mouth was dry as the Sonoran desert. He'd been fear-frozen in place, clamping his hand over the hole in his leg, but now he looked around. He had to take cover. But first, he needed his pistol.

He saw it lying in the sand and gravel a few feet away, and he lunged for it. As he wrapped his hand around the walnut grips, he heard the clipped screech of another large-caliber bullet and stared down in hang-jawed shock at the quarter-sized hole the bullet had punched through the dead center of his right hand over the handle of his Colt.

The heavy round had sort of flattened his hand out against the ground. As blood began to well up out of the ragged hole, looking like oil in the flickering shadows of the firelight, Charlie threw his head back and howled, "Oh, you son of a *bitch!*"

He was vaguely frustrated and disappointed that those were the only words he had at his disposal for expressing his consternation, fury, disbelief, and keen, heart-shriveling horror at what had happened here in what was probably less than two minutes' time.

He pulled his hand from the gun and clutched it like an injured bird to his chest, bawling, "Oh, you son of a bitch! Oh, you son of a bitch!" His voice trilling with sobs, his injured hand shaking as though with the palsy, he continued with: "Oh, you son of a bitch!"

He looked around. All his brethren were down. The coffee still sizzled on the fire, though not as intensely as before. The flames were dancing, shunting shadows this way and that. Aside from the crackling of the fire and the nervous whickering of the horses picketed in some brush near a spring to Kansas Charlie's left, an eerie silence had fallen over the bivouac.

Kansas Charlie wanted to run, but he was hurting too badly to gain his feet. It was a paralyzing kind of agony. He could tell his leg was only grazed—the bullet appeared to have clipped the outside of his thigh—but it hurt like hell, and his hand hurt even worse. Each beat of his heart felt as though someone were probing the wound just behind his knuckles with a rusty railroad spike.

On the downslope beyond the flickering, crackling fire, spurs chinked faintly.

The chinking grew louder until Kansas Charlie, staring hang-jawed over the flames, saw a moving silhouette gradually shape itself, growing taller and taller, into a broad-shouldered *hombre* with a broad-brimmed, tan Stetson. He wore a pinto vest over a blue shirt stretched taut across his chest and shoulders, and denim trousers clung to his muscular thighs. Tufts of dark-brown hair curled out from between the bone buttons of his shirt.

14

A big, pearl-gripped pistol was snugged down in an open-toed, brown leather holster thonged to his right thigh. The man was casually holding Killigrew's big Sharps rifle on his right shoulder. In his left what appeared to be a Henry rifle dangled low against his left leg. The barrel of the Sharps on his shoulder still smoked.

The big man was puffing the cigar sticking out one side of his mouth. He took a puff, rolled the stogie to the other side of his mouth, puffed again, and rolled it back to the other side of his mouth.

The man meandered around several black boulders and stopped at the far edge of the firelight. The light shone like copper in his wide-set eyes beneath the brim of his hat, which, Kansas Charlie could see now, was banded with snakeskin and silver *conchos*.

Kansas Charlie panted and groaned. "Oh . . . oh, shit. Now . . . now, you see, dammit—I just *knew* it was you!"

He hated the weakness he heard in his own voice.

The big man looked down and turned his head this way and that, apparently admiring his handiwork. Kansas Charlie hadn't heard a peep out of Mills for a while, but the outlaw leader now let it be known he was still kicking.

"Oh, oh, Christ," Mills said seemingly to no one in particular. "I'm gonna kill the son of a bitch . . . that done this to me. Gonna kill him *hard!*"

Casually, the big man on the other side of the fire dropped the Sharps in the dirt, palmed his big pistol with his right hand, turned, clicked the pistol's hammer back, and aimed straight out from his shoulder.

Mills said, panting, "I'm gonna kill him ha—"

But the pistol's loud report cut off his last word.

There was a shrill grunt and then the sound of a body hitting the ground. Spurs chinked for a time, as though Mills's legs were quivering, and then the chinking faded to silence.

The pistol was a big pearl-gripped, silver-chased LeMat. It appeared the size of a wheel hub in the man's big hand as, holding the popper straight down against his leg, he walked around the fire to Kansas Charlie.

He stopped and stared grimly down at Charlie, the salmon light of the fire sliding across the clean lines and hard, flat planes of his handsome face that wore a two- or three-day growth of beard shadow. His black hair was thick and curly as it folded over his ears beneath his light-tan Stetson. An ivory diamondback was carved into the rear stock of the handsome Henry rifle resting on his shoulder.

Sure enough. It was him, all right. The LeMat. The Henry rifle. The pinto vest and the snakeskin-banded Stetson. Charlie dribbled down his leg.

"You're him—ain't ya?" he said, the words coming of their own accord as he stared up at the tall, dark, menacing *hombre*. "You're Mike Sartain—the Revenger?"

Sartain rolled his cigar from the left side of his mouth to the right, blowing smoke out his nostrils. He nodded slowly, once.

"You got it right, Charlie."

He swung his right boot back and up, and it connected soundly with the soft underside of Charlie's chin, shattering his teeth and laying him out cold as winter mountain granite.

CHAPTER TWO

Mike Sartain, the Revenger, stared ahead along the meandering trail he was following toward a shelving red mesa hunched beneath a blue sky tufted with low, puffy clouds.

A hundred yards ahead, at the mesa's base, sat a small ranch whose roughhewn humility was part and parcel of this vast, parched Great Bend area of western Texas. The ranch was of the "shotgun" variety, and it was comprised of an adobe brick shack, a slightly larger mud barn flanking it, two rail corrals, and a round stone breaking corral near the barn. A windmill fronted the cabin. A narrow, brush-roofed stoop sagged off the cabin's front wall.

A chicken coop sat off to the right, surrounded by woven creosote branches for keeping predators out. The white- and copper-colored objects moving around the yard near the coop and the shack's front porch were chickens.

A few dusty cottonwoods and one lone oak offered meager shade against the relentless Texas sun. Wildflowers blooming amongst the rocks and sotol and prickly pear cactus offered the only color aside from that vivid sky and the red, brick-like stone wall of the mesa flanking the ranchstead.

The blades of the windmill turned lazily in the hot, dry breeze. As Sartain's big, rangy buckskin, Boss, clomped closer to the ranch yard, the shaggy-headed Cajun could hear the soft clattering of the windmill's wood paddles and the quiet splashing of the water into the stone tank at its base.

"Where the hell are we, Sartain?" asked Kansas Charlie Sale, riding a skewbald mare six feet off Boss's slowly switching, black tail.

Charlie's hands were cuffed, and the chain linking the manacles was tied to his saddle horn. Still, he managed to hip around a little in the saddle, looking behind and around him, scowling. "We ain't nowhere near Bittersweet. Shit, there's Baldy atop Mount Livermore over there . . . Shit, Bittersweet's to the north. What the hell are we doin' way out *here*?"

"I ain't takin' you to Bittersweet, Charlie," Sartain said, staring straight ahead over Boss's ears. "Never said I was."

He was watching a young blond woman in a drab brown and cream dress who'd just filled a wooden bucket with water from the tank beneath the windmill. She was carrying the bucket from the windmill to a small rise to the right of the shack. A straw *sombrero* trimmed with a red feather shielded her face from the glaring summer sun.

Water slopped over the sides of the bucket as she walked up the slight rise toward the large oak standing at its crest. The dress billowed against her long legs as she walked.

Kansas Charlie was confused. "I thought you was takin' me to Bittersweet to turn me over to Sheriff Chaney and claim the ree-ward."

"Did I tell you that, Charlie?"

"No, but I just assumed."

"You know what they say about assumin', Charlie."

"Kiss my ass, Sartain. Where the hell are you takin' me?" Behind the Revenger, Charlie fell silent for several seconds. Then a nervous trill entered his voice as he said, "Hey, wait a minute. Wait just a minute. That's the Red Mesa relay station up ahead, ain't it?"

" 'Bout time you recognized it, Charlie." Sartain glanced over his shoulder at his weary prisoner, giving a wry, crooked half-smile. "But then, it was night when you were here last, wasn't it?"

Charlie's broad, freckled face, framed by bushy red mutton-chop whiskers swelled with fear and anger. "What the hell you takin' me back here for, you Cajun son of a bitch? The sheriff's over to Bittersweet. You gotta take me to Bittersweet and turn me in to the sheriff. There's a ree-ward on my head, Sartain. Five hundred dollars! Might be higher now since we killed them marshals!"

"I don't believe in cashin' in on someone else's misery."

"That's real sportin' of ya."

"I believe in lettin' miserable sons of bitches like you cash in your own chips."

"What's that supposed to mean?"

Trailing Kansas Charlie's mare by a long lead rope, Sartain put Boss under the wooden portal straddling the two-track wagon trail, which also served as a stage road between Fort Davis and the little desert settlement of Bittersweet. The portal's wooden crossbar announced FERRIS RANCH & RED MESA STAGE RELAY STATION.

Kansas Charlie said in a quavering, skeptical tone, "Sartain, I asked you a question. What'd you mean by that? 'Lettin' the miserable cash in their own chips.' What the hell does that mean?"

"You'll find out soon enough, Charlie."

"Damn you, Sartain! You take me to Bittersweet! I wanna see the sheriff in Bittersweet. It won't be no picnic for me, if that's what you're worried about. The town—hell, the whole damn county—is run by Sheriff Chaney and his brother, Waylon. Now, take me there and let them deal with me! I got rights, by god!"

Sartain stopped Boss just inside the ranch yard. He slipped his big LeMat from its holster, clicked the hammer back, and swung around to aim the big popper casually out behind him at

Kansas Charlie's head. Kansas Charlie flinched, turned his face to one side, scowling.

"Hey, now . . . be careful with that big ole hogleg, Sartain."

"Charlie?"

"What?"

"Another word out of you and I'm going to blow one of your ears off."

Kansas Charlie flinched again, as though he were imagining the proposed pain. He already had a painful leg and an even more painful hand. Sartain himself had sewn both wounds shut with catgut and bandaged them, though Kansas Charlie thought it odd to be doctored by one as savage as the Revenger was known to be.

When Kansas Charlie had asked Sartain why he was bothering to bandage his wounds, when Sartain was known for *killing* men, not *doctoring* them, Sartain had just given one of his infuriatingly oblique, mock-affable smiles, and winked.

That wink had sent chills down Kansas Charlie's spine. He hadn't wanted to think about what it meant, but he couldn't help thinking about it now.

Sartain booted Boss on ahead. As he did, he watched the young blond woman stop at the top of the rise, beneath the sprawling oak, which was about the only living thing large enough to sprawl out here in this desolate valley. A crude wooden cross angled up from the sandy ground beneath the tree.

Fronting the cross was a mound of rocks in the shape of a grave, which was fitting since it was, indeed, a grave, Sartain knew.

It was the grave of the young woman's husband, young Gunther Ferris, killed by Kansas Charlie Sale. A red flower of some kind had been planted at the base of the cross. The young blonde was watering the flower from the wooden bucket. Apparently hearing the slow clomps of the horses entering her ranch and stage station yard, Maggie Ferris turned to look over her left shoulder.

She straightened abruptly, dropping the bucket, her right hand immediately sliding into a pocket of her dress. She pulled out something small and black and aimed the pocket pistol at Sartain. She shaded her eyes with her free hand. Sartain reined Boss to a halt near the windmill. He smiled and waved across the distance between himself and the woman.

Maggie Ferris must have recognized her visitor. She returned the pistol to her dress pocket, picked up the bucket, poured the rest of the water out on the ground around the oak and the flower with which she'd decorated her murdered husband's grave, and started walking down the hill, meandering around the clumps of sage and cactus.

The Revenger stepped down from his saddle and slipped Boss's bit from his teeth so the horse could freely drink.

"What you got in mind here, Sartain?"

Kansas Charlie stared at the young woman walking toward them, the breeze rustling her fine, long, straight, wheat-colored hair. Her dress was worn and plain, but somehow its bedraggled quality accentuated the sumptuousness of her body.

The simple frock was low-cut, and her breasts jiggled as she walked, betraying the fact she wasn't wearing a corset or probably much of anything else beneath the dress. Why? She lived alone out here, and the stage only rattled through once a week.

She was barefoot. All of her exposed skin had been deeply tanned by the west Texas sun; its dark tone accented the icy blueness of her eyes and the white-bleached highlights of her hair.

"I don't have nothin' in mind, Charlie. I've done my duty. The rest is up to the woman you raped and whose husband you gut-shot when you hoorawed this place the other night." While

Boss dipped his muzzle in the stone water tank, Sartain freed the horse's *latigo* and then went over and freed Kansas Charlie's mare of the same trappings, so the mare, too, could drink, which she did, merrily switching her tail.

Her rider wasn't nearly as happy.

"Hi, Maggie," Sartain said as the woman approached. She was tall and long-limbed, heavy busted.

She wore no expression at all. Like the shabby dress, the lack of expression seemed to increase her beauty by contrast. She had the face of a stony-souled Nordic goddess.

"Hi, Mike."

"Brought you a present."

Twenty feet away from the windmill, she let the bucket drop straight down to the ground. She continued walking, swishing her hips ever so slightly, curls of dust licking up around her bare feet, and stopped within ten feet of Sartain and Kansas Charlie.

Maggie Ferris stared blandly up at Sartain's prisoner. "I see." She had a slight gap between her two front teeth.

"Sartain . . ." Kansas Charlie said, eyeing the woman as though she were a rattlesnake coiled and ready to strike. "What in the hell'd we come here for?"

"Don't you like it here?" asked Maggie Ferris blandly.

Kansas Charlie scowled back at her. "Come on, Sartain. I get it now. I get the joke. You can take me on over to Bittersweet now."

"What's in Bittersweet?" asked Maggie Ferris.

"The county sheriff!" Kansas Charlie barked. "I need to be taken there and locked up and tried legal-like, by a court judge. That's my right. That's the right of any man, though I understand how's you wouldn't see it that way, Mrs. Ferris."

"Why wouldn't I see it that way, Kansas Charlie?"

Charlie scowled down at her, his own sun-bleached brows crawling down over his fleshy eye sockets. For a few seconds,

Sartain thought the big, paunchy, red-haired outlaw was going to break down and cry.

Sartain pulled his Barlow knife from the well of his right boot and cut the rope tying Kansas Charlie's cuffs to his saddle horn. "What're you doin', Sartain? I'll stay right here where I'm at."

"I don't think so, Charlie." Sartain backed away from the mare, slipped his LeMat from its holster, and cocked the weapon. "Climb down, Charlie. Been a long, hard ride. We're gonna stay here a spell, give the horses a blow, let 'em drink and eat and stomp around the yard. Have us a little visit with Mrs. Ferris."

Kansas Charlie looked at Maggie Ferris. For the first time since Sartain had known her—and he hadn't known her long; just since a couple of days after the West Texas Hellions had ridden through here, killing and raping, in fact—he saw her smile. It was an icy smile that didn't quite make it to her eyes, but it was a smile just the same.

It made the Revenger realize how beautiful a real smile would be on such a deftly crafted face, though he doubted he'd ever see a real one on Maggie Ferris.

At least, not for a long time.

"Climb down, Charlie," Sartain ordered. "Or I'll shoot you down."

Charlie sighed. "Aw, shit." He leaned forward and grimaced painfully as he swung his bandaged right leg over the cantle of his saddle and gently lowered it to the ground. He got his cuffs hung up on the horn, and when he jerked them loose, he stumbled back, tripping over his own heavy boots, and fell on his ass with a thud, dust wafting around him.

"Oh, shit! Oh, hell," he cried. "My leg! And this hand is grievin' me somethin' awful, Sartain. You gotta get me to

23

Bittersweet. That's my right. I wanna go on to Bittersweet, god-dammit!"

Maggie Ferris stared down at him. "What's wrong with my place, Charlie? You and the others seemed to like it well enough the other night. You seemed to enjoy stripping me right out here in the yard and forcing my dear husband to watch while you grunted around on top of me like the fat, ugly goat you are.

"While my poor, dying husband and the others watched, your friends cheering you on. You seemed to get a big kick out of forcing me to do something *awful* after you raped me. Instead of allowing me to go and lend comfort to my beloved Gunther. By the time I reached Gunther, he was dead."

Her tone was stony, but a faint sheen had grown over her eyes, which were crinkled at the corners as she spoke, staring down at Kansas Charlie and flaring her nostrils.

"Even the others seemed a little horrified, after all was said and done. You raping and doing . . . that . . . to me in front of my dying husband. Not that they didn't enjoy watching. I reckon they couldn't get their blood up much after they saw Gunther was dead, though. I guess the only good thing to come out of that night was that I wasn't raped by the lot of you . . . and probably murdered, like you murdered Gunther."

"Look, Miss," Charlie said, staring up at her.

"It's Mrs. Ferris, and don't you forget it."

"R-right. Mrs. Ferris. I know. I just wanna take this op-portunity to apologize for—"

"Shut up," Maggie said.

She looked at Sartain. "I think it would only be fair if he was stripped naked, Mike. I'll pay extra if you strip him naked, like he did to me. Strip him naked and leave him to season out here in the sun to pontificate on what's gonna happen to him next, in a couple of hours, while you and I go inside and eat some beans and drink a glass or two of whiskey."

"I told you, Maggie," Sartain said. "I don't do what I do for money. I do what I do for the satisfaction of havin' folks like you get justice. Stripping ol' Kansas Charlie and leavin' his ugly carcass out here to season in the sun seems about right, to my way of thinkin'."

Kansas Charlie's eyes flashed raw horror. "Sartain, you wouldn't!"

Sartain looked at Maggie and chuckled. Then he walked over to his horse and pulled a railroad spike out of a saddlebag pouch.

CHAPTER THREE

"Sartain, dammit, you take me to Bittersweet!"

Kansas Charlie saw the railroad spike Sartain held and tried to gain his feet and run. The Revenger kicked the man's boots out from under him, and Kansas Charlie fell hard on his fat gut.

Sartain kicked him over onto his back, lifted his cuffed hands above his head, and impaled a chain link with the railroad spike. He used a rock to hammer the foot-long spike into the hard-packed ground and tested it.

Kansas Charlie wasn't going anywhere.

Charlie kicked at Sartain and bellowed like a bull in an abattoir. Sartain pulled out his Barlow knife, grabbed the front of Charlie's grimy shirt, and cut it down the center. He ripped the shirt off Charlie's back and tossed it away.

"Sartain, goddammit—you can't do this!" Kansas Charlie railed, jerking on his cuffs and kicking both legs, but mostly just kicking the left one, as he'd opened up the wound in the right one. The white bandage behind his trousers was spotted with blood, and the spot was growing. The wound in his hand, cuffed and held fast to the ground above his head, appeared to have opened up, as well. Blood trickled out from beneath the bandage and down his wrist.

"You can't do this, Sartain. I got rights. I might be an outlaw, but I still got rights, and the law says you gotta take me to the sheriff in Bittersweet so I can—"

"I know, I know—I done heard you the first time, Charlie," the Cajun said, rolling out his long, flowing vowels in a way that brought a taste of the bayou to everywhere he traveled. "So you can be tried by a judge an' jury . . . legal-like." He pressed a knee down hard on the fat man's belly, causing the air in Kansas Charlie's lungs to gush out in a loud, bellowing curse.

As he set to work ripping Charlie's greasy denim trousers open, he said, "But you know that ain't my style, Charlie. I don't work that way."

With one hard tug, he pulled the outlaw's trousers down his legs, revealing the grubby, tattered summer underwear reaching down to Charlie's pale, dimpled knees. He ripped off the man's trousers and then the underwear, exposing Charlie's soft, winter-white flesh to the merciless west Texas sun.

Cursing like a gandy dancer, Charlie kicked his bare legs this way and that, trying to get at Sartain, causing his bulging belly to jiggle. His chest and belly were carpeted in thin, sweaty strands of curly red hair.

"Now, Charlie, you killed the poor woman's husband. You raped her in front of the dying man, and when I was passin' through here last week, on the way to Mexico for a leisurely sojourn away from the law and the bounty hunters I got doggin' my trail, she asked me if there was something I could do about that."

Staring stonily down at the flopping Kansas Charlie, bunching her lips and swelling her nostrils, a single tear rolling down her cheek, Maggie Ferris said, "I knew the law wouldn't do nothin'. The West Texas Hellions got a way of evadin' the law, of always slippin' down into Mexico when a lawman gets close. Or they kill him and send his body back to wherever he came from, tied belly down over his saddle. Besides, there ain't no telegraph out here."

She shook her head in frustration.

"So I told Mrs. Ferris that, yeah, I thought I could do somethin' about her woes."

"You take me to Bittersweet, Sartain!"

The Revenger looked at Maggie. "How do you want to handle this?"

"I say we let him season out here for a while." Maggie Ferris glanced at the sky. "Sun's still high. Got several hours of heat left. We'll go inside for some beans and whiskey, and I'll put some thought into how my Gunther should be properly avenged."

"All right, you go on in and break out the tangleleg. I'll tend the horses and join you in a few minutes."

"Sartain!" Kansas Charlie cried from between his elbows, trying to pull the stake out of the ground. It wasn't budging. The ground was nearly as hard as stone. "Sartain, you take me to the marshal in Bittersweet. I got rights!"

"No, you don't, Charlie." Sartain grabbed up the bridle reins of Boss and the mare. "You see, that's where you're wrong. When I come into the picture, you cease having any rights right then and there. The only one who has any rights out here is Mrs. Ferris. It is an undisputable fact what you did to her and her husband, so by the power vested in my by myself and with casual disregard for the laws of this country of ours—laws that benefit the criminals far more than they help the criminals' victims—I deem Maggie Ferris your judge, your jury, and your executioner."

Sartain pinched his hat brim to Kansas Charlie. "Because of what you did to her and her husband, your fate is in her hands now."

Maggie Ferris gave another rare smile, turned away from Kansas Charlie, and started walking to her cabin. Sartain began leading the horses around the windmill toward the barn.

"Sartain, you're crazy! You got no right to do this!"

Without looking back at his naked prisoner, Sartain said mildly, "Maybe no legal right, but I'm doing it, Charlie. And remember—you had no right to do what you did out here the other night, neither."

"Sartain, you crazy Cajun devil!"

The Revenger chuckled at that as he led the horses around the adobe shack to the barn. When he'd finished graining the mounts, he rubbed each down carefully and thoroughly with a scrap of burlap, curried them, checked their hooves for stones and thorns, and then turned them into the corral with Maggie's single horse and mule.

Boss ran around the pole corral, whickering and kicking up dust, staking out his territory, as the stallion was wont to do. Out in the yard beyond the shack, Kansas Charlie was still bellowing, but his voice was getting hoarse. Sartain knew, from having witnessed it many times in the past, that when a man yelled that long and loudly, his voice would soon die. Sartain and Maggie Ferris could enjoy some peace and quiet while they . . . and Charlie, of course . . . anticipated the final execution.

Sartain slapped his hat against his denims as he made his way out of the corral, where he left the horses munching hay, and headed around to the front of the shack. Charlie was still kicking, but not with nearly as much vigor as before, arching his back and grunting and groaning as he tried to pull the stake out of the ground.

Sartain stepped onto the shack's narrow, sagging front porch, dippered some water from the *olla,* took a long drink from the hanging clay pot, and then stepped through the plank door Maggie had propped open with a stone. She sat at the table just inside the door, on the table's far side. A pot of beans was bubbling on the small range behind her.

She sat sideways in her chair, a tin cup and a stone jug in front of her. She stared through the door and into the yard with the same vague, flat expression as before.

Sartain glanced into the yard at Charlie.

"The bitterness," she said. "Does it ever go away?"

Sartain doffed his hat and hung it on a wooden peg by the door. He kicked a chair out and slacked into it with a sigh. "No. It never goes entirely away. But doin' what you're doin' helps."

Maggie nudged the crock jug toward Sartain. "Help yourself. My husband's own corn whiskey. Twice distilled behind the barn. He was from Alabama, and his pa taught him how to make it. The recipe's an old one, been in the Ferris family for years."

"Obliged." Sartain splashed some of the clear liquor into the tin cup she'd set on his side of the table.

"You say it helps, and I think you're right," Maggie said. "I'm feelin' better already . . . with that dog chained naked in my yard, the sun burnin' down on him. Look at him kickin' out there. Squirmin' an' groanin'."

She lifted her brightening eyes to Sartain. A flush had risen into the nubs of her tan cheeks, making her even prettier. "You know it from experience—don't you, Mike? That it helps. You don't just do this for others, do you?"

"Runnin' down men . . . sometimes women . . . who've done bad things to others? No, I don't do it just for other folks who've been wronged and can't exact justice on their own without help. I do it because I know the kind of bitterness you feel, Maggie. I still have it deep inside me, but it helps knowin' that the men . . . the soldiers who killed my girl . . . are dead. They died hard. Maybe not as hard as what they done to Jewel, but . . ."

Sartain swallowed, stared down at the table, the pain like a lance in his belly again. But that was all right. He needed to feel it now and then, to remember what had happened so that he could sympathize with others who had endured . . . were enduring . . . *had yet to endure* . . . the same kind of horror.

"Maybe them soldiers didn't die as hard as they should have, but they died hard just the same. Screamin' an' bellowin' like Kansas Charlie out there now." Sartain raised his cup and looked over the rim at Maggie. "And, yeah, it helps. It don't take away the pain and the bitterness altogether, but it's a hell of a lot better than havin' 'em out there, runnin' free as mustangs and stompin' with their tails up."

He sipped the whiskey. It was like liquid fire. He could feel the burn in his cheeks and in his eyes, but it tapered off quickly and left a soothing glow, instantly filing the afternoon's sharpest edges. He stared down into the clear liquid.

"Good stuff."

Maggie sipped her own drink and then reached across the table to place her left hand on the Cajun's. "I'm sorry about Jewel, Mike."

Sartain's eyes glazed, as they usually did when he thought of his young wife, all the broken promises, and he threw another drink back to cover the swelling in his throat. "Thanks, Maggie." He set the cup down and placed his right hand over hers. "And thank you for letting me help you."

"It helps you, too, don't it?"

"It does indeed."

Outside, Kansas Charlie gave a particularly loud bellowing cry.

Maggie smiled. "You hungry?"

"I'm so hungry my belly's thinkin' my throat's been cut."

"I'm going to feed you, and then I'm going to make love to you, Mike."

Sartain arched his bushy, black brows. "Maggie . . ."

"Oh, it's not for no payment for what you done," Maggie said. "I know you don't accept payment. It's because my husband's dead, and he won't be comin' back to me ever again."

She brushed a tear from the corner of her left eye. "And because I'm a woman with a woman's needs, and you're a kind, handsome man, and there won't be too many more of those around here, most like."

She pulled her hand out from between Sartain's, rose, and stared out the open door behind him. "Besides, this whole revenge business is plum gettin' me all worked up!"

She laughed and turned to the range.

CHAPTER FOUR

Sartain and Maggie Ferris ate beans in which she'd stewed chicken meat, and some crusty corn bread. They washed the simple but tasty meal down with whiskey and water.

Halfway through the meal, the breeze through the door chilled considerably. Thunder rumbled. The yard beyond the stoop darkened, and Sartain could smell rain on the wind.

"Sartain!" Kansas Charlie bellowed, but not nearly as loudly as before. "You best bring me inside, Sartain! Gettin' cold out here. Startin' to rain!"

"We could do with a rain," Maggie said, setting her fork down and sipping her whiskey. She rose, said, "I'm going to put the chickens in. Sometimes they scatter during a storm, and it takes me forever to find 'em. No, you sit and finish your meal, Mike. It'll just take me a minute."

Sartain settled back into his chair as Maggie walked out of the cabin. He could hear her bare feet tapping against the hard-packed yard as she broke into a run. A few minutes later, the rain started coming down hard, rattling on the roof. It felt good against Sartain's back as he sat at the table, loading the last of his beans and chicken onto his fork with a swatch of cornbread.

When it started to come down harder, he rose from his chair and donned his hat, intending to go out and help Maggie with her chickens. But he stopped on the stoop when he saw her striding toward him through the white javelins of slashing rain.

The quarter-sized raindrops splashed in the puddles around

her bare, muddy feet. She was soaked, and the rain basted her dress against her so that it looked like a second skin, through which Sartain could see nearly every part of her.

As she strode past Kansas Charlie, the naked outlaw said just loudly enough for Sartain to hear above the storm's low roar, "I think you liked it, Mrs. Ferris." Charlie laughed. "Yeah, I think you liked it real good!"

He raised and lowered his heels, howling with laughter as the rain came down, turning the ground around him to mud.

Maggie stopped in her tracks. She stood staring at Sartain, who started down the steps to move toward her. He stopped when she shook her head and raised both hands to her chest, palms out. She continued walking forward, climbed the porch's three steps, brushing past Sartain, her breasts swaying and jostling beneath the dress, and disappeared into the cabin.

When she came out, she was holding an old cap and ball revolver. The gun was an old Confederate-model, iron-framed Griswold & Gunnison. Maggie held it in both hands, staring down at it. "This is what he used to shoot Gunther. He took it away from him when Gunther pulled it to protect me, and he shot Gunther in the stomach with it."

Sartain pulled her toward him and planted a tender kiss on her forehead.

She dropped down the steps into the yard. Holding the old Confederate cavalry pistol straight down by her side, she walked out to where Kansas Charlie lay naked in the mud, staring toward her, laughing.

"Sure enough, you liked it!" he bellowed, kicking his small, soft, white, bare feet. "You want some more of it, Mrs. Ferris, now that I got your husband out of the way?"

She stopped near his feet and stared down at him.

Kansas Charlie kicked and laughed, straining against the cuffs holding his hands above his head. She aimed the heavy revolver straight out in both hands and slanted it down at the fat man's head.

"Right between the eyes, Maggie—there ya go!"

Maggie shook her head. She wasn't ready for his misery to end. Not yet. She lowered the barrel, aiming at his crotch.

"No!" Kansas Charlie shouted, jerking at his cuffs.

The old gun belched flames and fire. Sartain had been worried it would misfire on account of the rain—his own similar revolver had often misfired during the war—but Maggie's didn't.

Kansas Charlie threw his head as far back as he could and screamed like an owl with one wing caught in a trap. He rolled the lower half of his body to one side, drawing his knees up to his belly.

"Oh, you bitch!" he cried. "Oh, you bitch! You bitch! You *bitch!*"

She lowered the weapon and took long strides back to the porch. She stopped at the bottom of the steps and stood to let the rainwater sluicing off the porch roof tumble over her, until her dress became transparent. For all intents and purposes, she was standing before Sartain naked.

Kansas Charlie's bellows lowered to agonized mewls and sobs as he kept his knees drawn to his chest.

Sartain's heart thudded as he stared down at Maggie. Maggie tipped her head back, swiping her wet hair behind her head and opening her mouth to drink the rain. She looked at Sartain. Then she looked down at herself. She walked slowly up the steps and stood before him, staring up at him, passion smoldering in her eyes.

Sartain glanced at the rise behind her, at the red flower and her husband's fresh grave. "You sure?"

She reached down, grabbed her dress, and lifted it up and over her head. She tossed it onto the porch floor, took Sartain's hand, and led him into the cabin.

Leaving the door open to the fresh damp breeze, hearing the rain pattering on the roof, Sartain followed the naked woman around the table to a bed at the back of the room, abutting the far left wall. There was a small parlor area with a rocking chair, a rope rug, and a small, mud-brick hearth to the right of it.

She stopped beside the bed and stood staring at him, her full breasts rising and falling heavily. They were lightly freckled.

Sartain moved heavily toward her. She rose up on her tiptoes and kissed him.

"This time it's my idea," she said just loudly enough that he could hear her above the rain.

Lightning flashed. Thunder rumbled. The rain wasn't hammering as hard as before but making a more peaceful rhythm on the roof and against the walls and windows. Beneath it, Sartain could hear Kansas Charlie crying while he clamped his viscera between his thighs.

He rolled off of Maggie Ferris, sweating, breathing hard.

She climbed out of bed and tromped naked out onto the porch. He followed her out there. She drank from the *olla*. She dipped up some more water and offered it to him, holding it up to his mouth. He drank it all, and when she dippered some more, he drank that, too.

There was an old wicker chair on the porch. He sat in it, and she sat on his lap. They sat there together, gently kissing and caressing and listening to Kansas Charlie's dwindling wails beneath the even rush of the rain that turned the yard to gauzy silver, the intermittent lightning flashes reflected in the puddles.

Maggie went in and poured fresh whiskey into a single cup, and they sat together in the wicker chair, snuggling and sipping the whiskey. The rain dwindled slightly but continued to come down. Kansas Charlie was a vague shape in the dark, silvery mud, curled on his side, his back to the cabin.

Maggie took another sip of the whiskey, ran her tongue across her upper lip, and looked up at Sartain. "Tell me how you came to do what you do, Mike. Tell me about Jewel."

"Yeah, she's a part of it," Sartain said, staring out into the rain-washed yard. "It was a long time ago. But sometimes it seems like only yesterday. I came home from the war, became a galvanized Yankee—"

"What's that?" Maggie asked, looking up at him from beneath her brows.

"Since I'd been a grayback, fought on the side of the Confederacy during the War of Northern Aggression, I had to swear allegiance to the federal army . . . in order to join the frontier cavalry, you understand. It's called becomin' 'galvanized' to the federal ways."

He shrugged a shoulder. "I had nowhere to go after the war and knew really only one thing—fightin'—so I decided the cavalry would be the best place for me. Fightin' in the Indian Wars out west. Besides, I'd never been any farther west than New Orleans. So I swore allegiance, got stationed at Fort Huachuca in the Arizona Territory . . ."

His gut tightened with the dread of those sharp-edged memories. Maggie's gentle hands took some of the teeth out of the horror that, despite the pain, was good to remember from time to time. Good to remind himself why he was here, doing what he was doing . . .

"My patrol was ambushed one afternoon by a Chiricahua war party. The entire patrol was wiped out . . . save myself. I was badly wounded. Somehow, when the squaws were sent in to finish off the wounded soldiers, they didn't find me lying in the brush and rocks. I must have been shaded or somethin' . . . I don't know. An old prospector and his granddaughter . . . Jewel . . . found me, nursed me back to health."

"Jewel," Maggie said, nuzzling his neck. "Pretty name."

"She was a pretty girl," Sartain said, wincing at the pain of the memories. "Pretty as a jewel, she was . . ."

"Was she your girl?"

"Yeah. She came to be my girl. Became . . . well, she got in the family way."

"Oh," Maggie said, sadness in her tone.

"I'd gone out hunting one afternoon. On the way back I spied five bluebellies—federal soldiers—riding fast. Viewed 'em through my spyglass. They were whoopin' and hollerin' like Apaches on the warpath. Later, when I got back to the camp, I discovered why those five renegade bluecoats had been stompin' with their tails up. They'd plundered the old prospector's cache of gold. Killed the old man. Killed Jewel . . . after they'd raped her. Each one of 'em, most like."

The Cajun tried to swallow down the hard knot in his throat, felt the warm wetness of tears rolling down his cheeks. "One after another . . ."

Sartain squeezed his eyes closed against the bloody images.

"And then what happened, Mike?" Maggie asked.

"And then I hunted them all down—all five—and killed them bloody," the Revenger said tightly. "And now I do the same thing for others who can't do it for themselves."

Maggie wrapped her arms around his neck and pressed her lips to his cheek. "Thank you, Mike. Thank you . . . for . . . bringin' Kansas Charlie to me . . . so he could pay for his sins. It don't bring my dear Gunther back, but . . ." She shrugged a shoulder.

Sartain ran a hand gently up and down her smooth thigh. "Revenge is a dish better served cold," he said, winking. "But it tastes right sweet, don't it?"

CHAPTER FIVE

Kansas Charlie must have rolled onto his back just before he died.

He lay on his back now, bloody and muddy, his wide, glassy eyes staring at the soft, dawn sky. His lips were stretched back from his yellow teeth in a death snarl.

A magpie had been sitting on his forehead when Sartain had ridden up, but it had flown as the Revenger had approached. There was a spot of blood in the corner of Kansas Charlie's right eye, where the bird had pecked him.

Kansas Charlie was nothing more than food for the carrion eaters.

"Couldn't have happened to a nicer guy."

Sartain removed his lariat from his saddle as he swung down from Boss's back and wrapped an end of the rope around Charlie's waist, slip-knotting it. He pulled the railroad spike out of the ground, removed Charlie's handcuffs, and returned both the spike and the cuffs to his saddlebags.

He climbed back into the saddle, dallied the lariat around the horn, and booted Boss toward the ranch's wooden portal and the main stage trail.

Kansas Charlie's pale, lumpy, muddy, bloody body was jerked around by the rope and pulled head first behind the horse, splashing through puddles and gouging a wide furrow in the muddy yard. As Boss plodded along toward the trail, Sartain glanced over his shoulder at the cabin cloaked in early morning

39

shadows, rain from another pre-dawn shower dripping from its eaves.

He'd left Maggie slumbering, exhausted from their night of lovemaking while the storm had swirled over the ranch yard, and Kansas Charlie's howls gradually dwindled to silence. Sartain pinched his hat brim in somber farewell at the sleeping woman and felt a pang of loneliness, as he often did when parting ways with a woman whose bed he'd shared.

You'd think a man like the Revenger would have a stone-cold heart, but that wasn't true for Sartain. He loved hard and he hated hard, and losing the love of his life a handful of years ago to renegade soldiers kept him riding hard along the vengeance trail, as though with each killer he killed, he was still avenging the killers of Jewel and his unborn child . . .

He felt lonely for Maggie, as well as for himself. She'd likely stay out here and tend the ranch and the relay station for the rest of the time allotted to her, tending her beloved husband's grave simply because she had nowhere else to go, and that was the kind of woman she was.

The world was a hard, unforgiving place.

Sartain dragged Kansas Charlie's worthless carcass several hundred yards from the Ferris ranch and rolled it into a deep ravine. A man like Kansas Charlie didn't deserve a decent burial, nor did he deserve any words said over him. Sartain merely rolled him into the ravine, coiled his lariat, and stepped back into the saddle.

He continued on, taking the southern trail, which he hoped would eventually lead him to Mexico. From having perused a map in a Wells Fargo office up in the Panhandle, he knew that the town of Carmen was to the north and the larger settlement of Bittersweet was to the south, between the Davis Mountains and the Del Carmen Range just across the border in Mexico.

He'd ride through Bittersweet in a few hours, he judged. He

usually tried to steer clear of smaller towns where he might be recognized from the "Wanted" dodgers bearing his likeness that had circulated through the West, announcing the two-thousand-dollar government bounty on his head for killing the soldiers. But Bittersweet would be the last town before the vast wastes of Old Mexico. He needed to lay in trail provisions for the long ride.

He'd ridden along on the muddy trail for a good hour when a clattering rose behind him. Instantly, his hand went to the big LeMat holstered on his right thigh, and he turned to stare back along the trail. There was no dust because of the mud, but he thought he could make out a fast-moving wagon coming around a bend maybe a quarter mile back and obscured by scrub oaks and sotol cactus.

The wagon was moving at a fast clip, clattering to beat the band. Now he could hear someone hoorawing whatever poor animal was pulling the contraption.

Sartain turned Boss off the trail and rode around behind a large, cabin-sized boulder and stopped on the far side of the boulder from the oncoming wagon. He waited, his hand on the LeMat.

The clattering of the wagon grew steadily louder as did the loud hoorawing of the driver and the thuds of the galloping puller. The wagon dashed past the boulder in a tan and red blur, divots of mud flying up from the horse's hooves and the wheels. Sartain saw through the creosote scrub between him and the trail that a girl was driving, standing in the driver's boot, feet spread wide. She was whipping the reins over the skewbald paint horse pulling a battered, dull-orange farm wagon.

It wasn't her clothes that had given her sex away, for she wore the felt Stetson, hickory shirt, brown belt, and denims of a man. It was her slender figure with the feminine curves, and the high-pitched voice trying to coax more speed out of the galloping paint that told Sartain she was a girl. Many men wore their hair long, but hers, which was as black as night, hung down to the small of her back, and it owned a feminine shine.

The girl wasn't what interested the Revenger most about the fast-moving wagon, however. As she'd dashed past him, he'd caught a glimpse of what appeared to be a body covered by a brown and yellow Indian blanket. At least, the figure beneath the blanket was shaped like a body, and he thought he saw the top of a head and one arm flopping out to one side.

A body, all right. Most likely a dead one. Any injured man would have been killed by the girl's violent driving along the chuck-hole stippled stage road curving through the west Texas desert.

Curious, and because the girl was obviously in distress, Sartain pulled Boss out onto the trail and put the buckskin into a rocking canter, keeping about seventy yards between him and the girl as they continued along the trail, heading nearly due south. The Del Carmens rose dark and mysterious in Old Mexico, straight ahead of the trail and above the bristling chaparral brushed with occasional cloud shadows.

As hard as the girl was pushing her horse, Sartain expected the paint to blow out both lungs at any moment, or for one of its hooves to plunder a gopher hole. If that happened, the girl would be a goner, crushed beneath a toppled wagon.

He suppressed the urge to catch up to her and slow her down. Though it rankled him to see a horse abused the way she was abusing the paint, her business was her own. Besides, he thought they were probably within a mile or so of Bittersweet.

A few minutes later, he saw the mud adobe dwellings of the ranch- and mine-supply settlement crawl into view between two steep ridges. He wouldn't have recognized it as a town if he didn't know a town was out here. From this distance of a third of a mile, it was a few scattered brown shapes amongst boulders and cactus and scrub oaks and *piñons* climbing the lower slopes rolling up toward the base of the steep, sandstone cliffs. The cliffs towered a good two thousand feet over the town.

Only a town this small could be a county seat in the vastness of the Great Bend.

Sartain followed the wagon around a long bend in the trail, until he could see the tall, false-fronted business buildings lining the trail, which became Bittersweet's main street.

Flanking the mud-brick and shabby gray business buildings, the small, pale adobes remaining from the town's Mexican origins rolled up in the brushy, rocky hills, where the Revenger could hear lambs and goats bleating, a few cows lowing, and dogs barking. There was the smell of privies and trash heaps, as well as animal dung moldering in the harsh sun and ubiquitous heat.

There were also the rich, spicy smells of Mexican cook fires, and they started Sartain's stomach rumbling. He hadn't had breakfast at Maggie Ferris's place, though she'd offered to cook for him the night before. She'd been sleeping so deeply that morning, he hadn't wanted to awaken her.

Likely her slow, satisfying execution of Kansas Charlie had been a load off her shoulders, and she'd finally been able to get a good night's sleep, though her and Sartain's riotous coupling probably had something to do with that, as well.

The Revenger smiled, remembering it fondly.

Ahead of him, the wagon lurched and jounced into the town. As it did, the tailgate jerked open to lie flat, one broken chain dangling toward the trail. The wagon swung toward the right side of the street and stopped. Sartain halted Boss at the edge of the town, near a blacksmith's hut from which rose the clangs of a hammer striking an anvil.

The Revenger poked his hat brim back off his forehead as he

frowned curiously, watching the girl with long, black hair jerk the wagon's brake forward, engaging the blocks against the wheel, and then climb down out of the driver's boot, on the wagon's right side. She yelled something that Sartain couldn't hear, and then she shouted louder as she mounted the boardwalk fronting a large adobe brick building whose sign jutting into the street announced BROWN COUNTY COURT HOUSE.

A sign beneath that sign read simply: COUNTY SHERIFF.

"You bastard!" the girl's cry echoed. She'd stopped to shout into a window to the right of the courthouse's front door. "You killed him, you bastard, and I brought him here so you could take a good look at him!"

The front door opened, and an older man in a black, three-piece suit and spectacles stepped out, holding a fat stogie in his hand.

"Carleen!" the older man said, Sartain able to hear better now as he put Boss ahead along the street.

There'd been a dozen or more people milling about the shops, and they all turned their attention to the courthouse. Shop doors were opening, and men as well as women were stepping out to investigate the commotion.

Several dogs had come running out of alleys to sniff and mewl and wag their tails around the wagon. A building similar in bland, bulky style to the courthouse stood to Sartain's left. One of its several signs boasted "free blowjobs between 5 and 7 every Friday night with the purchase of a whiskey," so it likely had little to do with officious government grindings—except when the county officials were not taking advantage of the specials.

A large sign stretched across the upper story balcony read simply: NORA'S.

Doves in their fluttering finery were bleeding out onto the

rickety-looking balcony to peer over the ironwood rail toward the source of the commotion.

The black-haired girl hammered on the window to the right of the courthouse door, yelling, "Sheriff Chaney—you in there? You murdered him, you bastard! I know you did! I brought him here for you to look at!" She hammered on the window again, until Sartain winced, fearing she'd break the glass and shred her fist.

The old man in the three-piece suit, looking chagrined and befuddled, moved up to her as though to grab her arms, exclaiming, "Now, Carleen, pipe down before you cause a scandal, dear child!"

"Me cause a scandal?" Carleen shrieked so loudly that one of the dogs near the wagon put its tail down and dashed under the wagon bed.

To Sartain's left, a man shouted, "What in tarnation is goin' on over there? Who's yellin' so's to wake the dead? Carleen, is that you caterwaulin' over there?"

A tall, black-haired man had just walked out the front door of Nora's place, knotting a string tie around his neck.

He yelled, "Goddammit, girl—you pipe down, or I'll pull your pants down and blister your naked ass!"

CHAPTER SIX

The tall man stepped into the street, the doves looking down at him from the balcony above. He was dressed in the black suit and slouch hat of a card sharp, complete with gold watch chain drooping from a pocket of his paisley vest. A stylish brown slouch hat shaded his soft but handsome face.

His white linen shirttails drooped over his wide, black cartridge belt glittering with brass-cased rounds for the big Peacemaker sitting high and for the cross-draw on his left hip. The thongs on his holster dangled toward his high-heeled, undershot black boots.

A five-pointed sheriff's star glittered on his vest.

The girl had swung around to face the man. She glowered at him from the boardwalk fronting the courthouse. "Ha! I should've expected you'd be whore-mongering, you guttersnipe! Get your cowardly ass over here and say good-bye to your brother, Warren! He's dead, and don't try to tell me it wasn't you who shot him in the back, neither!"

"What're you talkin' about, girl?" the sheriff said, finished tying his necktie and striding slowly forward. The street had suddenly gone so quiet that Sartain could hear one of the horses tied to a hitchrack fronting Nora's place plop apples into the street.

"Get over here and say good-bye to your brother, Warren!" The girl thrust her arm out toward the blanket-covered dead man in the back of the wagon.

46

Her voice had been quavering with emotion, and now her knees buckled, and she collapsed in the street, her long hair dancing down her arms. She clamped her hands to her face and sobbed. "You killed him! You finally killed him just like you been wantin' to do ever since he came back to Bittersweet!"

She sobbed into her hands, shoulders jerking, her hat falling off her head and tumbling into the street.

Everyone watched, including Sartain, as the tall, slender sheriff with hair nearly as dark as the girl's strode over to the wagon. He stared down at young Carleen, and then he turned to the bundle in the wagon box. With one hand, he tugged the blanket down to reveal the man's face. Then he froze before squaring his shoulders and staring into the wagon for a full minute.

No one said anything. The only sounds were the occasional snorts of a horse and the girl sobbing into her hands as she knelt in the finely churned dust of the street.

The older gent in the three-piece suit had come down off the boardwalk to tentatively peer into the wagon. He winced again and shook his head. "It's Waylon, all right. Sure enough. May god have mercy on his soul." He turned to Carleen and clucked. "Oh, you poor girl!"

"He did it!" Carleen lifted her head and pointed at the sheriff. "He might not have pulled the trigger, but he saw to it that his brother was killed, sure enough!" She rose and lunged for the tall man before her. "You killed your own brother, an' you'll burn in hell, you son of a bitch!"

She tried to punch him, but he grabbed her arms. He was far bigger and stronger than she, and she was no match for him. A short Mexican in buckskins had slowly stepped up to the wagon. He'd come from the direction of the blacksmith shop behind Sartain, and he moved slowly but deliberately up behind the girl now and took her in his brawny arms.

"There, there, Carleen," the burly Mexican said sadly, enfolding the crying girl in his arms and pulling her back away from the sheriff. "There, there . . . come away from there, now."

"Let me go, Vicente!" Carleen yelled, struggling in the burly man's grip, kicking out at the sheriff, who stood sullenly before her. "I'm going to kill that bastard! He killed his own brother! His own *twin brother!* He killed my father, and I won't rest until he's dead, too!"

"Come now, Carleen. I take you home. Vicente will take you home."

"I don't wanna go home. There's nothin' there for me anymore . . . with Pa dead, murdered by his own brother!"

Suddenly Carleen managed to wriggle out of the stocky Mexican's arms. Sobbing, tears rolling down her cheeks, she stumbled into the middle of the street. "I, Carleen Chaney, daughter of Waylon Chaney, who was murdered by his twin brother, Warren Chaney—*Sheriff Warren Chaney*—am, as of right now, offering five hundred dollars to the man or men who kills this killer standing before me now!"

The sheriff whipped his head around, his right hand automatically driving across his belly to close around the grips of his Peacemaker. He spun as though to make sure no one was taking the girl up on her offer, and then he spun back to her, thrusting an arm and castigating finger at her. "Goddamn you, Carleen—you simple *bitch!*"

With that, he struck the back of his right hand across her face with a resolute smack. The girl screamed, spun, and fell in a heap.

Red-faced with fury, the sheriff bounded toward the girl, his eyes fairly bulging out of their sockets. Sartain knew unbridled rage when he saw it.

"Come on, Boss!" He booted the buckskin ahead, shucking his LeMat from its holster.

As the sheriff jerked his right boot back, apparently intending to drive it into the girl's belly, Sartain let a bullet fly. The .44-caliber slug plumed dirt and horse shit about six inches to the left of the sheriff's left boot. The Revenger turned Boss full around and halted him, dust billowing around horse and rider.

Sheriff Warren Chaney had lunged back, tripped over his own boots, and fallen in the street with an indignant yelp. His enraged eyes blazed up at Sartain, and again his hand went to the Peacemaker.

Sartain drove another .44 round into the dirt near the man's hat, which tumbled off his head and, cocking the big popper once more, narrowed an eye as he aimed down the barrel at the bridge of the dark-haired, blue-eyed man's nose. "The next one's gonna earn me that five hundred dollars right quick!"

Chaney froze, his Peacemaker half out of its holster. He stared up at Sartain with bald fury, the nostrils of his peeling, sun-blistered nose expanding and contracting. His sharply chiseled, clean-shaven face was mottled red.

The crowd had moved a little closer to see over and around the wagon. A shocked rumble rose. At the first roar of Sartain's LeMat, the three dogs had high-tailed it into alleys, but a shaggy, burr-laden black and white collie peered from over a pile of lumber, grinning as though this were the most interesting thing to happen in Bittersweet in a month of Sundays.

The girl stared up at Sartain from the dirt. Her mouth hung open—a pretty, full-lipped mouth it was, too—and her eyes were wide. Her man's flannel shirt had torn open, revealing the top of the deep, alluring valley between her breasts.

The stocky Mexican stood staring with much the same expression as the girl, his coffee-brown eyes flicking back and forth between Sartain's smoking, pearl-gripped, silver-chased LeMat and his eyes. A woman's voice yelled, "Warren!"

She came running out of the crowd—another black-haired

beauty, only this one was better appointed, in a burgundy gown with a wasp waist and pleated skirt, a little straw hat trimmed with fake berries and leaves on her classically beautiful head. She was shielding that beautiful head from the sun with a parasol that matched the gown.

As she ran toward the wagon, her corset jostled becomingly. She was still a good twenty feet from Sartain when he could tell that she was blood related not only to the sheriff, but to the girl, as well. In fact, Carleen appeared merely a slightly younger version of the woman, who was maybe twenty-five or twenty-six, only a few years younger than the sheriff.

"I heard the yelling, and . . . Carleen, it is you!" She stopped near the wagon and looked around at Chaney and Carleen and then at Sartain, who had lowered the LeMat slightly while keeping it cocked and trained on the sheriff.

Now the woman turned to peer into the wagon. "Oh!" she said, clapping a hand to her cleavage visible at the top of her stylishly low-cut gown. She took a halting step backwards. Her fine lower jaw hung, and her ruby lips parted in shock. "Oh, god! Waylon?" She moved forward slowly, dropped the parasol, and closed both her white-gloved hands over the top of the wagon's side panel.

"Go on home, Celeste." Keeping a close eye on Sartain's LeMat, Chaney gained his feet. "Go on home. I'll tend to him."

"Who did this?" Celeste asked, her cheeks pale. Otherwise, she looked more angry than sad. There were no tears in her eyes, and her fine jaw was firm. She was staring at Chaney. "Who did this, Warren?"

"He did!" Carleen exclaimed, gaining her feet, her hair in her eyes. "His own twin brother murdered my father. I found him dead in Cobalt Canyon. Back-shot!"

Chaney glanced around self-consciously and said tightly through his teeth, "Carleen, I didn't murder my own goddamn brother, and if you don't stop sayin' it . . . !" He glanced at Sartain, as did Carleen.

She acquired a smug look as she switched her gaze back to Chaney. "What're you gonna do, Warren? Looks like there's a new dog in town. One with a bigger gun and bigger balls than the soft little marbles you got danglin' between *your* legs."

A man laughed loudly, briefly, as several others amongst the crowd snickered with sheepish delight. Chaney turned to the man who'd laughed loudest, and the man turned his head away and brushed a fist across his nose.

Celeste moved toward Carleen. "Come, Carleen. Let me take you to the house, get you cleaned up and—"

"No." Carleen backed away. She glanced at the stocky Mexican standing behind her. "I'm going with Vicente. He's the only one around here who stayed loyal to my pa. He was more a brother to him than you ever were, Warren, you yellow-livered, murdering bastard!"

She sobbed again and turned to the stocky Mexican, who wrapped his thick arms around her, gave her a quick hug, and muttered something into her ear. Then she turned away from him and walked over to the wagon's left side, and climbed into the boot. The Mexican walked off down a wide break between buildings on the west side of the street.

"Carleen, where are you taking him?" Celeste asked, frowning up at the girl whom Sartain assumed was her cousin. "Your father should be buried up at the house. His own father will want to see him one last time."

Carleen disengaged the brake. "I'm burying him up in the mountains, far away from here and everything Chaney. You Chaneys killed him. Warren just finished it. I only brought my father to town so everyone could see Warren's handiwork. So they could see what he did to his own brother."

She raised her voice and looked around the crowd of stockmen, drummers, painted ladies, burly prospectors, and apron-clad shopkeepers, as well as several round-faced, domesticated Apaches who likely did menial labor in and around the town.

"You've all seen what Sheriff Chaney did to his own brother. The reward stands. I will pay in gold dust as soon as I've been given confirmation that Sheriff Chaney is dead! *Hi-yahhh!*"

Several men dashed out of the way as she shook the reins of the paint in the traces, and horse and wagon and its slack cargo dashed off down the wide break between buildings, on the heels of the stocky Mexican, Vicente.

Chaney glowered at Sartain. The corners of his mouth rose with a devilish smile. "You can toss that big hogleg down in the dirt, now, stranger."

"Can I?"

A deep, rumbling voice behind Sartain said, "Yeah, you can."

The Revenger heard the unmistakable click of a gun hammer being cocked.

CHAPTER SEVEN

Sartain looked over his right shoulder.

A big, savage-looking *hombre* in a too-tight three-piece suit that made him look even more savage by contrast stood about ten yards behind the Revenger. Wearing a deputy sheriff's tin star on his left lapel, he was aiming a double-barreled Greener straight out from his right shoulder, his head canted slightly over the barn-blaster's rabbit-ear hammers, both of which were rocked back to full cock.

He grinned, showing two gold front teeth.

Sheriff Warren Chaney smiled with satisfaction. "Toss it down here in the dirt, or my deputy here, Mr. Amos McCluskey, is gonna blow a hole the size of Texas through your brisket."

Sartain tightened his grip on the heavy revolver and offered a snide grin of his own. "I never toss my weapons in the dirt. Scratches the finish and fouls the action."

Chaney's smile faded. His left nostril twitched. Another angry flush rose in his cheeks.

Sartain broadened his own smile as he kept the LeMat aimed at Chaney's chest.

"This piece has a hair trigger," he warned. He didn't have to add that if Deputy McCluskey's Greener went off, the LeMat would go off, as well. Sartain might get his spine turned to shards, but a .44 pill drilled through Chaney's heart would kill the sheriff just as dead.

Chaney's left nostril twitched again. A murmur rose from the crowd still staring at the hubbub from up and down the street. The sheriff's rage shifted to embarrassment, then back to rage again with a good touch of frustration added.

He glanced around Sartain at his deputy. "Amos."

"You got it, boss."

Sartain heard the shotgun's hammers click softly down. Sartain curveted Boss and then backed the horse to the left side of the street so he could have both Chaney and big Amos McCluskey in his view. McCluskey let the Greener hang down at his side.

Sartain offered an affable grin and depressed the LeMat's hammer.

"All right, then," he said.

A couple of people in the crowd sighed as though they'd been all worked up for action, and now that it didn't look like they were going to get any—at least any *more*, now that Miss Carleen had made her exit—they were disappointed. The crowd started to disperse, murmuring their chagrin at having to return to the humdrum workaday world without having gotten to see any blood shed.

Chaney looked around cautiously. Sartain knew the man was thinking about that bounty Carleen had put on his head. He was wondering who, if anyone, was going to try to collect.

And if they weren't going to collect it here—where?

Sartain would be wondering the same thing, as would most men. He had to smile at Chaney's predicament. He was constantly in predicaments like that himself, and he knew it was like living between two steam-saw blades.

Besides, while he knew little or nothing about what had just occurred here on Bittersweet's main street, he sensed that Chaney deserved the position he was in. What made it even more satisfying was that the arrogant lawman had been placed there by a young woman who thought the sheriff was responsible for her father's death.

"You'd best mosey, *amigo*," Chaney said, staring hard at Sartain. "You'd best mosey real fast-like. We ain't even met, and I can tell I don't like you. And when I don't like a man, I tell him to leave. And if that man's smart—and you don't look overly stupid—he leaves."

"Thanks for the high compliment," Sartain said. "I was just gonna stay long enough to do business with your mercantile. But now you done piss-burned me, and, while it's not for me to say how smart or stupid I am, I can tell you that I am sensitive. Bein' told to leave a place just sorta makes me wanna stay on. So I think I'll hang around a while. And if you decide to do somethin' about it, I can almost double-dee-guaran-damn-tee you it's gonna be a *pair* of Chaneys bein' buried."

He looked at the big, stupid-looking deputy with the two gold front teeth. "Or a pair of Chaneys and one deputy sheriff."

The big deputy gritted his gold teeth in fury and stepped forward, raising his shotgun. Sartain's LeMat roared, and the big man groaned as he brushed a hand across his cheek. He looked at the blood on his hand, and his face turned red.

"Why, you son of a . . ."

Sartain said, "I wasn't whistlin' 'Dixie.' "

Chaney glared at him, opening and closing his hands at his sides. "Who are you, mister?"

"I'm just a son of a bitch lookin' for a livery barn."

With that, the Revenger holstered his LeMat, pinched his hat brim to the sheriff, touched spurs to Boss's flanks, and rode off down the street. The Federated Livery and Feed Barn sat two blocks up and around a bend from the courthouse.

An old man with a straggly goat beard and smoking a corncob pipe stood outside, watching Sartain approach. Apparently, he'd been watching the festivities out in front of the courthouse.

"Boy, you sure piss-burned Warren Chaney good, mister."

"I did, didn't I? Will you stable my hoss? He's an owly son of a bitch around the fillies, and he eats like a blue-ribbon bull."

"My fillies can handle him. They're west Texas fillies, don't ya know."

As Sartain swung down from the saddle, the old man stepped forward, puffing his pipe. "Was that really Waylon Chaney lyin' in the back o' that wagon?"

"That's what his daughter said."

"I'll be damned. Waylon dead after all these years."

"What does that mean?"

Taking Boss's bridle reins, the old man studied the horse's rider. "What do you mean—'what does that mean?' "

"Sounds like Waylon Chaney cut quite a swath through these parts."

"You obviously ain't from here, young fella. Louisiana?"

"How did you know?"

The old man snorted. "Bayou Country, by the 'lect."

"Gulf Coast. New Orleans. French Quarter to be exact."

"Oh, shit. I know who you are."

"Yeah, well keep it under your hat, will you Mister . . . ?"

"Pap Chisolm. Yeah, I'll keep it under my hat but"—Chisolm gave a mock-devilish grin as he knocked the dottle from his pipe—"I ain't gonna promise I won't try to collect on that bounty you got ridin' your shoulders. What is it—two thousand?"

"Thereabouts. And thanks for the warning. I'll be watchin' for you." Sartain smiled at the oldster, who looked arthritic and frail, his shoulders hunched, his face bristling with warts and liver spots.

Chisolm shoved his pipe into a shirt pocket and reached under Boss's belly to unbuckle the *latigo*. "I used to have a pistol around here somewhere . . ."

"Make the first shot count." Sartain shucked his Henry from

56

its scabbard and hiked a hip on a water barrel. "Is the girl right, Chisolm? Do you think Sheriff Chaney killed his brother? I know it's none of my business, me bein' a stranger here an' all, but I'm naturally curious."

Chisolm turned to him. "Listen, young fella: it don't matter who you are or how good you are with that LeMat and Henry, or how many people you killed. Bein' curious, natural or otherwise, is dangerous business around here. I don't recommend it. And I ain't one to go flappin' my lips to folks who is over curious, neither. Talkin' too much and bein' curious—both'll get you killed faster'n you can shake a dead skunk!"

"Good advice." Sartain slid off the barrel, hiked his Henry on his shoulder, and poked a cigar between his lips. "Thanks, Chisolm."

"You ain't gonna take it to heart, are ya?" Chisolm asked as he led Boss up the barn's wooden ramp.

"Probably not," Sartain said fatefully.

Chisolm merely shook his head.

Sartain walked out into the street and looked around. He saw a sign for a café—at least he figured it was a café, for the sign read TEN CENT MEALS in crudely painted letters—and after investigating and discovering it was indeed an eatery run by a fat Mexican couple, he sat down to a filling meal of *carne asada* preceded by a big bowl of thick *menudo.*

He washed the spicy grub down with a couple of bottles of *cerveza.* The fat Mexican man had hauled them up from a deep root cellar, so the Mexican suds were cool and refreshing.

While the Cajun ate, he went over in his mind all that he'd encountered here in Bittersweet. It had been, and probably still was, *TROUBLE* in capital letters, and he admonished himself to lay in trail supplies and continue on down to Old Mexico, as he'd planned. Bounty hunters as well as lawmen were starting to clog up his back trail.

The trouble was, *TROUBLE*—in capital letters—had a way of attracting Mike Sartain, despite his troubled past.

He was just too damned curious about Waylon Chaney to pull his picket pin just yet. His curiosity probably had as much to do with the dead man's comely daughter, but there it was. He'd stay at least the night and see what he could turn up about the Chaneys and Miss Carleen and Miss Celeste. If there was a party here who needed help—Well, helping a person who couldn't help himself or *her* self was his business.

He tossed coins onto the table, nodded his gratefulness to the Mexican woman, donned his hat, and headed on outside. He stood on the boardwalk fronting the tiny adobe place and relit the stogie he'd been smoking earlier, the smells of the Mexican cooking and the eatery's warm air wafting out from behind him.

A couple of Mexican horsebackers were just now passing in the street before him. They turned down a side street where he'd seen another whorehouse earlier, when he'd been looking for food. It was a colorful little *adobe* with a wood frame and stone addition to one side, and the window shutters had all been brightly painted different colors.

Likely a Mexican-run establishment.

Sartain considered heading on over there, buying himself a chubby Mexican whore with whom to while away the waning hours of the afternoon, and maybe learn some gossip about the town in general and the Chaneys in particular.

But then, if he was going to visit a whorehouse, why not the big one nearly right across from the sheriff's office? He'd probably have a larger covey of painted ladies to choose from. Besides, it being so close to the sheriff's office, and with the sheriff having patronized the place earlier, he might learn more about the Chaneys there.

Something told Sartain that Sheriff Chaney was a regular.

Yeah, that's the brothel he oughta patronize. He wasn't nearly as interested in having his ashes hauled, since he'd had them hauled so well the previous day and night, as he was in learning a few salient tidbits about the Chaney brothers.

Puffing the stogie, he peeked back into the barn to check on Boss. Satisfied that Pap was tending the horse properly, giving the mount a good, thorough rubdown, he crossed the street and walked back in the direction from which he'd come. He glanced at the sheriff's window in the courthouse.

A *CLOSED* sign had been hung in the curtained window.

The sheriff must have had enough excitement for one day.

Sartain stepped up onto the broad stoop that fronted the whorehouse. Both windows right of the door had red velvet curtains drawn across them, and more curtains were also drawn across the door's top window panel.

He couldn't hear any noise from inside. Hoping that all the whores, having grown bored with the drama on the street, weren't now slumbering in the mid-afternoon, he tripped the door's latch and stepped inside.

CHAPTER EIGHT

He was instantly met with the fresh-cut timothy smell of marijuana tinged with the ground-cinnamon smell of opium. The room before him was nearly dark save for a foggy red glow from the sun shining through the heavy curtains.

The room lay three steps away from the door, and it was carpeted in wine red with black dragons breathing yellow fire flying and flapping their bat-like wings. The room was a cozy, well-appointed parlor, though its furniture was somewhat in disarray. Three barely dressed girls lounged singly in plush chairs and on couches while two others were entertaining men.

One girl and one man waltzed slowly on the room's far side. A baby grand piano sat under a large oil painting of a naked black girl riding a white horse, but no one was playing it. Judging by the heaviness of the aromatic smoke in the room, the dancers were probably waltzing to music issuing from inside their own heads.

Another girl lay on a sofa, her head in the lap of a rangy, middle-aged cowboy who sat up straight, staring toward Sartain, though it didn't appear the cowboy was seeing much of anything. His watery blue eyes were opaque from the drug coursing through his brain.

The girl lying with her head on his lap was as naked as the day she was born but a whole lot better filled out. She was talking vaguely, softly, as though to herself. Sartain couldn't make out what she was saying. She seemed to be holding a very mundane conversation with herself, and the cowboy had no interest in it whatever.

"Well, lookee here," came a woman's voice, this one deeper, fuller than the girl's voice. "If it ain't the tall drink o' water who tied a knot in Sheriff Chaney's britches!"

The woman strolled toward him from the misty rear of the long room. She was short and fat, and she wore a red negligee that revealed too much of her. She held a wooden cigarette holder in one hand and a delicate wine glass in the other.

Sartain doffed his hat and moved down the stairs, feeling a little awkward bringing his rifle into such a room, but the Henry was a security blanket of sorts. He figured that, with all the men hunting him, he had a right to such security. The woman didn't seem to mind. She drifted over to him, the negligee swishing around her fat, pale body, and smiled up at him.

"Welcome to Nora's, cowboy. Or should I say, welcome to Nora's, Vengeance Man!" She winked and sipped her wine, letting her round, brown eyes trail him up and down.

"Well, I'll be damned if I'm not tired of my reputation precedin' me wherever I go," Sartain said, chagrined. "When did you recognize me?"

"When you fired that first shot with your big LeMat. Very distinctive pistol on a very distinctive man. You're handsomer than I expected. You got you a rakish southern charm. I done read about that in the papers, but them scribblers failed to give your appearance the credit it's due."

"Well, shit, now you got me blushin'. I wish there was a horse apple I could kick."

"I was hopin' you'd find your way to my place, Mr. Revenger. I'll enjoy the notoriety of servicing such a noteworthy and, may I say, *notorious* customer?"

"I'd just as soon you kept my identity under your hat, Miss Nora. Not that it matters overmuch, as the liveryman also called me by name, and I wouldn't know him from Adam's off ox."

"Of course! Indeed!" Nora tapped ashes from her cigarette into the wine glass she'd just drained. "My girls and I pride ourselves on our ability to be discreet, though I must say it would be good for business to know a man of your fame scrubbed his boots on my door mat."

She chuckled and looked him up and down again, puffing on the cigarette. "What's your pleasure? I got me a dozen girls available. Two are down with buns in their oven, so they're out of service and bein' tended by the Chinaman down the street, but the rest are open for business. They're clean as April rain, to boot. I know that for a fact because I just had the local sawbones in here last week, and he had him a good long peek up the pussies of every one!"

She laughed loudly, though it didn't seem to disturb any of the others in the room. In fact, none even seemed to have heard.

"You like 'em young, old, small, fat like myself, or tall like you? I got two with shaved bushes. Got a mulatto with a silver tooth and the softest blowjob lips this side of the Mississippi River."

"Now, Miss Nora," Sartain said, joshing the woman, "how would you know that?"

She laughed again. "Oh, mister, I do love that dew-on-the-Kentucky-bluegrass accent of yours. My second husband talked like that, and he could make me come just by callin' my name. Ha!" She sobered suddenly, almost tearing up, even. "Poor man died in the Little Misunderstandin', don't you know?"

"Many did."

"What kind of a girl would you like this afternoon, Mr. Samuel?" She winked, jovial again and coquettishly pivoting around on her broad hips. "That's what I'll call you: Mr. Samuel."

"Well, Miss Nora, Mr. Samuel's been foggin' the lonely trails of late. How 'bout a girl given to waxin' poetical, or at least one that likes to talk. I like a mattress dance as much as any man, but when you spend as much time alone as I do, it's nice to talk a while afterwards—you know, instead of just donnin' my hat and hittin' the trail again before the bedsprings have stopped singin'."

Nora smiled and blew peppery smoke into his face. "I have just the girl for you. A real talker. And a pretty girl, too. Go on up to our 'honeymoon suite,' but don't let the name spook you into jumpin' out a window. Ha! The name's a joke, but the room's our very best. We reserve it for special guests."

"Like the sheriff?" Sartain didn't want to be nosey right off the bat, especially with Miss Nora, in whom he detected a cunning skepticism, but he couldn't help asking the question.

Nora's right nostril flared, and she turned her mouth corners down. "No, not him! He's over here all the time. Nothin' special about him. I'm just always grateful when he doesn't get drunk and break up the place, just like his brother used to do to my old place. The governor's been to the 'honeymoon suite' more than once."

She chuckled and winked. "Go on up. Third floor, right end of the hall. Frankie will be with you soon. Probably dead asleep, but I'll wake her."

"I do hate to disturb the girl's slumbers, Miss Nora."

"Oh, hell—she'd sleep all day and all night, given her way. They all would. I'll give her some smelling salts. Go, now. Go, Mr. Samuel! There should be some water in the pitcher if you'd like to tidy up a bit. And I keep a good bottle of whiskey up there, as well!"

"Obliged, Miss Nora," Sartain said, lifting his hat to the woman and resting his rifle on his shoulder as he made his way to the stairs at the room's right rear corner.

Climbing the carpeted stairs, Sartain could hear soft sounds rising from around him. Soft female sounds of low talking, water pouring for a bath, the occasional giggle—the sounds of girls likely helping each other prepare themselves for the coming night ahead.

He could smell them, as well. Beneath the natural, subtle, delicious potpourri particular to the sex, he could detect an intoxicating elixir of perfumes and soaps and scented waters, as well as tobacco and marijuana smoke and the incense tang of opium.

As he walked down the third-story hall, crudely paneled in pine and with no carpet on the floor—by the time the jakes got this far, they were no longer paying attention to the furnishings—he ran into a couple of semi-naked girls talking to each other from open doors on opposite sides of the hall.

They immediately stopped talking when they saw the big man in the pinto vest walking the dim hall lit only by a window at each end. One girl wore only a thin pair of lace drawers and a towel over her head. The other was clad in a man's over-sized wool shirt. Spying Sartain, both girls looked him up and down, giving him the critical, suspicious eye.

One twisted a lock of hair around her index finger and said softly, "Hi."

Sartain dipped his chin. "Ladies."

He continued down the hall to the Honeymoon Suite, which was how the plain wooden door was ornately labeled in painted letters across a varnished pine plank. As he turned the doorknob, he glanced back down the hall. Both girls were still looking at him.

"The Honeymoon Suite, eh?" said the one with the towel on her head, in a slightly funning tone. "Who're you?"

"Horse buyer's my guess," said the other girl. "You buy horses, mister? You're damn near as big as a horse."

"How did you know, darlin'?" the Revenger asked, winking. "I don't remember having had the pleasure of your company, and"—he brashly raked her up and down in the same manner both girls had done to him—"I got a feelin' I'd remember."

The girls snorted.

Sartain went into the room and closed the door behind him. It was a large room with a large mountain-lion rug on the varnished oak floor by the four-poster bed. It was nothing like you'd find in one of the better Denver or Cheyenne brothels, but it would do for this far out in the tall and uncut. The air was a little pent up and gamey, he thought, so he pulled the red velvet curtains aside and opened a window to a cool, late afternoon breeze.

He was washing at the washstand when the door clicked. He hadn't heard the door open but only heard it close. The little blond standing there in only a camisole that reached to the tops of her well-turned thighs pressed her back to the door and widened her eyes as she stared at Sartain.

"My, my—what have we here?" The girl was pretty but not beautiful, and her hair was slightly tangled. But she had exotically shaped gray eyes. Her breasts pushing against the cotton camisole were full and pointed. "Sorry—I reckon I shoulda knocked, but Miss Nora said we had a secret guest so I didn't wanna make a big to-do."

Sartain gave a wry snort. So much for secrecy. Probably every girl in the house was talking about the "secret guest" in the Honeymoon Suite.

The girl came toward him, placing one bare foot down in front of the other. She had a sexy way about her—from the swing of her breasts and hips to the playful flashing in her eyes. A farm girl, the Revenger guessed. He'd grown up around farm girls who could curl a boy's hair with their earthy demeanors and practical, untethered approach to lovemaking, and he'd bet the seed bull that Frankie was one of those.

She rubbed her temple against his shoulder. She looked up at him sidelong, narrowing a playfully suspicious eye. "Nora said you wanted to be called Samuel."

She canted her head to indicate down the hall. "Betty thinks you're Jesse James. Henrietta says you're the spitting image of pictures she's seen of Black Bart." Frankie giggled. "Yeah, that's who you are. At least, for tonight. Don't worry—I won't tell, Mr. Bart."

"Thank you, Frankie."

"Ma says you been on the trail a while."

"You can bet the farm on that." Sartain hadn't really been on the trail all that long. Mainly, he'd just been curious, and there was nothing like a doxie to fill him in on the lay of the land. But there was something about this girl he found intoxicating.

"Been a while, has it?"

"A few weeks, yeah." Sartain nuzzled the girl's neck and slid the strap of her camisole off her right shoulder. He slid the other strap off her left shoulder, and the entire garment whispered straight down her body to pile up on the floor around her ankles.

She was indeed beautiful. Pink and plump and beautiful . . .

CHAPTER NINE

Sartain unsnapped the keeper thong from over his LeMat so that the pistol was ready to go in case anyone, namely a bounty hunter or a federal lawman who might have spied him on the street earlier, decided to kick his door down and enter firing.

He had to admit, however, the added danger did add to the allure of the imminent transaction. Nothing like a little extra tension to add a spark or two.

He climbed onto the bed, mounting the girl, who spread her knees for him. She wrapped her arms around him, and, propped on his outstretched arms with elbows locked, he kissed her hungrily. She entangled her tongue with his and then pulled her head back slightly, chuckling.

"You kiss whores, Mr. Bart? Some men don't, you know."

"They're missin' out on the best part."

She giggled again. "I like you, Mr. Bart. Despite how many innocent people you likely robbed, and how many lawmen you probably killed . . . *ohhh*, I like you *indeed!*"

They'd been causing the bedspring to sigh for a long time when the Revenger saw a shadow move under the door. Alarm bells immediately began tolling in his head. He'd been ambushed so many times that part of his brain was always on alert, even when his other senses were otherwise disposed. He kept an eye on the shadow.

It was still under the door.

That meant someone was standing out there.

It could just be one of the other girls, but Sartain couldn't afford to think so.

Despite the distraction of the shadow under the door, he felt his blood rise. He calmly, slowly reached up to slide his LeMat from its holster and lay it beside him and the girl on the bed.

Frankie's eyes were closed, so she didn't notice.

Sartain glanced at the floor beneath the door again. The shadow was still there, setting his nerves on edge. He brushed his lips across Frankie's right ear and whispered.

The girl fell silent and stared up at him, wide-eyed.

Sartain winked and nodded at her.

She glanced toward the door and then threw her head back on the pillow and continued to groan and mewl like a mare with a stallion bucking against her. She flopped around on the bed, making the headboard spank the wall and the leather springs screech like hunting owls.

Meanwhile, Sartain grabbed his LeMat, got off the bed, and walked to the door. Clicking the LeMat's hammer back, he pressed his left shoulder against the wall to the left of the doorframe, nearest the knob. He looked at the floor. The shadow was still there, unmoving.

He frowned, curious.

If the person in the hall was a bushwhacker, what was he waiting for? You couldn't get a man in a much more defenseless position than when he was enjoying a mattress dance.

Frankie continued to mewl and groan and kick her legs and punch the mattress with her fists, doing a damned good imitation of the deed of topic. But then, most whores were good at faking their pleasure, though Sartain doubted she'd been faking the passion of only a minute before. After all, he'd been taught by the best whores in New Orleans, if not all the United States and its territories.

Sartain placed his thumb over the keyhole. A startled gasp

sounded on the other side of the door. He switched the LeMat to his left hand, turned the doorknob, and pulled the door wide. Celeste Chaney stumbled backward, slapping a hand to her chest. Her face was red as burnt clay.

Standing naked in the doorway, Sartain aimed the big LeMat at her, snarling, "You're damn lucky I didn't blow a twelve-gauge wad of buckshot through the door while you were peeping through the keyhole, Miss Chaney. Would you like to come inside and watch? You'd have a better view."

Behind Sartain, Frankie snickered.

"Oh, god!" Celeste said, stammering. "I-I . . . I don't quite know what to say. I was just . . . I was just wondering when you were going to be finished . . . so we could talk, Mr. Sartain."

Behind him, Frankie said incredulously, "Sartain? I thought he was Black Bart!"

"Black who?" Celeste said, looking around Sartain. She was busily trying to keep her eyes off his naked body, and he enjoyed her discomfort. That's why he just stood there—tall and naked and nearly filling the doorway before her.

"I see," Sartain said. "I guess we weren't making enough noise for you." He chuckled and stepped back, while Celeste stood there, hand to her chest above her well-filled corset and looking as though she were about to faint with embarrassment. "My offer stands."

"What offer?"

He lowered the pistol and stepped back into the room. "Come in?"

"Uh . . ." She glanced around. "Oh, well . . . perhaps. I was hoping to speak to you alone."

When she'd stepped into the room, looking straight down at the floor now and toying with the black choker to which was attached a small, gold medallion, Sartain closed the door. "Frankie and I have no secrets."

Celeste looked at the girl now lying on her side on the bed, smiling with interest, her head propped on the heel of her right hand. Her hair was sexily mussed and tangled.

"Oh, no—I'd best come back later." Celeste turned to the door.

"We could chat through the keyhole if it'd make you feel more comfortable."

Celeste swung around, angry, her cheeks turning red all over again. "Oh, damn you! Would you please . . . ?" She let her voice trail off, uncertain as to how to continue. She seemed to want to defend herself but knew deep down there was really no way to explain peeping through a keyhole. Her tongue might as well have been tied in a knot.

She looked at Sartain. He stared back at her, one brow arched. She looked at Frankie. The pretty whore arched her own brow skeptically.

"Don't worry about it," Sartain said, returning the LeMat to its holster. He donned his underwear and sagged into a chair. "We all got our . . . peculiarities."

"I'm mortified," Celeste said quietly, staring at the floor. She held a beaded reticule in both hands, the straps dangling from her left wrist. "There is no defense for what I did. I was voyeuristically watching you couple through the peephole, and you caught me, and that's that."

She swallowed and met Sartain's eyes. "I did come up here to speak to you, Mr. Sartain."

"Does Miss Nora always let folks stroll up here to talk to her customers while said customer is . . . uh . . . bein' entertained?"

"Miss Nora defers to me," Celeste said. "You see, I . . . er, we—the Chaneys—own this place. Nora's own place went bankrupt, so we started this place, and Miss Nora works for my father and brother now."

"Oh, I see," Sartain said. "So you can peep through a keyhole any damn time you want. Ain't that convenient?"

"Mr. Sartain—I have tried to apologize!" Tears of shame dribbled down the young woman's cheeks as she stared in horror at the floor.

"Now look what ya done!" Frankie scolded him.

She crawled off the bed and wrapped an arm around Celeste. "It's all right, Miss Chaney. I don't mind. You can come around here and watch me whenever you like. I know how folks are. We're all sewn from different cuts of cloth, and all that does is make the world more interesting."

Her words seemed to somewhat cheer Celeste, who brushed a hand across her nose and smiled at young Frankie, who was about Celeste's height.

"Why, thank you, Frankie," Celeste said, still blushing. She touched her hand to her temple and looked at Sartain. "Oh, this is just too embarrassing. Perhaps you and I could go somewhere . . . perhaps grab a bite to eat . . . and talk? It really is a very serious matter, Mr. Sartain."

Sartain glanced at Frankie, who shrugged a shoulder. The young doxie was beginning to look bored.

Sartain turned back to Celeste. "All right. But only if you call me Mike."

Celeste smiled.

Sartain and Celeste departed the upper story by a rear stairs. They left the brothel by a rear kitchen door that opened onto a back alley, so that no one in Bittersweet—especially Celeste's brother, the sheriff—would start to suspect where she'd been keeping herself.

"I'd invite you to my father's house for supper, Mike," Celeste said as they made their way around the near-dark street, maintaining a discreet distance from each other, "but I've probably missed supper. We have a wonderful cook, Mrs. Ivan, but my father and brother eat promptly at five. They're probably all wondering where I've been. I'm going to have to make up a story, I'm afraid."

She clapped both hands to her mouth and laughed. "Oh, Lord—what a devil I've become!"

Sartain was puffing a stogie. "Now, now, Celeste, let's forget all that."

"I really should be married, Mr. Sart—I mean, Mike. At my age. Instead, I . . . *oh!*"

"Some girls wait until they're married, but I'll guarantee you that most do not, despite what they might tell you."

"Most? *Really?*"

"Well, maybe not most. But a good many of 'em. I can assure you of that. Especially them who make it for as long as you have without getting hitched. It's a natural act. Nothin' to be ashamed of. That said . . . I reckon we'd best have our discussion and then part ways before someone sees us together."

They were at the edge of town, near where a trail twisted up a crease between barren bluffs. Behind them, the lantern-lit windows of Bittersweet splashed dim yellow and amber light out onto the dusty boardwalks.

Horses at hitchracks stamped and blew. A vagrant breeze shunted a couple of tumbleweeds along the street.

Two pianos could be heard pattering away in separate saloons. The main street was nearly abandoned, most everyone either home or enjoying drinks in one of the town's several watering holes or the doxies in one of the several brothels, though Sartain doubted any man could be having as good a time as the one he'd just enjoyed.

He was exhausted and just wanted to find a hot meal and a pile of hay to slumber in . . .

The Chaney house loomed tall against the starry sky atop one of the bluffs along whose slope the trail meandered.

Celeste placed her hand on his forearm. "Come."

Sartain followed the young woman up the path. About halfway to the house, a wooden bench sat beneath a lone, sprawling oak.

"My father had this placed here some time ago," Celeste said. "He always walked to and from town via the path, and by then he was getting old enough that he needed a place to stop and rest."

She sat on the bench. Sartain looked around to make sure they were alone out here, and then he sat beside her. Somewhere in the dark bluffs around them a couple of coyotes were yammering away, tuning up for the night.

"All right, Celeste. What is it you wanted to visit with me about? I'm assuming it's your brother."

"Oh, yes. I wanted to talk to you about Waylon, all right." Celeste gave a wry snort. "I suppose it's awful crass, the way I've commemorated the day he was killed."

She looked at Sartain. "But Waylon and I were never very close. Just as Warren and I were never very close, though for different reasons. I came late to Bittersweet, as I told you, Mike. For as long as I knew him, Waylon was a tough nut. He was tough all his life, I understand—oddly heartless, mean, and cruel. And he never respected authority. Our father kicked him out of the house when he was fifteen, and he galloped down the wrong path, as they say."

"Became an outlaw?"

"That's right."

"His daughter seems to have loved him. She was pretty broken up."

"She worshipped him, Carleen did. Her mother died when she was quite young, and she fell in love with the romance of her father's lawless early life. Waylon put an end to his outlawry and came back to raise Carleen when Kathy, his wife, died. Kathy was living out on her father's little shotgun ranch, and Waylon took the place over, Kathy's father having preceded her in death. I don't think Carleen ever really got to know her father. That's why she loved the wicked man so."

"Maybe he wasn't so wicked in his later years."

Celeste gave another snort. "Does a zebra change its stripes?

He was wicked, all right. I've heard the stories about him. Even as Warren's deputy sheriff, he was wicked. Often played judge, jury, and executioner right out on the range. At least, the outlaws came to respect him."

"And Warren . . . ?"

"Warren was our father's pride and joy. He was a young George Chaney. He managed our family's ranch before we sold it. The selling of the ranch and the mineral rights to an eastern syndicate made my father quite rich indeed. When we moved into town, Warren ran uncontested for sheriff and won, of course. When Waylon returned and couldn't scratch out much of a living on that little ranch out their near Cobalt Canyon— though he did mine a little gold—Warren hired him as deputy."

"So you had a good brother and a bad brother."

"I guess you could look at it that way, though Warren is far from 'good.' He drinks too much, and he frequents fallen women, though I am no longer one to judge him on that score!"

She laughed. She had a beautiful, rich, throaty laugh. She sagged back on the bench, crossing her long legs beneath her skirt and then leaning forward to entwine her hands around her knee.

"My god—I still can't believe what I just did with you and Frankie." She pondered her misdeed in silence, smiling back at the town.

She shook her head as though to wave away the distraction. "Anyway, yes, Waylon was not a good man. I like to think he was a better man than before he'd left Bittersweet, because he seemed to have done a good job with Carleen, though I've never come to know her very well. I think Waylon turned her against Warren and me.

"You see, Warren gave Waylon a job mostly because he wanted his twin brother on his side. He didn't want him to turn outlaw again, because Waylon had made a formidable outlaw indeed.

Besides, Warren needed a tough deputy, this being a tough country hosting all manner of outlawry. We still have Kiowas and Arapahos running wild off the reservations from time to time and murdering ranch families. And then there's the *banditos* who ride up from Mexico."

"You mentioned that you and Warren didn't get along, either. In what way, if I may ask?"

"That was mostly my fault, I think. I was jealous of Warren for the freedom of his sex. Being a boy, he could do most everything he wanted, while I was pretty much restricted to the house. Also, he was so obviously our father's favorite. But he played himself up to be the favorite, because he knew exactly how he would benefit by being George Chaney's favorite son. As soon as Waylon left, Warren convinced Father to write Waylon out of the will and to make him, Warren, executor of his estate.

"Father started to lose his mind just before Waylon returned, and that played to Warren's benefit. Father no longer had the capacity to consider changing his will to include Waylon as a beneficiary, and Mother was dead by then, from cancer, so she wasn't around to convince him to change it. And, while Father loved me and relied on me, especially after he started losing his memory, he never respected me enough to listen to me about anything regarding business or legal matters."

"So Warren had his brother written out of the will and didn't want him written back in even after Waylon returned and led a somewhat straight-and-narrow life—despite some loose interpretations of the law."

"Oh, god—those two boys were always at odds with each other. No, Warren would never have wanted Waylon to get a dime. Warren had given Waylon a job—and he loved being his brother's boss, believe me!—but he would have died before he'd have allowed Waylon to be written back into our father's will!"

"Then why shoot Waylon? Why go to the trouble?"

Celeste sighed, shook her head. "I don't think Warren would do that. I know they hated each other, and I think Warren worried that Waylon was getting too big for his britches, acquiring too much power. But I just don't think Waylon would shoot his twin brother." She shuttled a beseeching look at the Revenger. "But I'd like to know for sure. Would you look into it for me?"

"How did you know who I was?"

"I recognized you the minute I saw you. I'm pretty much homebound, taking care of Father and all, despite that we hired a private nurse for him a few weeks ago to take some of the strain off me. He's virtually bed-bound these days and recognizes no one, including me. In other words, I have plenty of time to read." She gave a sheepish shrug. "Mostly dime novels and illustrated magazines, I'm afraid."

"I see." Sartain removed his hat and twirled it on his finger. "Then I reckon you know that I ride mainly for revenge, Celeste. I'm not a private detective. I kill for a living. Kill for those who can't kill for themselves."

"All right." Celeste nodded. "I will pay you one thousand dollars—if I can get into Father's safe, that is—to exact justice for my brother's killing. True, Waylon and I never got along. But they say blood is thicker than water, and I think that's true. I would like to see the coward who killed my brother—shot him in the back—dead!"

"What if it's . . . ?"

"Warren?" Celeste stared at Sartain, pensive. Then she said resolutely, "Then my brother deserves to die for killing his twin."

Sartain whistled and looked at the young beauty in a whole different light. "That's a tall order of revenge for such a sheltered woman, Miss Chaney."

"I may be sheltered, Mr. Sartain, but I'm still a Chaney. That means I have a good bit of ruthlessness in me, as well. Ruthlessness as well as . . . craven desires." She looked off, apparently thinking it through, the breeze playing with her hair.

Finally, she looked at Sartain once more. "No—whoever shot Waylon Chaney deserves to die. If that's Warren Chaney, so be it."

"Were they identical twins, Celeste?"

"Yes. About as identical as twins can get. In fact, for years the only way my mother could tell them apart was Waylon had a bright red birthmark—a stork's kiss, she called it—on the very back of his neck." She smiled pensively as she touched the back of her own neck. Finally, she rose. "I'd best be getting home. I . . . I don't know quite how to thank you for . . . earlier."

"Thank me?" Sartain chuckled, took Celeste in his arms, and pressed his lips to her forehead. "Thank you."

"I wish I could invite you up to the house. My father wouldn't know, but his nurse would, and it would be all over town by sunrise. Warren might be there, as well. He usually has supper with Father and me, and sometimes he sits with Father for a while afterwards, but mostly he goes over the ledger books in Father's study."

"No need to apologize. I'll look into Waylon's murder and get back to you."

Celeste threw her arms around the Cajun and kissed him. Then she gave him a bright, parting smile, the starlight and lamplight from Bittersweet dancing in her eyes. She swung around and continued on up the trail toward the large house sitting like a jewel against the night sky.

Sartain relit his cigar, rested his Henry on his shoulder, and headed down the trail in the direction from which he and Celeste had come. He'd look for a hotel and get a good night's sleep. He needed it after today. Tomorrow he'd get started investigating Waylon Chaney's murder, not only for Celeste but also to satisfy his own natural curiosity.

He walked into the ragged, dark outskirts of Bittersweet, puffing the stogie and thinking through the Chaney situation. He was hugging the street's left side, habitually letting the shadows of the buildings conceal him. He'd just stepped down off the boardwalk fronting a barbershop when a light flashed ahead and to his right.

He'd recognize the flash of a gun anywhere, anytime.

The rifle cracked wickedly a half second later, on the heels of the flash.

Sartain stopped, tucked the stogie into the corner of his mouth, pumped a live round into the Henry's action, and fired at the spot he'd seen the flash. A man yelped. At the same time, another gun flared and barked straight ahead of Sartain. The man ahead and left yelped again, and there was the creaking thud of a body falling on a shake-shingled roof.

The gun ahead of Sartain blazed again, barking loudly. The bullet curled the air inches from Sartain's right ear before it smashed into an awning support post over the Revenger's right shoulder. He cursed, ejected the spent cartridge, seated a fresh one in the chamber, and fired at the gun flash straight ahead of him. He fired two more times, the empty cartridge casings arching over his shoulder and pinging onto the boardwalk fronting the barbershop.

Beneath the Henry's roars, Sartain heard a man curse. Boots thudded and spurs chinked. A shadow flicked in the darkness near where the gun had flashed. The shooter had bolted down a break between buildings.

Sartain pumped another round into the Henry's action and took off running. He didn't like running in the dark where men lurked who were out to kill him. The thing about stalking a man in the darkness—you had to take your time so you didn't walk into a bullet.

He jogged a block, squinting into the darkness ahead of him.

He was vaguely aware of men shouting in the distance around him—likely saloon patrons who'd heard the gunfire. When he kicked what must have been the ambusher's cartridge casing against an awning support post, he turned into the next dark alley mouth and quickly dropped to one knee, half expecting another gun flash, another bullet hurtling toward him.

The shot didn't come. Sartain jogged down the alley, gritting his teeth when he kicked an empty airtight tin or got a spur caught on a tumbleweed. He ran out of the alley and found himself in a relative clearing backing up to the rear of the main street buildings. There were a couple of what looked like stables and stock pens back here, and one lone, dark, log cabin hunched low to the ground—likely an old prospector's shack.

The shack's tin roof reflected the starlight.

Gravel crunched somewhere around the shack. A boot clipped a rock, and a spur chimed softly. The sounds had come from the shack's far side.

Sartain jerked forward. His own spurs rang. Quickly, he kicked out of his boots, picked up both boots in his left hand, and then ran toward the shack in his stocking feet, wincing at the pebbles and thorns nibbling at him.

He stopped at the far front corner, edged a look around to the other side. A man-shaped shadow was just then turning the corner to walk behind the shack. Sartain set both boots down carefully, so the spurs wouldn't ring, and ran silently to the rear of the shack and around to the other side.

He could see the ambusher moving away from him, toward the front of the shack. The man moved slowly. He'd heard Sartain's spur ring before the Revenger had removed his boots, and he was keying on that sound.

Sartain strode quickly forward. He slowed when his quarry stopped at the shack's front corner and aimed a rifle straight out ahead of him, sliding the barrel this way and that, looking for the man he'd tried to dry-gulch. His back was squarely facing Sartain, who came up behind the man and rammed his Henry's forestock soundly against the back of the man's right knee.

The man screamed, triggered his rifle into the ground before him, and dropped to both knees. He twisted around, trying to bring his carbine around as well. Sartain stepped forward and rammed the Henry's brass butt plate against the man's left cheek. There was a solid smacking sound.

"Oh!" the ambusher said, falling back on his butt and dropping his rifle. He wobbled on his hips, dazed, raising one heavy hand to his face. "Oh—*Christ!*"

A five-pointed star winked on his paisley vest.

"Not even close, Sheriff," Sartain said through a growl. "But you're about to see the pearly gates, you son of a gutless bitch."

CHAPTER ELEVEN

Warren Chaney froze as he stared up at the big man towering over him. The sheriff had lost his hat, but his face was shadowed. Starlight gleamed in his dark hair, off his eyeballs, and off the brighter threads in his fancy vest.

"You," Chaney said. "Christ—I should've known it was you. The Revenger! I realized who you were after we parted ways this afternoon." He spread his arms, palms out in supplication. "Well, you gonna finish me?"

"Finish *you*?" Sartain chuckled, letting the Henry go slack in his hand but keeping it generally trained on the sheriff. "I didn't start this thing, you son of a bitch. You're the one who took a shot at *me* back there."

Chaney didn't say anything for a second. "Didn't you take a shot at *me*?"

"I was shooting at the fella on the other side of the street. He shot at you. Then *you* shot at *me*."

"Who was he?"

"I figured you'd know."

"I figured you were in with him. But that was before I knew it was you, Sartain, gunnin' for me. Everyone knows you work alone."

"I wasn't gunnin' for you, Chaney."

"That what you say!" The sheriff was fingering the cut Sartain's brass butt plate had gouged beneath his left eye. "Christ, I think you damn near busted my face!"

82

Running footsteps sounded. Sartain saw a thick man running down the same gap between buildings that he and Chaney had taken. The big man stopped suddenly and extended a long gun from his right side. "Hold it right there!"

Raising his Henry slightly toward Chaney's chest, Sartain said quietly, "Call off your bulldog, Sheriff."

Chaney glanced over his left shoulder. "Hold up, Amos. It's me. And Sartain," he added, looking up angrily at the big man before him.

"Sartain, huh?"

"Nice to see you again, Amos."

"Screw you!"

"Ouch."

Chaney slowly heaved himself to his feet, digging a handkerchief out of a back trousers pocket and holding it to his bloody cheek. "Someone bushwhacked me," he told his deputy, who was slowly walking up, holding his Greener at port arms. "I thought the Revenger here was in on it. Maybe cashin' in on that bounty my charming niece put on my head."

"How do you know he wasn't?" the big deputy asked. He was fifteen feet away, but Sartain could smell the sour sweat stench of the man.

"I don't. But under the circumstances"—Chaney glanced at Sartain's rifle—"I reckon I'll have to take his word for it. For now," he added, threateningly. He glanced at McCluskey. "Did you see the other shooter?"

"Yeah, he's lyin' in the street in front of the millinery. Bone Mitchell from the Triple L-Connected."

"Ah. Should have known *he'd* try to take Carleen up on her offer. The little bitch. Mitchell was always more outlaw than cow puncher." Chaney looked at Sartain. "You mind if I walk back to my office? I need a shot of whiskey to quiet the dog yappin' in my cheek. I might have an extra one, if you'd care to join me."

Sartain shrugged and lowered the Henry's barrel, depressing the hammer to the half-cock position.

"I'm going to pick up my carbine," Chaney said.

"Go ahead. Just don't cock it or aim it at me. Amos, you can lower them two rabbit ears on that Greener, too."

"Go to hell, Sartain!" the big, belligerent deputy fairly shouted. "You got a two-thousand-dollar bounty ridin' on your head!"

"If you'd like to try and claim it, do it now, or lower those hammers and shut up about it, or I'll gut shoot you and leave you here, howlin'."

Amos glowered at Sartain.

Chaney picked up his carbine. Dusting it off against his pants, he turned to his deputy. "Go on an' haul Mitchell off the street. Take him over to the undertaker's and then continue on with your rounds. If you see anyone else in town who you think might try to collect on Carleen's five hundred dollars, let me know. Don't try to take 'em down alone. You're my last deputy, and I hate the hirin' process."

"You got it, Boss." Amos lowered the Greener's hammers and sauntered off through the dark alley.

Sartain followed Chaney along the alley and over to the courthouse. The sheriff dabbed sullenly at his cheek. He carried his carbine low in one hand. He looked the picture of dejection. A whipped, angry dog. Sartain wasn't going to let his guard down. Such dogs were often the most dangerous.

Sartain followed the man into the courthouse and then through the first door on the right side of the hall. In the sheriff's office, Sartain watched as Chaney sat down heavily in the swivel chair flanking a flat-topped, cluttered desk sporting a low-burning Rochester lamp with a red chimney. The door to the cell block stood in the wall behind the desk. It had a small, barred window in it.

Chaney turned up the lamp's wick, spreading a warm glow across the sparsely furnished room, which smelled of Amos Mc-Cluskey's sour sweat, whiskey, and gun oil.

"Christ, this is gonna leave a goddamn scar," Chaney said, still dabbing at the cut on his cheek and jerking open a desk drawer. He not only dressed like a Fancy Dan, but he had that air about him. "You like to have killed me."

"Well, then, I reckon I'd be five hundred dollars richer." Sartain sank into a Windsor chair against the wall to the right of the office's closed door, near a gun rack with a chain drawn through the trigger guards of all the rifles and two Schofield revolvers.

"I reckon you would." Chaney pulled a glass out of the same drawer from which he'd drawn a half-empty bottle. He hauled another glass down from a stack of "Wanted" dodgers on top of what appeared to be bound county tax ledgers and splashed whiskey in both glasses, half filling each. "You want any water."

"I done had a bath."

Chaney slid the glass across the desk. Sartain rose, sat with a hip on the front edge of the desk, and lifted the glass. He sniffed, able to tell by the fragrance it was of the top-shelf variety.

"You drink well way out here," he said, sipping.

Chaney threw half his own drink back and set the glass on the desk. As he dabbed an end of the handkerchief into the glass, he said, "What were you doing out on the street this time of the night?"

Sartain figured that Chaney hadn't been up to his father's house. Otherwise, he would have known his sister had been late for supper, and he probably would have suspected she'd been out with Sartain. Sartain didn't care what the man thought about him, but that wouldn't have been in Celeste's best interest. He didn't want to get the young woman into trouble.

"I was looking for a hot meal and a soft bed. If I'd been gunning for you, you'd be dead."

"Why are you still here?"

"Because a lot of men died to make this a free country."

"You're curious, ain't ya? Curious about my brother."

"Yes, I am."

"Why?"

"Because I'm the curious sort." Sartain drew a fresh cigar from the breast pocket of his shirt, bit off the end, spat the end on the floor, and touched the tip of the stogie to the chimney of the Rochester's lamp, lighting it. "I hear you and your brother were like night and day." He rolled the cigar tip against the chimney, lighting the edges and puffing smoke. "Him bein' night and you bein' day."

Chaney scowled as he dabbed at the cut with his whiskey-dampened handkerchief. "Who told you that?"

"Some old coot in a saloon this afternoon. Didn't catch his name."

"Yeah? So? We didn't get along. That doesn't mean I killed him, and who are you to be asking me these questions, anyway?"

"Why did you give him a job?"

"Because he was my brother and he needed one."

"Some think you killed him because you thought he was getting too big for his britches, that he was a tougher lawdog than you, and he was showing you up."

"Hogwash. He was a tough son of a bitch—that's true. But I wouldn't kill my twin brother; I couldn't do that." Chaney chuckled ruefully. "*He* could have done that. Waylon could have done that to me. But I couldn't have killed my own brother. Shot him the back? Hell, no!"

"Who do you think did it, then?"

"I don't know. He was out looking for claim jumpers around

Cobalt Canyon. Them claim jumpers could have ganged up on him. But, shit, there's owlhoots of every stripe around here. Throw a rock and you'll hit a likely candidate."

Sartain puffed the stogie, sipped his drink. "Have you been investigatin'?"

Chaney threw the handkerchief down on his desk and sipped his own drink. "No, but I'll head out there tomorrow, have a look around."

"You don't sound too urgent about it."

Chaney cursed loudly. "I give you a belt of my good whiskey, and you just sit there blowin' smoke at me and accusin' me of killin' my own brother. If I ride out there now, someone'll likely follow me an' bushwhack me for that damned bounty my lovely niece put on me head! Now I'm tired of explainin' things to a man with a two-thousand-dollar federal bounty on *his* head, so, if you'll forgive me, I'd like to call it an evening!"

"I understand." Sartain threw back the last of his drink and donned his hat. "Thanks for the whiskey. Went down smooth."

"You're welcome. Now, are you gonna leave town tomorrow?"

Sartain sauntered to the door, picked up his rifle, and rested it on his shoulder. "No. Can you recommend a good restaurant? I'd prefer a quiet place that knows how to properly cook a steak."

"Yeah, there's a place like that down in Juarez. Pablo's. It's on the main drag. A little pink adobe. You can't miss it. If you leave tonight you'll be there in three days!"

Sartain pinched his hat brim to the angry lawman. "All right, then. Good night, Sheriff. Be seein' you around."

"Jump yourself, Sartain!" the Revenger heard the man bellow as he left the courthouse and stepped into the street.

He did find an eatery that served a satisfying steak and beans even at this late hour. It was on a side street near the Mexican brothel from which loud voices emanated, including the jeering laughter of women.

A couple of gunshots sounded, but Sartain didn't doubt that they, too, came from the brothel. There was a three-piece band playing over there, as well, and it only wavered a little at the gunfire.

The middleaged gent with a handlebar mustache who ran the eatery even served Sartain a nice ale to wash the steak and beans down with. The proprietor stooped to peer out the front window at the brothel and rolled a stove match from one side of his mouth to the other, shaking his head. "Now that Waylon Chaney's dead, them greasers think they can get away with whatever they want."

He cursed and straightened.

"Oh? They're not afraid of Warren and Amos?" Sartain said between mouthfuls of steak and beans.

"Hell, no. Waylon, now, he was keepin' a cork on the Mexican side of town. He never cared much for Mescins and he didn't mind the Mescins knowin' it, neither. Ah, shit—why worry about it? Nothin' I can do. I just hope Warren can hire another deputy half as good as his brother was."

The proprietor started to walk back to his kitchen behind a louvered door but stopped when Sartain swallowed a mouthful and said, "You think Warren killed his brother like his niece thinks?"

The man thought about that, chewing the stove match. "Nah. Warren doesn't have the balls. He might have sent Amos, though. Ah, hell—I'm not gonna worry about it. All I can do is get up every morning an' put my shoes on an' fetch firewood to start the range. I can't worry about things that are out of my control!" He pushed a shoulder against the kitchen door, stopped, and glanced back over his shoulder at Sartain. "And hope I don't get shot by a stray bullet fired from over in that greaser brothel!"

He canted his head to indicate a bullet hole in the wall to his left.

"That one missed by a snake's whisker."

He disappeared into the kitchen, and Sartain could hear him knocking pans around and cursing.

After the meal, tired and weary, Sartain went over to the Federate Livery & Feed Barn, which was closed at this late hour but not locked. He opened a big front door and slipped inside, climbed up into the hayloft with his Henry and his bedroll, and slept like the proverbial dead dog, occasionally half waking when he heard gunfire from the Mexican side of town.

CHAPTER TWELVE

In Cobalt Canyon the next day, Sartain saw the sun flash in the corner of his right eye, and, having seen similar flashes before and knowing what nine out of ten of them meant, he kicked free of his stirrups and hurled himself over Boss's right wither.

He hit the ground hard on his right shoulder with an anguished grunt. At the same time, a bullet screeched through the air over Boss's saddle and hammered a boulder with a wicked-sounding *spang!*

As the rifle's flat report reached his ears, Sartain heaved himself to his feet, jerked his Henry out of his saddle scabbard, and yelled, "High-tail it, Boss!"

The buckskin didn't need to be told twice. As Sartain racked a round into the Henry's action and dove behind a boulder, the horse reared, whinnied shrilly, and bolted off down the trail in the direction from which he and Sartain had come. Another bullet blasted against the side of the boulder the Revenger had just dived behind, the ambusher's echoing report following a half second later.

Sartain gained his knees and picked up his hat. He ran out from behind the boulder to another one and then immediately began climbing the side of a low, boulder-strewn escarpment that formed a wall of the narrow chasm. The ambusher fired two more rounds, but both bullets flew well short of the man's quarry, which meant the son of a bitch had lost track of Sartain amongst the cabin-sized boulders comprising the slopes of

Cobalt Canyon.

The chasm was appropriately named, the Revenger had seen when he and Boss had first ridden into it, following the directions of the liveryman, Pap Chisolm, back in Bittersweet. The chasm itself was all dull yellows and burnt oranges of wind- and sun-blasted basalt sculpted as if by a mad god entertaining himself. But the sky hanging over the fissure high in the Davis Mountains was a velvety, flawless, cobalt blue.

The sky appeared close enough that a man could rip some of the blue out of it by just reaching up with his hand, and deep enough that it made him feel giddy, as though it were trying to suck him out of his boots and send him reeling into the cosmos beyond it. It was like staring into an ocean above his head.

The sun and heat pulsated off the rocks around Sartain, who was hunkered now in a niche on the shoulder of the scarp, overlooking the canyon floor, a winding ribbon of flood-scalloped sand littered with the glowing, white bones of recent cattle and deer and, most likely, ancient dinosaurs, whose bones were forever being carved from the rock by spring storms.

On the opposite ridge, which was as rocky as the one Sartain occupied, and tufted with short, wiry brush and stunt oaks and creosote shrubs, a man moved out from behind a wagon-sized, flat-topped boulder and scurried behind another one. The Revenger raised his rifle but jerked it back down to avoid the same sort of sun flash that had given his attacker away.

The man was out of sight.

With the fleeting glimpse and the sun glare, it had been hard to tell much about him. He appeared to be wearing a brown hat and a checked shirt, which told Sartain next to nothing about him.

The Revenger snaked his rifle around the right side of his covering boulder. Squinting through the sun glare, he made out a rifle barrel bristling from the top of the boulder the sharpshooter had ducked behind. Sartain fired three quick shots, watching his first bullet blast rock dust from the front of the boulder, just beneath the son of a bitch's rifle barrel.

The rifle barrel was pulled back out of sight, and Sartain's second and third shots blew more rock dust from the face of the boulder. Sartain bounded out from behind his own boulder, ran through a narrow channel curving up the escarpment, and then ran down the other side.

He was in the open here as he made his way toward the canyon floor, and his assailant soon found him.

Lead hammered behind him. One clipped his left spur and nudged his heel. Sartain went to ground behind a low hump of sand and gravel from which a sotol jutted like a quieting finger, and the shooting stopped.

He looked at his left spur. It was missing a point from its rowel.

Sartain whistled. Three inches closer and he'd be sporting a hole through his ankle. Whoever was out to get him—a bounty hunter, possibly a lawman who'd picked up his trail in Bittersweet, or maybe Warren Chaney himself—was a damned good shot. Sartain would have to tread carefully.

He removed both spurs and stuck them in his back pocket, where they wouldn't jangle.

He racked a fresh round into the Henry's breech. He picked up a rock a little larger than his fist and lobbed it down the slope. As the bushwhacker fired at the movement, Sartain whipped his Henry up over the top of the gravelly mound, picked out the dark rifle barrel and the pale oval face beneath the brown hat, and cut loose with three more quick shots, the Henry belching, the empty cartridge casings winging out over his right shoulder and pinging onto the rocks behind him.

Amidst his own thundering shots, he heard a man yell. The rifle, the face, and the hat disappeared behind a boulder about halfway up the opposite ridge shrouded by the throbbing glare of the sun.

Sartain wasted no time in hightailing it out from behind the gravelly mound. He sprinted downhill, following a winding course between boulders and brush snags. Near the bottom of the canyon, he stopped behind a block-like boulder and glanced up the slope toward where he'd last seen the shooter.

There was a high, eerie sounding whisper.

The bullet hammered into the boulder with an angry, snarling crash, blowing sharp rock slivers and dust every which way. Sartain cursed and ducked his head, squeezing his right eye closed against dust that had slipped behind his eyelid. That eye burned, watered. The shards peppered his hat and his pinto vest.

"You son of a bitch," he raked out, blinking his burning eye.

The ambusher's rifle spoke twice more. The bullets hammered the face of Sartain's covering boulder. The Revenger snaked his own rifle over the top of the boulder, fired twice, then ran straight to his left.

He slipped behind another boulder and then ran from behind that boulder and into the flood-scalloped sand at the canyon bottom. Sensing a bead being drawn on him, he stopped suddenly and was instantly glad he did.

A slug screeched through air where he would now be standing if he hadn't stopped and blew a branch off the madrone tree to his left and behind him. He jerked the Henry up and fired at the puff of gray smoke still dancing in the sunshine. He pulled the rifle back down and ran up the ridge, meandering in the general direction of the ambusher.

He took his time now, moving slowly, twisting his way through the large rocks and humps of sand and spidery shrubs and cacti. No shots rang out from above. That made him wonder if he hadn't wounded the man too badly for him to continue the fusillade, or even killed him.

He'd prefer the former. He wanted to know why the coward was after him.

There was also the possibility the man was waiting for him in silence.

Sartain moved even more slowly.

He stopped beneath a slanted ceiling of basaltic rock and peered out from beneath the overhang, stretching his glance up the broken slope. He saw what he thought was the boulder the shooter had last used as cover.

There was no movement. The only sounds around him were the monotonously whining cicadas. Occasionally a hot, dry breath of breeze scratched dry brush together or there was the soft padding of a kangaroo rat.

The air was as hot as a cookshack at noon.

Sartain dropped to a knee. He leaned his rifle against that knee, doffed his hat, and ran a hand through his thick, sweat-damp hair. His heart beat slowly but heavily.

Was the ambusher waiting for him up there? Or maybe the man, having a better vantage from the high ground, had slipped down around him.

Maybe he was moving up behind him.

Sartain glanced over his right shoulder. His heartbeat quickened when a round, white-faced Montezuma quail slipped out from behind a rock and disappeared behind a clump of Spanish bayonet. Sartain drew a deep breath, calming himself.

Then he quietly slipped the Henry's loading rod from the tube beneath the barrel and filled the rod from his cartridge belt. When he'd snapped the rod back into place and locked it, he moved from beneath the slanting roof of rock and continued slowly up the narrow channel between boulders and humps of sand and gravel and the occasional twisted gray oak with its dusty leaves buffeting lightly in the hot breeze.

The large, teardrop shaped boulder from which the shooter had last fired at him grew slowly ahead and above him. A sotol fingered up at its left side.

Even more slowly, Sartain approached the boulder, expecting to see a rifle jut toward him from either side. His own rifle was aimed straight out from his right shoulder, and he slid the barrel from left to right and back again.

His muscles were coiled like a snake's. He was ready to aim and squeeze the trigger.

He moved up the slope and around the boulder's left side. Crouching, he jerked the barrel toward the backside of the boulder.

The shooter wasn't there.

Sartain looked around carefully. He looked up slope and down and to both sides, his muscles still drawn taut and ready to spring. When he saw no imminent danger, he walked into the niche between the teardrop boulder and the slope rising steeply behind it. On the ground were several fresh scuff marks and four empty cartridge casings. A small patch of blood stained the sand near one of the casings. The casing had a couple of crimson spots on it, as well.

A shadow slid over the casing.

Sartain's muscles uncoiled instantly. Crouching low, he aimed the Henry high and fired. The man standing atop a boulder thirty feet above him flinched. The rifle the man was aiming from his thick right shoulder jerked slightly to Sartain's right. Smoke and flames stabbed from the barrel, just ahead of the crashing report.

The bullet slammed into the teardrop boulder two feet to Sartain's right, spraying rock shards and dust.

The man grunted and stumbled backward nearly out of Sartain's field of vision. Then the man stumbled back into it and dropped to his knees. The rifle fell from his hands, clattered onto the steep slope, and fishtailed toward Sartain.

Clutching his chest, the shooter leaned forward. He rolled over the edge of the boulder he knelt on. He turned one complete somersault in the air and was just starting another one when he struck the incline with a grunt, pluming dust. He rolled wildly. His head and shoulders struck a boulder, and then he was sliding feet-first down the slope.

Fifteen feet above Sartain, he turned again and rolled to within six feet of the Cajun's boots.

Amos McCluskey lay on his back, groaning and wagging his head slowly as blood pumped out of his chest. More blood oozed thickly from both corners of his mouth. His gold front teeth glistened in the sunlight.

Sartain walked up to him and stared down at the fast-dying deputy.

"Chaney send you?"

McCluskey's eyelids fluttered. Then they stopped fluttering, and he stared up at Sartain. Slowly, a smile twisted his thin, cruel mouth. "Yeah," he said.

"You damn fool."

McCluskey blinked once. "No more than you are."

"What's that supposed to mean?"

"You'll know soon enough," the deputy spat out, blood dribbling down his chin.

He smiled again, and then his fleshy, bloody chest fell still, and his eyes turned opaque but just as mocking as before.

CHAPTER THIRTEEN

Sartain found Amos McCluskey's horse tethered to some brush in a notch canyon not far from where the man had died. The Revenger tied McCluskey's corpse belly down across his saddle, tied the mount's reins to the saddle horn, and fired his LeMat over the beast's head.

The copper-bottom dun lunged down the canyon floor, heading in the general direction of Bittersweet. It would likely be back in town within the hour, and Chaney or someone else could see to the bushwhacker's disposal. Sartain hoped the body would send a message to Chaney and others who thought bushwhacking him was a good idea.

Boss had returned to his rider's side when Sartain had whistled for him, and now the Revenger and the big stallion continued to walk along the floor of Cobalt Canyon, looking for the spot where Waylon Chaney had been shot in the back. That's what Sartain had been doing when McCluskey had thrown that first slug at him—looking for blood.

He'd been looking around for over an hour, and he'd found nothing—no blood, no scuffmarks, no cartridge casings, nothing.

Now, after another hour of searching, he still found no sign to indicate where Waylon Chaney had been shot.

He'd thought there might be a chance he could track the killer from the spot of the shooting. But while Cobalt Canyon was not an overly large piece of ground, it was a rugged one.

His chances had been slim, and now he realized the only way he'd be able to find the spot would be to ask Chaney's daughter. He hadn't wanted to involve the grief-stricken girl, but if he was going to find out for Celeste who had killed her brother, the girl's father, there was no other way.

He'd learned in town that Waylon Chaney's small ranch was less than two miles north of Cobalt Canyon. Sartain followed the snaking trail through more rugged country—low buttes tufted with sage and cactus and sparse clumps of fescue—and up a gradual rise toward a steep ridgeline. A few longhorn cattle grazed here and there around him in the distance, most clinging to the sparse shade of lone post oaks or rock outcroppings.

Sartain had also learned in town that the ridgeline he was heading for was known as Owl Mountain. Now the mountain was catching low, dark, fast-scudding clouds as a storm moved in from the west. As Sartain continued along the trail, he occasionally heard the rumbling of distant thunder. Cloud shadows swept the country around him, and a fresh breeze was rising.

He topped a plateau and saw the ranch straight ahead of him, dwarfed by the tan, rocky bluffs around it and the ridge looming behind it. If he hadn't known it was out here, he wouldn't have seen it yet, for it was just a single mud cabin and mud barn flanking what appeared to be a rickety windmill.

There were a couple of connected rail corrals and an orchard fence, and that was all. The entire place looked the size of a postage stamp amidst the rugged country stretching all around it and the cobalt sky arching over it.

There was a low rise to the right of the ranch yard, and, as Sartain and Boss kept moving toward the cabin, he saw a wagon parked at the bottom of the rise. A saddled horse stood behind the wagon, its head down. A few minutes later he saw two figures atop the rise, under a couple of mesquites and post oaks whose branches nodded in the rising breeze.

Sartain turned Boss toward the rise, and soon he saw the girl, Chaney's black-haired daughter, sitting on a rock on the rise.

She watched the stocky Mexican, whom she'd called Vicente in town the day before, shovel dirt onto what was most likely a grave—her father, Waylon Chaney's, grave. The girl rose from the rock and adjusted a makeshift cross poking out of the ground at the head of the mound.

Vicente stopped shoveling and stood leaning on his shovel, staring down at the grave. The girl did, as well, the rising wind blowing her black hair around her head.

Vicente turned his head toward Sartain. Then the girl did, as well. Sartain stopped Boss near the wagon and stared up the rise at the girl and Vicente, who stared down at him. They were a somber looking pair, and Sartain wished he hadn't come here now, when they were just finishing burying the girl's father. He wished he had waited until later.

But he was here now, so he might as well stay and find out what he could as delicately as he could.

The beefy sorrel tied to the wagon gave a whinny at the newcomers, and Boss returned the greeting in kind. The horse in the wagon's traces nodded its head and switched its tail.

The girl and the stocky Mexican set rocks from a pile they'd gathered over the grave, to keep predators away. The girl slapped her hands together, dusting them off, and smacked dust from the thighs of her denim pants. She started down the hill toward the wagon, the stocky Mexican following, the shovel resting on his shoulder.

"I'm sorry," Sartain said as she neared the bottom of the hill. "I didn't mean to intrude."

"You're not intruding, Mr. Sartain. We were just finishing up." Carleen Chaney stopped to lean against the side of the wagon and glanced at the Mexican walking up behind her. "Neither one of us are much good at funerals, I'm afraid. Vicente knows the Lord's Prayer, so he said it, and that's that."

She brushed tears from her cheeks with the backs of her hands and shook her head, trying to be tough.

Vicente set his shovel in the wagon and looked at the sky, over which dark clouds were sliding quickly, catching and tearing at each other. "I'd best be getting back to town," he told the girl, placing his hands on her shoulders and giving her a sympathetic squeeze.

"You're gonna get caught in it," she warned.

"If so, I'll hole up. Gotta get back to town. Work to do. I'll be out to check on you again in a couple of days." Vicente pulled his straw *sombrero* up from where it had been hanging down his back, set it on his head, and heaved his heavy bulk into the sorrel's saddle, the leather squawking beneath his weight. He gigged the horse ahead and glanced once more at the girl. "You sure you want to stay out here all by yourself, Carleen?"

"Where else would I go?"

"You could come and stay with me."

"In that bear den you call a cabin?" She dipped her chin and smiled wryly.

Vicente chuckled. "Invitation's open." He looked at Sartain. "You the Revenger?"

"That's what they call me."

The Mexican pondered this, and then he nodded and canted his head toward Carleen. "If anyone needs revenge now, it's her. That bastard killed her pa."

His fleshy, mustached face turned ruddy with anger. Vicente turned the sorrel around and batted his mule-eared boots against its sides, heading for the trail.

Somberly, Carleen watched him go. "My pa's best friend," she said, the first raindrops falling, her black hair snaking around both sides of her face in the wind. "They knew each other since they were just boys . . . ridin' roughshod around these parts. They both settled down at about the same time. After Ma died, Vicente helped raise me." She chuckled. "If you could call it 'raising.' "

She looked at Sartain. "Would you like a drink, Mr. Sartain? My Pa always kept a few jugs of mescal around. Set store by it, in fact. Called it his 'medicine.' "

Sartain winced and reached around to the small of his back. "I do feel a mite on the creaky side."

"Follow me. You can stable your horse yonder. There's parched corn. Then we'll go on over to the cabin, and I'll fix you up." She gave him a warm smile and then climbed into the wagon, her taut denims caressing her firm rump and well-turned thighs.

When he'd tended Boss and turned the stallion into Carleen's corral, Sartain followed her back to the cabin and sat on the porch while she went inside to fix a couple of drinks.

She came out a few minutes later no longer wearing her man's checked wool shirt and skintight denims and stockmen's boots. She wore instead a plain but nicely formfitting cambric frock—cream with pale-blue flowers that matched the deep blue of her eyes. Her hair was freshly brushed to a high shine as it flowed across her shoulders and hung down to the small of her back.

Beneath the hem of her dress, Sartain could see that she was wearing low-heeled black shoes and frilly stockings.

Sartain stared up at her in surprise as she handed him a tumbler half-filled with the colorless mescal. She did not return his gaze, but he could tell by the flush sitting high in her perfect cheeks that she was aware of his scrutiny.

She sat in the string-bottom chair to the left of his own. He

101

assumed she and her father had sat out here in these very chairs, probably to watch the late-summer afternoon rain come down as it was falling now, the small drops tossed by the fresh breeze that smelled of sage and brimstone.

It was not as violent a storm as the one a few days ago. The thunder merely rumbled and lightning flashed in the northwestern distance as the bulk of the storm bypassed the ranch. The droplets fell to curl the dust of the hard-packed yard.

Carleen sipped her drink and shook her hair back from her cheeks. "So, tell me, Mr. Sartain: what brings you out here? Not that I mind, of course. At such a time it's nice to have company, though I can't say I was expecting a man of your fame."

"Or infame, as the case might be," he corrected her.

"Possibly to some. But not to folks like myself who've been wronged." She took another sip of the mescal and turned to him. "Are you here to look into my father's murder?"

"That's right, Miss Carleen. I am." Sartain frowned. "How did you know who I am?"

"Oh, it didn't take long for word to spread around Bittersweet. I stayed in town last night with Vicente. I just drove in to give Warren a good look at his brother's body, and to let him know that I know he killed my pa in cold blood. Backshot him in Cobalt Canyon, the bastard!"

Sartain sipped the mescal, which was so strong it instantly made his eyes water. But it was good stuff, and he knew mescal. It both tasted and smelled like the southwestern desert in full spring blossom.

"Are you sure it was the sheriff who killed your pa?"

"Of course I'm sure." Carleen's voice had turned bitter, and her cheeks were now red with anger as she glared at the light rain thumping into the yard. "Of course, I didn't see it. I can't prove it. But I know. He's the only man who'd have the nerve to back-shoot Waylon Chaney. It was either him or he sent his deputy, that fat moron, Amos McCluskey."

"Well, that would fit. McCluskey tried to trim my wick out in the same canyon less than an hour ago."

She jerked a startled look at him. "Really?"

"He's dead." Sartain took another sip of the potent liquor and let it loll on his tongue for a time before he swallowed it. It tasted especially good with the desert rain falling, the fresh air tanged with sage easing up under the porch roof.

"Whoa." Carleen sat back in her chair. "He must've followed you out to Cobalt Canyon and wanted to make sure you didn't find anything."

"If that's true, he gave up his ghost for nothin'. I didn't find anything. In fact, that's why I decided to pay you a visit at this delicate time, Miss Carleen. I'm wondering where you found your father. I'd like to see if I can track the killer or killers away from the area."

"I'll show you tomorrow. Storm doesn't look like it's gonna stay long, but by the time it's done rainin', it'll likely be too late to get started and back before dark." Carleen frowned curiously. "Who sent you out here, Mr. Sartain? You just come to help a girl in need?"

Sartain shrugged, threw the last of the mescal back, and smacked his lips. "I don't reckon there's any reason to keep it a secret. Your aunt, Miss Celeste, sent me."

"Celeste?"

"She said she wanted to get to the bottom of your father's murder."

"That's odd."

"How's it odd?"

Carleen shrugged a shoulder. "She an' my pa were never very close."

"She said as much. But she also said she wants to know if Warren murdered him. If he did . . ."

Carleen arched a brow.

"She'd like me to handle it."

"Would you kill him, Mr. Sartain?"

"If I find out he killed your pa, I would."

She gave him a pensive smile, probing him with her gaze. "Because that's what you do for folks, isn't it? Avenge them who can't avenge themselves."

"I figure your aunt fits into that category." The Cajun smiled. "I got a feelin' you can take care of yourself, however."

Carleen pursed her lips, nodding. "Poor Celeste. Cooped up in that house all alone with that crazy old man. Catatonic, the doctor calls him. Just sits in his chair all day, shittin' an' pissin' himself."

"That's a terrible way to live. For both of 'em."

"Hell, that old man don't even know what's goin' on. It's Celeste who had it hard. And then"—Carleen's voice hardened with anger as she stared down at her near-empty glass—"Warren got the old man to change his will just before he went totally crazy. Convinced him that . . ."

The girl shook her head and let her voice trail off.

"Convinced him of what?" Sartain gently prodded.

Carleen sighed. "Let's just say that once the old man's dead, Celeste ain't gonna be taken care of nearly well enough for all that old man has put her through for the past five, six years. Most of the money—hell, *all* of the money and property and business interests—will go to Warren."

"And your father wouldn't have gotten any of it, either . . . had he lived, I mean?"

"Nope. There's been no chance of that since Pa got wild. Never mind that he came back and walked the straight and narrow. Even went to work for Warren, gettin' paid next to nothin', though he did all the heavy liftin'."

"Why do you suppose the old man's bein' so hard on his daughter?"

"Well, because Celeste is just a silly young woman, ya see, and wouldn't have sense enough to spend the money wisely. So Warren will have to see to her, and—Oh, don't get me goin'!"

Carleen rose and turned to Sartain. "Do you think I'm pretty, Mr. Sartain?"

Sartain looked up at her. She filled her dress out in all the right places. The frock was high necked, but it was drawn taut against the full swell of her bosom.

"Indeed, I do, Miss Carleen."

She smiled. "I like the way you talk. You talk like a real southern gentleman."

"I like to think of myself as a gentleman."

"Does that mean you wouldn't frolic with a girl you just met?"

Sartain hesitated. He wasn't sure he'd heard her right. As he pondered it, Carleen crossed her arms, grabbed the dress beneath her bosom, and lifted it up and over her head.

Her long, beautiful hair floated messily back to her shoulders as she dropped the dress to the floor and stood before him— willowy, pink, and perfect.

CHAPTER FOURTEEN

Sartain silently opined that there must be something in the water around the Davis Mountains that made all the women hotter than Colt .45s on Saturday nights in Abilene. Or maybe the Chaney women were all so repressed that their carnal desires came out in craven spurts, with nary a nod to the niceties of their female station.

"Well, I'll be jiggered three ways from sundown, Miss Celeste, but ain't you a forward little thing."

"I'm a lonely little thing, Mr. Sartain. Lonely as these mountains, but a whole lot younger." She reached behind her neck and lifted her hair in a messy ball above her head. "So when I see an opportunity to be not quite so lonely for a time, I leap on it. Besides, my daddy's gone now, and I'm tired of grievin' already. And"—she let her hair tumble down around her shoulders and bosom—"I don't wanna think about the heartache anymore today or tonight. Besides, the weather's good for snugglin' by a mesquite fire—don't you think?"

"You don't give a man much choice."

Sartain rose from his chair. He felt a little wobbly. He'd been desiring this girl even before she'd taken her dress off and he'd seen that she was wearing nothing more underneath it than her aunt had been wearing under her own burgundy frock.

He doffed his hat, wrapped his arms around her shoulders, and kissed her.

She fairly melted in his arms, returning his kiss as hungrily as he was giving it.

Pulling away suddenly, she said, "Do you think me terrible? Carrying on like this after . . . after . . . ?" She turned to stare up the rise upon which she'd buried her father.

"Ah, hell," Sartain said. "You're alive. Might as well enjoy it. He's not gonna know."

She smiled up at him, pressed her breasts against his chest, and wrapped her arms around his neck. She kissed him, and he returned it, and later, when they were both exhausted, they shared a bottle of mescal.

She sat back against the porch rail, resting an elbow on a raised knee, giving him a smoky smile, and smacking her lips.

"Damn," she said.

"Yeah," he said, sighing and taking another pull from the bottle.

Later, she fried venison steaks and potatoes from her irrigated garden, and then they slept with the door propped open to the cool breeze that was both fragrant and fresh on the lee side of the rain.

Sartain didn't let himself fall into a deep sleep, waking about an hour after Carleen had drifted off, exhausted. By the moonlight angling through her bedroom window in the cabin's half-story loft, where she had a small bed and a chest of drawers, he checked his Waterbury.

One forty-five A.M.

Carefully so as not to wake Carleen, he rose, gathered his clothes, and crept down the creaky stairs, gritting his teeth against the complaints of the rotting planks. He dressed in the kitchen, wrapped his shell belt and LeMat around his waist, donned his hat.

He walked out to the barn to retrieve one of the shovels she and Vicente had used to dig her father's grave. He climbed the rise with the shovel on one shoulder, the Henry on the other. A half-moon angled a gauzy light over the wet ground. He tried to stick to the shadows so Carleen wouldn't see him if she happened to wake and look out a window.

At the top of the rise, he leaned his Henry against a mesquite. He looked around carefully, listening, to make sure he was alone out here. There were only the wan stars and the moon and the distant yammering of a coyote. Occasionally, an owl hooted from somewhere nearby. The air was cool and still damp from the rain, though the ground was barely soggy.

Sartain set to work removing the rocks from Waylon Chaney's grave. He was going to feel like a fool if his suspicions were wrong, but he felt compelled to investigate.

When he'd removed all the rocks covering the grave, he set to work with the spade. Fortunately, Carleen and Vicente hadn't buried the body very deep. Only about fifteen minutes after he'd started shoveling, Sartain's shovel thumped on a wooden casket lid. Apparently, Carleen had boxed up her father before leaving Bittersweet.

That fact made the Revenger begin to doubt his suspicions.

Still, he cleared the dirt, dry at this level, away from the wooden lid so green that he could still smell the pine resin wafting up along with the metallic smell of the desert clay and sand. He stabbed the spade into the dirt, dropped to his knees, and slid his fingers around the sides of the lid, feeling for a hold.

When he had one, he pried the lid up off the box, and his eyes watered from the sour smell of rot. He recoiled slightly when the moonlight reflected off the two eyes glaring up at him. He hadn't gotten a good look at Waylon Chaney when he'd been lying in the back of Carleen's wagon, but now, despite the swollen face and lips stretching back from yellow teeth, he saw the similarity to Sheriff Chaney.

Carleen hadn't dressed the man for his funeral. He wore a

brown wool vest over a calico shirt, a ratty red cloth knotted around his unshaven neck. She hadn't even combed the man's hair, for it was sticking up in tufts all around his head.

Nor were his eyelids sewn shut, as was often the practice when a body was being prepared for formal burial. The coppery stench of blood mingled with the cloying sweetness of death as Waylon Chaney continued to glare, sneering angrily, at Sartain.

The Revenger wrestled the body over onto its belly in the casket. He lifted Chaney's thick, black hair up above the collarless shirt and yanked the neckerchief down, exposing the man's pale neck. And there it was—red as a fresh sunburn against the otherwise pale skin.

A birthmark in the shape of a feather.

Celeste had said that when the boys were younger, the only way that even their mother could tell them apart was by the birthmark on Warren's neck.

"Well, well, well," Sartain said, slowly shaking his head. "I do believe I been hornswoggled, Mr. Chaney. Sheriff Warren Chaney, that is." He stared down at the eyes that looked more anguished and befuddled now in his recognition of the man's true identity. "Your bad brother do this to you, Sheriff?"

He looked down toward the cabin, wondering if Carleen knew. She certainly hadn't made love like a bereaved daughter.

Behind him rose the crunching sound of a foot stepping down on gravel. A shadow flicked over the dirt mound in front of and just left of Sartain. A girl grunted.

As Sartain jerked his head around, he glimpsed the blade of the shovel hurtling toward him a sixteenth of a second before it smashed across his temple and sent him sprawling back against Sheriff Warren Chaney lying dead in his casket, and a vague voice whispered into the Revenger's ringing ears, "Yep, she knew, all right . . ."

CHAPTER FIFTEEN

The girl's foot had slipped slightly as she'd brought the shovel down, and the back of the steel blade had caught Sartain's right temple a glancing blow.

It hurt like hell, and it dimmed his lights momentarily, but he regained his faculties quickly. As Carleen lunged toward him, raising the shovel once more, Sartain saw that she was naked, the moonlight shifting shadows around beneath her jostling breasts. Her hair swung wildly out behind her shoulders.

As she started to bring the shovel down once more toward Sartain's head, he scissored his right leg, sweeping her feet out from under her. She screamed and dropped the shovel as her legs came up and her ass hit the ground.

"Ahh, *damn!*" she intoned.

Sartain realized that he'd been hearing the low drumming of galloping horses. The drumming was growing louder, and he started to hear the clank of bits and bridle chains.

"Carleen—that you?" a man's voice shouted.

As Sartain heaved himself up off the dead, bloated corpse of Warren Chaney, Carleen sat up and twisted around to stare down the rise in the direction of the cabin.

"Sheriff!" she screamed. Then she looked at Sartain, and in the moonlight, he could see her grin delightedly. "Sheriff, it's Sartain!" She thrust her finger and arm out, pointing wickedly. "It was him all along! He killed my father and tonight he raped me! Oh, Uncle Warren, it's terrible! Please stop him!"

Sartain stood, crouching. The lunging silhouettes of a good half dozen—maybe closer to a dozen—horseback riders were galloping up from the yard, tack squawking and flashing in the moonlight. They were spread out in a shaggy line.

"He killed Amos, too!" a man shouted. "Sent him back to Bittersweet tied belly down across his saddle. That son of a bitch!"

"He's pure crazy!" exclaimed another one of the posse. At least, Sartain assumed it was a posse that "Warren" Chaney had sent out after him, likely knowing that sooner or later the Revenger would figure out the trick the imposter and his daughter were playing on the town.

Warren Chaney as well as Amos McCluskey probably had enough tough-nut friends in town they could call on for help. Sartain could sense the blood lust in these men, who appeared to have taken personally the death of the big deputy.

"He raped me, Uncle Warren!" Carleen ripped out on a phony grieved wail. "Oh, god—you should have seen the things he made me do!"

"Get down, girl!" shouted a man whom Sartain took to be Waylon Chaney in the guise of his twin brother.

As Carleen threw herself belly down on the ground beside the open grave, Sartain ran down the backside of the rise. Knowing he was badly outnumbered, he'd already picked up his Henry and was hightailing it. Good thing he had. Behind him, pistols crackled like hot grease on a giant skillet.

Bullets screeched through the air above his head, a couple spanging off rocks beyond him.

Sartain ran hard, pumping his arms and legs. He couldn't see much out here on the backside of the rise, but that meant his pursuers wouldn't, either.

He kept running, trying to avoid the gauzy moonlight, zigzagging around rocks and cacti slanting shadows across the gravelly turf. Behind him, the posse riders were yelling and hoorawing. They were probably drunk, and that would account for the speed at which they kept coming regardless of the danger to themselves and their mounts.

They were topping the rise now and heading down the backside toward their quarry, pistols flashing and belching.

As the drumming grew louder and bullets landed closer to Sartain, he whipped around and lowered the Henry. Firing from his right hip, he cut loose with four quick shots, pumping and triggering the sixteen-shooter, flames stabbing from the barrel.

Immediately he heard the screams of men and horses. As he ejected the fourth cartridge casing, he pumped another live round into the action and triggered off four more shots.

More screaming. He heard the thuds of horses and men falling, tumbling, rolling.

"God*dammit!*" a man shouted shrilly.

Others kept coming, but he could tell they weren't coming as quickly as before. Having slowed them at least a little, he turned and continued running, heading across a rocky flat toward the black shapes of what he took to be buttes humping up in front of him.

He came to the first butte and climbed, pulling at small, wiry shrubs and lunging off the balls of his feet. The riders were galloping behind him but keeping their distance. The shooting had stopped. At least, it had paused, which meant that for now the posse had lost its prey.

"There!" a man shouted.

Sartain cursed as he gained the crest of the bluff. Someone must have seen moonlight flash off the Henry's barrel, perhaps off one of his spurs. He hunkered down behind the ridge crest and pumped another cartridge into the Henry's chamber.

"Where is he?" another man yelled.

"On top o' that bluff!" shouted another. They were riding side by side—two shadows growing larger in the darkness, flanked by the other jostling shadows of the posse riders.

Sartain had no desire to kill innocent townsmen who'd been hornswoggled by Waylon Chaney. But they weren't about to hold fire while he explained the situation. They knew he'd killed Amos McCluskey and probably thought he'd done so in cold blood. They were also under the false impression that he'd raped Carleen Chaney.

They didn't realize that the man leading them was an imposter.

Sartain aimed at the left lead rider, hoping it was Chaney. He fired. The shadow leaned back and to one side, and the horse's eyes flashed in the moonlight as it leaned to the same side as its rider. The horse nearly tumbled on its side before the rider fell free of the saddle and rolled, grunting. Then the still-galloping horse swung hard right and away, trailing its bridle reins.

"Now that bastard's killed Tiegen!" shouted the other man. "Surround that bluff, boys! If we get him surrounded, he's ours!"

Shit, Sartain thought. That was the same voice he'd heard earlier and which he'd attributed to the bastard, Chaney.

He aimed the Henry and fired at Chaney, but Chaney had swung his own horse hard left and was riding wide of the bluff. Sartain couldn't tell for sure, but he didn't think any of the lead he flung until the Henry's hammer pinged empty hit its target.

Pulling the LeMat from the holster on his right thigh, he fired twice to try and hold the others at bay, then rose with the LeMat in hand, the empty Henry in the other, and ran down the backside of the bluff. Members of the posse were trying to work around behind him, and if they accomplished the maneuver, Chaney would have the last say.

And it was the wrong Chaney.

Sartain scrambled to the bottom of the bluff as two shadows moved toward him from his right and his left.

"There he is!" the man on the left shouted.

Sartain stopped and triggered the LeMat.

"Dammit!" the rider cried as Sartain saw the rider's shadow separate from the shadow of the galloping mount. There was a dull thud, a rattle of flying gravel, and the chink of spurs as the rider hit the ground and rolled.

The horse stopped, reared, and whinnied shrilly.

Sartain holstered his pistol, ran toward the beast, and reached for the reins, missing the sashaying ribbons as the horse wheeled and galloped away. "Mangy cayuse!" he raked out and ran up the bluff opposite the one he'd just descended.

Several guns barked behind him. Bullets kicked up dirt and gravel around him, spanged off rocks on the bluff above him. Wheeling, Sartain palmed his LeMat and squeezed off a shot. A horseback rider in the crease in the bluff below squealed and grabbed his shoulder.

Sartain turned and continued running. He bounded over the top of the bluff and hunkered behind a boulder. Breathing hard, he quickly reloaded the Henry, raked a round into the action, and lowered the hammer to half cock. The shooting had dwindled to occasional pops and barks, the bullets flying wide.

The posse seemed to have lost him.

He stared around the bluffs humping darkly around him. He saw a few jostling shadows and heard a few distant hoof thuds, heard a few men shouting, but most of the riders were now well below him. He must have climbed into a series of connected buttes up which none of the posse wanted to dare try climbing on horseback.

He looked behind him.

Ridges bulked against the dim stars, and the sky washed in the periwinkle blue of moonlight. A trail angled up the next ridge. He reloaded the LeMat, holstered it, snapped the keeper thong over the hammer, took the Henry in his right hand, and began following the trail through the jutting escarpments peppered with cedars and occasional mesquites and Spanish bayonet.

He continued to hear men shouting angrily behind him, the occasional drumming of hooves, but then the sounds of the posse faded below and behind him.

As he continued moving through this devil's playground comprised of crumbling bluffs, steep-walled mesas, and blocks and fingers of jutting basalt likely carved by some ancient, winding river, silence closed around him.

Occasionally, however, sounds intruded upon the silence. He couldn't quite make them out, but he suspected that Waylon Chaney's recruits were trying to move around him in the darkness.

At one point he heard the rake of a spur and a clipped curse. Both sounds were sharp and clear, but Sartain didn't think the man was close. At least, he wasn't within more than sixty or seventy yards. The silence of the night and the still air cleansed by the earlier storm gave all sounds an almost eerie crispness.

The Cajun kept moving, weaving amongst the formations, meandering around and through them and several times over them, hunching low so that his silhouette wouldn't be outlined against the stars and the moon-streaked sky.

Exhausted, he found a niche amongst the rocks, with sheer ridges towering around him, and leaned back against the stone wall behind him. He sank to his butt, rested the Henry across his knees, and closed his eyes. He intended to take only a catnap, but when he opened his eyes the sun was nearly up.

The rocky world around him was the copper of a newly minted penny.

A noise. Close by.

He'd only been half awake, but now he was fully awake and slowly climbing to his feet, raising the Henry and pressing his thumb against the hammer. Ahead were two boulders and a crooked passage between them. He moved into it, stopped.

The noise again. Someone was moving ahead of him, on the other end of the passage between the boulders.

He continued walking, stopped again when he heard a footstep, saw the front end of a hat brim and a boot move at the passage's far end. He darted to his right, pressing his shoulder into a niche in the boulder on the side of the natural corridor. He heard the soft scuffs of boot heels.

Then silence.

He could hear the man breathing at the far end of the passage.

He was peering into the chasm, in Sartain's direction.

Sartain held still. He could raise the Henry and shoot, but he didn't know how many other posse members were near. When the footsteps sounded again, moving away, Sartain hurried to the far side of the passage. The man stood eight feet ahead of him, on a ledge overlooking a boulder- and brush-choked canyon that was about fifty feet deep.

The man wore town clothes—a shirt, wool vest, bowler hat, and scuffed black half-boots. Sartain could see the bows of spectacles hooked over the man's ears.

The man had just dipped a hand into his right vest pocket and was pulling out a tobacco sack when Sartain moved soundlessly up behind him and pressed the barrel of his LeMat against the back of the man's right ear.

The man froze.

"One sound," Sartain warned, "and you're deader'n last year's Christmas goose. Understand? Don't say anything, just dip your chin."

The man slowly dipped his chin.

He was holding a Winchester carbine in his left hand. Sartain took it and tossed it into the canyon. Then he slipped the man's Remington revolver holstered high on the man's right hip and tossed that into the canyon, as well.

"What's your name? Say it nice and quiet. You call out, you'll die."

Sartain could hear the man swallow. Sweat trickled down the back of his clean-shaven neck beneath his close-cropped, sandy blond hair.

"Boyd." The man's voice trembled. "Raymond Boyd. I'm . . . I'm the mayor of Bittersweet."

"No shit? The mayor. Well, I'd best watch my language, then. I'm in the presence of royalty."

"Very funny."

"I'm gonna tell you somethin' else that's funny."

"What's that?"

"The man you followed out here ain't Sheriff Chaney. It's his brother, Waylon."

The man turned his head to the right, frowning. "Wha—? Can't be. Waylon's dead. You killed him, just like you killed Mc-Cluskey and sent him back to town belly down over his horse. He was my brother-in-law."

Sartain snorted at that bit of information. "Think about it, Mr. Mayor. What would possibly compel me to shoot Waylon Chaney? I didn't even know the man. Shit, I just rode into this country three days ago."

"Some old grievance, no doubt."

Sartain sighed. "All right. Try this on for size. If you go back to the Chaney ranch and look at Waylon's body, you'll see a birthmark on the back of his neck. Accordin' to his sister, Celeste, Warren's the one with the birthmark."

The mayor rolled his eyes around behind his glasses, perplexed. "Why . . . ?"

"Why would Waylon impersonate his brother? Think about it."

The mayor didn't have to think about it long. His lower jaw sagged. The morning light flashed on his spectacles as he turned toward Sartain, beetling his brows. "Because his father wrote him out of the will. As Warren, he'd inherit most of it."

"All of it—lock, stock, and barrel."

"Shit."

"Yeah. Now, why don't you have a little powwow with the other posse members, and all of you ride back to town and spread the news?"

The mayor nodded slowly as it all came together in his mind. "You know, I thought there was—"

A rifle thundered nearby.

The mayor's head fairly exploded, blood and white brain tissue spewing out the hole above his right ear. His glasses tumbled off his head as he sagged sideways and dropped into the canyon.

Sartain spun.

Waylon Chaney, dressed in the Fancy Dan garb of his brother, stood on a ledge about twenty feet above the Revenger. Grinning beneath the brim of his crisp, felt Stetson, he pumped another round into the chamber.

He was fast with a long gun. Before Sartain could raise the Henry and draw a bead on the man, Chaney's Winchester thundered. The slug ripped a hot line across Sartain's left temple.

Instantly, the Cajun's lights dimmed. He was half-aware of dropping his rifle as he stumbled backward. Then he was falling. Still half-conscious, he flailed out with his arms, grabbing at rocks and what appeared to be old tree roots angling out the side of the cliff wall. Agony ripped through him—he could feel the skin being torn from his fingers as he grabbed anything he could find to break his fall.

And then, mercifully, he stopped falling, and everything went dark as dusk.

He heard a rifle belching from afar, felt the vibration of bullets slamming into the ground around him.

And then everything went dark as night.

CHAPTER SIXTEEN

Misery hammered away at Sartain's head and body. Mostly at his head, but his body ached, too. The pain was like a deep pool, and several times he tried to swim out of the pool, but it was ocean-sized. The pain clung to him like a cold blanket.

Relentless.

Then he heard a man's voice from close by say, "Gotta get you up . . . get you outta here . . ."

He was aware of being lifted and half-dragged, half-carried. And then someone went to work with a sledgehammer against his head and his ribs, hammering both at the same time. Vaguely, distantly, he thought he might be lying belly down over a horse's rump, a saddle blanket cushioning him.

Then everything went dark and quiet again for a time, and he dreamed fleeting but vivid dreams.

In one, he was carrying the body of his dead lover, Jewel, killed by soldiers a handful of years ago in Arizona, across a blazing desert.

Wolves leaped at him from the rocks all around him. When he looked at one of the wolves lunging at him and the dead Jewel in his arms, he saw that the beast's fur was on fire. Flames even lapped from its eyes. He was overcome with the need to carry Jewel to safety, to find a place to bury her where the wolves would not find her and chew her and the baby in her belly to pieces.

Gradually, that dream died and there were others, less vivid and even more fleeting, until a man's voice said, "Looks like the fever's broke some."

Sartain was aware of something cool against his forehead. He reached up and touched a cloth.

"Jewel?" He jerked his head up hopefully and opened his eyes.

A ruddy, round, mustached face stared at him from a foot and a half away.

"Jewel?" asked the man. "Nah . . . I don't have no jewels, *amigo*. Other than the family jewels. Still got them, though they don't work so good as they used to." He spoke with a thick Spanish accent, and Sartain frowned at the man until he recalled the name of the stocky Mexican friend of Waylon and Carleen Chaney.

"Vicente?"

"*Si*. Yeah, that's better. You remember. Brain must not be too scrambled up. Jewel—that a name, or were you hoping to find a diamond or somethin' on your pillow?"

Sartain looked around. They were in a small stone cabin. Several candles and a bull's eye lantern flickered a watery light. The dark of night pushed at the small windows and seeped in through the door that was propped open with one of Sartain's boots.

The floor was hard-packed dirt. The ceiling over Sartain's head was brush. He lay on a small cot in his shirt and summer underwear and socks.

"Jewel?" he said, frowning.

"That's what you said—'Jewel'."

Sartain felt a pang of grief stab the backside of his heart, and he shook it off as he continued to look around the small, crudely furnished cabin. There was a small beehive fireplace. A cast-iron pot hung over glowing coals from an iron tripod. The pot bubbled, filling the shack with the smell of cooking beans and meat. Those smells mingled with the sweat, leather, and horse smell of Vicente and another, cloying, medicinal odor that Sartain couldn't identify.

Sitting in a hide-bottom chair beside the cot, the Mexican held a smoking tin cup on his beefy left side. He lifted the cup and arched his shaggy, salt-and-pepper brows. "You hungry? Your fever's broke, I think. Thought you might like a bite. Even if you don't feel like it, you might force a few bites down. Need to get your strength back, *amigo*. That bullet creased you pretty good.

"I brought my old mother out here, and she doctored your cuts and bruises and forced some tea down your throat. She doctored our whole family—nine kids—and only one o' them kids didn't make it into his twenties. That was Hector, but he fell off his mule and was bit in the chest by a diamondback. Dead before Mama could reach him."

"What's that smell?"

Vicente glanced at Sartain's forehead. "Some wild herb concoction she smeared on that bullet crease. Supposed to keep it from festering."

"Smells like mule shit."

"Who knows—it probably is." Vicente's heavy shoulders jerked as he chuckled, showing crooked, yellow teeth beneath his heavy, drooping mustache. He raised a spoon containing a few beans and a chunk of meat.

"Why not?" Sartain said. "Couldn't make me feel any worse."

He opened his mouth, and Vicente slid the spoon between his lips. Sartain ate a couple of bites and then realized his bladder was bursting.

"I gotta take a leak," he said, suddenly desperate. "Christ—how long I been here?"

"This was the second full day. This is the third night." Vicente set the cup down and fished a coffee tin out from beneath the cot. "Here you go. You gonna need some help?"

Sartain took the can and sat up. "I don't think so."

"That's good, brother." Laughing, Vicente ducked out through the low door to give the Cajun and his bursting bladder some privacy.

When Sartain had filled the can nearly to the brim, and Vicente had emptied it over a rock outside, Sartain asked him where in hell they were. The Mexican kicked Sartain's boot out of the way, shut the door, and replaced the coffee tin beneath the Revenger's cot.

"Old outlaw shack over Cobalt Canyon."

Vicente sat in a chair at the small, square table that was the only other furnishing besides the cot and a few chairs in the little shack. The chair creaked precariously beneath his bulk. He'd built a cornhusk cigarette outside, and he puffed it now and sipped from a tin cup on the table next to a half-empty, clear bottle that probably housed mescal or tequila.

"Me an' Waylon and a few others used it back when we were runnin' roughshod," the Mexican added, tapping ashes from the cigarette onto the floor. "Ten, twelve years ago now. When we were young an' stupid."

Sartain lay back against the wall, propped on the flour sack he'd been using as a pillow. He kept the cool cloth pressed to his forehead, over the stinky bandage. "How'd you find me? Why . . . did you help me?"

"I seen what happened. I seen Waylon shoot Boyd and then you. I was watchin' through field glasses. Didn't realize it was Waylon at the time, but then I knew. Only Waylon would pull a dirty trick like that. I had no use for his brother, but his brother wouldn't bushwhack a man with a rifle. His brother wouldn't kill his own brother so he could inherit his old man's fortune. Oh, Warren would have taken the money, all right. He wouldn't have cared a damn about cuttin' his brother and sister out, but

. . . what Waylon done was wrong."

"You didn't know he was gonna pull that trick?"

"Ahead of time? No. I didn't know Carleen was in on it, neither. Always knew she was wild. Didn't know she was as crazy, rotten-mean-wild as Waylon could be."

"Doesn't make sense," Sartain said, trying to ponder it all beneath the dull hammering in his temple. His hands were sore where he'd scraped skin off trying to break his fall into the canyon. "Carleen put a price on her father's head."

"I'm guessin' she didn't know it was Waylon till later that night, after she rode to town with Warren's body in her wagon. They had 'em a little powwow outside my shack. I didn't know what it was about, but her mood changed considerable after that. Took the venom out of her bite."

"Waylon didn't tell her what he was going to do beforehand?"

"My guess is Waylon wanted to see how she'd react to his death before he told her. Maybe he was testing her."

"He must've been right proud of that bounty she put on his head. He even managed to look afraid, jumpy."

Vicente said, "I thought when he came back from outlawin' up in Colorado and down in Mexico, he'd settled down like I had. Those wild ways are for young men that don't know better. When you get older, you respect people. You respect yourself and lawful ways."

He blew smoke out his broad nostrils, sighing and wagging his head regretfully.

"What you do," he continued, "ain't so bad. Some folks need help when they can't help themselves. That's why I came back for you, brought you here."

"Waylon doesn't suspect, I take it?"

"Nah. I rode back with him and the rest of the posse, rode back out to that canyon he left you in the next morning, brought you here."

"I'm much obliged, Vicente. My horse . . . ?"

"He's out back, in the stable. Carleen went to town with her old man. I think she's livin' up at the Chaney house with Celeste, still playin' like she's heartsick, eyes red all the time. Must chop a lot of onions."

The Mexican chuckled. "She missed her calling—should have joined a traveling theater show. That horse of yours—now, there's a stallion!" Vicente laughed. "He's worried about you, I can tell. Keeps lookin' toward the shack and sniffin', like he's lookin' for you."

"He just knows that anyone else besides myself wouldn't be stupid enough to put up with him."

Vicente laughed his rollicking laugh, ground out his cigarette on the table, flicked it out an open window, and rose. He nodded at a stone jug. "This here jug has water in it. There's a creek out back. Barely runs this time of year except when it rains, but it's got good, cold water. I'll leave the tequila. Might ease your pain."

He removed the iron pot from the tripod and set it on a flat rock near the beehive fireplace. "This pot's nearly full. That should do you till tomorrow night. I'll come back then and check on you."

"Much obliged for the help."

"You've helped your share of others, brother. I figure you were due some help yourself."

"Maybe I can pay you back some day."

"I hope not!" The Mexican laughed and crouched in the doorway, one hand on the doorknob. "Get some rest."

"Vicente?"

"Yeah?"

"What about Chaney? Carleen? What are they up to, you think?"

"Oh, yeah. Meant to tell you. The same day we rode back to

town, after Waylon shot you and the mayor, he went up to see his father. Ain't it funny how the old man breathed his last in his son's presence?"

A stone dropped in the Revenger's belly.

"Yeah, Waylon killed the old man, most likely," Vicente went on. "Probably put a pillow over his face. Funeral's tomorrow morning." Vicente laughed, but this time there wasn't an ounce of humor in it. "The will's gonna be read tomorrow afternoon in the judge's office in the courthouse."

Vicente wagged his head darkly, ducked out of the shack, and drew the door closed behind him. In a few minutes, Sartain heard the Mexican's horse drum into the distance.

And then he was left with the silence of the night and the fury of his revenge-oriented thoughts.

CHAPTER SEVENTEEN

The next day at two P.M., the last surviving members of the Chaney family gathered in Judge W. George M. Stall's office in the Brown County Courthouse, just down the hall from the sheriff's office.

The judge stood behind his large cedar desk as Celeste Chaney and her niece, Carleen, both dressed in somber, conservative frocks complete with dark bonnets and black gloves, sank into two of the three chairs angled in front of the desk.

Waylon Chaney, dressed in his brother's Fancy Dan three-piece suit adorned with his brother's five-pointed sheriff's star, stood back near the loudly ticking grandfather clock, twirling his hat on his finger. Carleen was a better actor than her father, Chaney silently noted. He just couldn't keep his enthusiasm under wraps. Against all odds, his scheme had worked, and he was about to be a rich man indeed, in spite of his brother's crooked hijinks.

He remembered the day he'd followed Warren out to Cobalt Canyon. Warren had gone out to try to pick up the trail of three claim jumpers reported to be in the area, and Waylon had seen that as his chance to put his plan into motion. While Warren had instructed Waylon and Amos McCluskey to stay in town and keep an eye on the saloons—as it was payday out at the Circle K, the largest ranch in the area, and the Circle K riders could really do some damage once they got a few drinks under their belts—Waylon had secretly followed Warren.

He'd run him down and threatened to shoot him unless he shucked out of his duds. Once Warren stood in only his short underwear, socks, and an undershirt, Waylon ordered him to turn around.

Warren had not been able to believe his brother would actually kill him. He hadn't thought Waylon would actually go through with it, though Waylon had enjoyed detailing his plan to his doomed twin. Warren had thought it would all turn out to be a joke, that Waylon was merely trying to humiliate him by making him return to town in his underwear.

"You ain't gonna do it, Waylon," Warren had said, smiling nervously and shaking his head stubbornly as he'd turned around. "I just know that even you, the low-down, mean an' nasty Waylon Chaney, couldn't squeeze the trigger on your own twin brother."

Waylon had laughed in delight at that.

Pow!

And then Waylon had stripped down, shot a hole through his own shirt and vest, about where he'd shot Warren, and exchanged clothes with his brother. He'd left Warren in Cobalt Canyon, where he figured someone would find him eventually. As it happened, Carleen herself had found the body the very next day, on her way to town to sell rattlesnake skins to a hat maker. Waylon had been delighted to see how upset she'd been, thinking her father was dead—killed by his own brother.

For who else but his cowardly brother, incensed by how Waylon was gaining more power around the county, would have shot Waylon Chaney in the back?

Warren Chaney valued power and respect almost as much as he'd valued money.

Too bad for him.

Waylon did, as well. But Waylon was smart enough to know

how to acquire and keep it.

"Sheriff, would you care to have a seat?" the judge asked Waylon now, glancing at the chair beside his "niece."

Chaney tossed his hat on a hat rack on the far side of the grandfather clock and plopped onto the judge's leather sofa. "Sure—why not?" he said, stretching out, resting his head against one arm of the couch, crossing his boots on the other arm. "Go ahead and read it out for us, Judge. I think I know what it says, but I reckon we'd better make it all formal and legal-like."

Celeste glanced over her shoulder at him, anger reddening her cheeks. Chaney grinned.

Carleen sat staring down at her hands in her lap, still playing the bereaved daughter, but he could tell by the way her ears had turned red, she was doing her damnedest not to laugh.

She was also likely imagining what she and her old man were going to do with the old bastard's fortune. For his part, Waylon was going to buy a few more businesses, possibly even the Circle K ranch and hire someone else to run it while he just raked in the money. He knew of a few mines he'd like to buy some interest in, as well.

Money and power.

Of course, he'd need a few more deputies. The Revenger had really hammered a dent in Waylon's deputy department. It thrilled him no end to think of the great Sartain lying dead at the bottom of that canyon, his bones probably being licked clean by coyotes and cougars.

Eventually, Chaney would get out of the lawdog business, but first he needed the position to wield his power—for the thrill as well as to build and maintain his properties, namely, more saloons and brothels. Booze and girls brought in the most money.

Money and power.

Soon, Waylon would have such a stranglehold on the town, the county, that its citizens would see him as a god. Or at least as the Jay Gould of Brown County, Texas.

He chuckled at that and then cleared his throat and brushed a fist across his nose to cover it.

The judge frowned at him.

"Get on with it, Judge—I got me a powerful thirst," Waylon intoned. He couldn't help loosing another chuckle.

Money and power: Just the thought of them had his proverbial cup filled to overflowing. He couldn't wait to get over to Nora's Place and eat and drink and tussle for the rest of the afternoon. Tomorrow, he'd start getting down to business.

The judge sank into his high-backed, leather swivel chair. He donned his reading spectacles, took up the single-page will in his hand, and began reading.

By the time he was finished, Celeste stared straight ahead. Even from behind her, Waylon could tell that her face was as white as a sun-bleached bone in the desert. Carleen said nothing, merely sat in her chair with her head down.

"All righty, then—thanks, Judge!" Waylon dropped his boots to the floor and rose.

"Well, Warren," the judge said, "you're a very wealthy man. Your niece and your sister, however, seem to have been left out in the cold."

Celeste bowed her head in dejection.

"My dear niece will be well taken care of."

Carleen smiled at him, winked. "Thank you, Uncle Warren."

Waylon returned his daughter's wink. He turned to the stricken Celeste. "Ah, don't worry, sis." He wrapped an arm around her shoulders. "We'll get you out of that big old house and into Mrs. Embry's boarding house in a few days."

Celeste turned to stare up at him in shock, eyes brimming with tears. *"What?* You're kicking me out of the *house?"*

"Gonna tear it down, build another one. A bigger one." Waylon opened the judge's humidor and helped himself to one of the judge's cigars. He struck a match on the mantel of the judge's Tiffany lamp, and the flame sputtered. "You don't need all that room. Hell, you'd get lost in a house the size o' the one I'm plannin'. Be much more comfortable in town. We'll get you a two-room suite—don't worry. Find you a job over at the millinery. You're a young woman, Celeste. You been pampered long enough. Time to get out on your own, make a livin' of your own. Toughen you up a little. You'll find life much more enjoyable, once you're toughened up and bringin' in your own bacon. Maybe you'll even find yourself a man before you get too long in the tooth."

"You bastard!" Celeste screamed, leaping to her feet and squaring her shoulders at her brother. "I've spent the bulk of my life, the best years of my life, taking care of our father! And you had the nerve, the gall, to convince him in his crazy, demented state to have me written out of the will!" She sobbed and rushed at him, swinging her arms, her fists. "You're pure *evil!*"

Waylon grabbed his sister's arms. "Celeste, you're overwrought. Pa's and Waylon's deaths an' all . . . I assure you, dear sister, I do not intend to see you starve. You will live quite comfortable. But, while I know it's gonna be hard at first, you're simply gonna have to start working—"

He stopped when someone knocked on the door.

"What is it?" the judged barked from where he stood behind his desk.

The door opened. The stocky Mexican, Vicente, stuck his head in the room and hooked a thumb over his shoulder. "Maybe you better come out here, Sheriff."

Waylon thought his brother's associate might have placed a

slight, ironic accent on "Sheriff." Or was Waylon just being paranoid?

"Why?" he asked his friend, whom Warren had never liked and whom Waylon no longer trusted. Vicente, who'd put his outlaw past well behind him, had turned into a goody two-shoes.

"Someone you know's out in the street . . . *Sheriff.*"

There it was again—unmistakable this time!

"Well, who in the hell . . . ?" Waylon let his voice trail off as Vicente pulled his head out of the room and clomped down the hall toward the courthouse's front door.

Waylon scowled as he grabbed his hat. "Goddammit, what the hell's goin' on?"

He headed into the hall. The judge came next, and then Celeste and Carleen. Waylon followed Vicente out onto the boardwalk fronting the courthouse and froze.

Vicente grinned at him, sneeringly, and sidestepped to Waylon's right. Meanwhile, the judge came out to stand between Waylon and the Mex. Celeste and Carleen stepped to his left.

Waylon heard the two women gasp at the same time.

Maybe he himself gasped, as well. He wasn't sure. He did know that his heart turned a quick, painful somersault in his chest.

"What the hell . . . ?" Waylon said, scowling at the big man standing directly across the street from the courthouse.

The handsome, dark-haired, clean-shaven man in the pinto vest and light tan Stetson, a heavy LeMat hanging low on his right thigh, was leaning against an awning support post of Nora's whorehouse. He frowned beneath his hat brim. A white bandage shone beneath the hat. The ends of his knotted neckerchief blew around in the mid-afternoon breeze that smelled like rain again.

Chaney shook his head in fury, bunching his lips. He stepped off the boardwalk and clamped a hand over the walnut grips of his pistol. "Who the *hell* are you? You aren't Sartain. I left him for bobcat bait in the bottom of a canyon. What are you up to, *amigo*? You know who I *am*?"

"I know who you are, Waylon," Sartain said with quiet menace.

"Waylon?" Celeste and the judge intoned at the same time.

"Waylon," Sartain said, pushing away from the awning support post, dropping his hands to his sides. He'd already released the keeper thong from over the LeMat's hammer.

Carleen slowly raised an arm to point at her father, sliding desperate gazes between the mayor and Celeste. "This . . . this is my uncle Warren."

Sartain curled his upper lip. "No, it ain't, honey. You know that as well as I do."

"Bullshit!" Waylon Chaney barked, taking one long stride toward Sartain, his dark-blue eyes fixed on the Revenger. "You killed the mayor and now you're here to kill me, 'cause you're a killer!"

"Ah, bullshit, Waylon," Vicente said, smiling. "I seen it all, Judge. I seen Waylon kill the mayor, and then he shot Sartain. The mayor was dead, but I fished the Revenger out of that canyon. He didn't rape Miss Carleen, neither. Shit, she prob'ly raped him."

He snickered.

Carleen wheeled on him, seething, but holding her tongue.

The judge turned to the imposter. "*Waylon* Chaney?"

Chaney glared at Sartain.

He slapped his walnut-gripped Colt, started to whip it up out of the leather.

Sartain wasn't particularly fast, but he was faster than Waylon Chaney by half a wink. And he was calmer. That's why his slug hammered Chaney's right arm, causing Chaney to trigger his own pistol into the dirt of the street, halfway between himself and the Cajun.

Sartain wanted Chaney alive.

Waylon yelped and grabbed his upper right arm.

"No!" Carleen screamed, bending forward at the waist.

"Give it up, Waylon," Sartain advised.

Chaney shoved his left hand into his vest pocket. Silver-chased steel glistened in the fading sunlight as he raised the derringer.

Sartain's LeMat spoke again. The bullet punched through Chaney's left side, throwing him back onto the boardwalk. He dropped the derringer and lay writhing and cursing like a gut-shot bobcat.

"No!" Carleen screamed again. *"Pa!"*

She ran to her father, dropped to both knees beside him. She whipped an enraged, hard-jawed glare at Sartain. "Goddamn you!" She looked at Vicente and repeated, "Goddamn you!"

Chaney slid off the boardwalk, trying to stretch his left hand out toward the derringer. Sartain had been striding toward him, and now he bent down to scoop up both the derringer and the Colt Peacemaker.

He tossed both pistols into an alley to the right of Nora's Place. All of Nora's girls were either on the second-floor balcony or on the front stoop, muttering in shock amongst themselves.

Celeste moved to Sartain. Tears wavered in her eyes. She threw her arms around him, pressed her cheek to his chest.

"I thought you were dead."

"Me, too. Would have been if Vicente hadn't hauled my worthless carcass out of that canyon."

Celeste glanced back at the mewling Chaney and the sobbing Carleen and then turned to Sartain once more. "Oh, I don't think it's all that worthless. Thank you."

"Ah, hell."

The judge moved as though in a daze down off the boardwalk, and stood before the Revenger, frowning in consternation. "You're . . . Sartain?"

The Cajun didn't say anything.

The judge glanced back at Chaney. "He's . . . *Waylon?*"

"You can dig his brother up from the grave out at the Chaney ranch. Celeste will confirm it's Warren out there, and that this here polecat is Waylon." He glanced at Carleen glaring over her shoulder at him. "But I reckon Waylon's daughter already done that."

"I'll be damned," the judge said, shaking his head in shock. "I reckon . . . I reckon I'll be sending a telegram to the U.S. marshal about this bit of nastiness."

"You'll be needing a new sheriff."

Sartain crouched over Chaney and ripped the badge off his vest. He tossed it to Vicente. "I can't think of a better man for the job . . . at least until you can run another election."

"If you want the job," the judge told Vicente, "it's yours."

Vicente shrugged. "For a week or two. What the hell?"

He pinned the badge to his shirt, grabbed the back of Waylon's coat, and began dragging the wounded owlhoot into the courthouse. Carleen ran to keep up with him, both she and her father cursing like banshees.

Sartain looked at Celeste. "You're next of kin."

"That means your father's wealth is now yours," the judge told her, "since Warren is dead and Waylon will likely hang. I'll get the county prosecutor on the case straightaway, and we'll get some deputy U.S. marshals in here to watch over the trial."

Celeste looked around at the town, as though she'd never quite seen it before.

"About Carleen . . ." the judge said, frowning at the window of the sheriff's office. "I'm not sure about her."

"I'll take care of her," Celeste said. "When she calms down,

I'll take her up to the house. If she wants a home there with me, she'll have one. For as long as she wants. I guess it's time what's left of the Chaney family starts to heal its considerable wounds."

The judge yelled for one of the many onlookers to fetch the local sawbones, then turned to Sartain. "As for you . . . if I remember correctly, you have quite a reward on your head, Mr. Sartain."

"That's right, Judge. I do."

The judge fingered his chin whiskers. "Best not let any grass grow under your feet in Bittersweet. That said, I'd be remiss if I didn't thank you for what you did here. I guess justice has been served . . . by a wanted man. Go figure."

"I think he serves plenty of justice, Judge," Celeste said, smiling up at Sartain. "May I offer you a glass of brandy, Mike? Perhaps supper?"

"Where?"

"Up at my house," Celeste said, as though it were a silly question. "Where else?"

Sartain turned and hooked his arm for her. She threaded her own arm through his.

"This ain't gonna look one bit proper," he warned.

"I don't care much about proper," Celeste said. "You know that as well as anyone, Mike." She kissed his cheek warmly.

They started walking together along the street, in the direction of the Chaney house. Sartain whistled, and Boss came running from where the Cajun had left him ground-tied a block north of the courthouse. The buckskin slowed to a walk and followed the arm-in-arm couple up the path to the large house on the butte.

Behind them, Waylon Chaney's screamed curses echoed.

* * * * *

GOLD DUST WOMAN

* * * * *

CHAPTER ONE

Hooves drummed in the distance.

Mike Sartain, the Revenger, sipped his tequila and turned to stare out the *cantina*'s open door toward the west, where a horseman was galloping down from a low ridge, heading toward him.

Horse*woman*, rather. A fine one at that, sitting smartly on a fine, sleek grullo.

She was silhouetted by the setting, blood-red New Mexico sun. The rays shone like liquid fire in her thick, blond hair tumbling messily across her shoulders and down the sleeves of her man-sized canvas coat. She rode straight-backed, lightly, with an easy hand on the reins, letting the grullo pick its own way through the prickly pear and Spanish bayonet.

Sartain took his gaze from the woman beyond the door, slid it toward the five men clad in dirty dusters, leather chaps, gaudy Spanish-style shirts, and billowy neckerchiefs standing at the bar of this little *cantina* on the outskirts of Fort Sumner. They stood six, maybe seven feet apart, one boot hiked on the crude wooden beam that served as a foot rail at the base of the wainscoted counter.

They'd come in together, had obviously been riding together, but were not speaking.

One was smoking a quirley, occasionally blowing smoke at the ceiling over the bar.

There was no back bar in the roughhewn watering hole, only

a few plank shelves with a dozen or so unlabeled bottles and a single, cracked mirror about the size of one you'd find mounted on your average hotel dresser. One of the five men standing at the bar glanced into the mirror. Sartain met the man's brown-eyed gaze, and the man quickly lowered his eyes to the bar. With a casual sigh, he lifted his shot glass to his lips and tipped his head back as he drank.

The man standing to his right glanced at him, drew on his quirley, glanced away, and blew smoke at the ceiling.

The only sounds in the room were the hollow ticking of a cuckoo clock on the wall opposite the bar, the occasional glassy thuds of a shot glass being set down on the bar, and the growing hoofbeats of the woman's grullo as she rode on into the yard and reined up before a peeled-log corral, scattering chickens.

One of the men turned toward the woman. The others did, as well, and then returned their attention to their drinks.

They all seemed to be purposefully keeping their hands away from the pistols holstered on their hips and behind which the flaps of their dusters had been tucked.

Sartain threw back the last of his own tequila and set the glass down on the table. He looked out the open door again. The woman was striding toward the cantina, batting her tan Stetson against her right thigh. She wore a blue chambray shirt under the canvas coat and blue denims tucked into her high-topped riding boots. A red neckerchief fluttered in the breeze beneath her fine, assertively sculpted chin.

Her thick, curly hair, sparkling gold with hints of red, winnowed behind her in the cool autumn breeze that skidded yellow leaves this way and that about the hard-packed yard littered with pieces of watermelon rind pecked clean by the chickens.

The men at the bar had all turned to watch the woman approach the cantina, mount the small, rickety stoop, and stop in the doorway. One of them chuckled softly, with sneering, goatish approval.

The man nearest her turned full around to face her, his chin dipping as he studied her up and down. He said, "Say, now— ain't you lovely."

One of the others snickered softly.

The man nearest her held up his shot glass. "Miss, you come to the right place. I'm gonna buy you a drink."

The woman looked at him and the others standing at the bar. She turned to Sartain, who was one of only three men seated at one of the six tables to the left of the bar. The other two were old, bearded Mexicans involved in a game of checkers behind the Revenger, near the bottom of the narrow staircase that rose to the *cantina*'s second story. Pungent smoke from their slender, black cigars peppered the air in the room.

The bartender had excused himself from the *cantina* a few minutes ago. A middle-aged Mexican with a young family, he'd muttered that he'd needed to check on his children. They were alone in his shack flanking the *cantina,* as his wife had gone into town to sell eggs. He'd demurely, almost regretfully, put his customers on the honor system. Sartain had silently opined that the barman had not liked the way the climate inside the *cantina* had changed when the five pistol-packing riders had entered a few minutes behind the Revenger himself.

The woman glanced once more at the man who'd offered her a drink and then strode toward Sartain, meandering around the tables, nudging a chair with a nicely rounded hip.

"All right," said the man at the bar. "How 'bout you buy *me* a drink?"

The man who'd snickered now laughed openly.

The woman stopped before Sartain, her back to the bar and the five men who'd all turned to follow her with their appreciative gazes. Their eyes had lowered to appraise her backside, which, judging by their glassy stares and eager smiles, was not unfavorable.

"Are you Sartain?" the woman said loudly enough for everyone in the saloon to easily hear.

Sartain inwardly winced and glanced behind her at the men, who now stared at him instead of her. Their appreciative grins dwindled.

The woman pulled a chair out from the table and sat down. She glanced over her shoulder toward the men at the bar, then folded her arms on the table and leaned toward the Cajun. She kept her voice lower this time.

"You're the Revenger?"

Her face was only two feet from his. God, she was pretty. A brown-eyed blond with a light spray of freckles across the nubs of her tanned cheeks. She was no spring chicken—there were lines around her eyes and at the corners of her mouth—but some women retained a youthful beauty despite their years and the unforgiving southwestern sun. Her mouth was wide and practical, her eyes brash and earnest. She was probably thirty, maybe a few years older than that, with a few extra pounds on her. Still, the man who'd been raised by toothsome, sexually astute young doxies in the wilds of the New Orleans French Quarter found her as alluring as any woman ten years younger than she.

Still, she was the last person Mike Sartain wanted to see at the moment.

"Miss . . . er, ma'am . . . this, uh, may not be the right—"

"You got my note, I take it. You are Sartain, correct? I have a job for you, Mr. Sartain. It is very urgent."

She frowned at him, saw that his eyes were not on her but on the men standing at the bar, who now faced him, staring at him, their faces blank. A few of their hands had come down to sidle up against the grips of six-shooters.

"Ma'am, could we discuss this later?"

She glanced, puzzled, behind her, then returned her gaze to his. "I don't have much time, Mr. Sartain. I have to get back to my ranch. First, before we discuss my problem, I'd like to know how much you charge for your . . . services. I need you to know that I am not a wealthy woman, so—"

"That's all right, Miss, uh . . ."

"*Mrs.* Chance. Maggie Chance."

Keeping his tone mild, his voice low, Sartain said in his slow Cajun drawl, "Missus Chance, would you mind goin' on upstairs for a bit? I'm in room five. Middle of the hall on the left. We'll discuss payment shortly."

Maggie Chance stared at him, her eyes widening a little with surprise. "Oh." She looked down at the table. "So . . . so that's how it is."

"Yes," Sartain said, smiling, keeping his gaze mostly on the men behind her still staring at him like wax statues. "That's how it is."

"I had no idea."

Her tone becoming angry, she leaned toward him, frowning. "So, then, Mr. Sartain—how does this work? If you require . . . uh . . . *payment before* you take on an assignment, how can I be sure you'll actually fulfill your obligation?"

"I always fulfill my obligations, Miss Chance. Now, then, as I was saying . . ."

"I'm sorry," the woman said, staring down at the table, troubled. She nervously brushed her hand across the table's grainy surface and said quickly, indignantly, "I didn't realize that would be the sort of payment required. I had no idea, Mr. Sartain. I'm afraid I came quite unprepared for such an arrangement. While I do require your help, quite desperately, in fact, I am not . . . well, I am not that kind of—"

"Maggie?" Sartain said.

She snapped her startled gaze to his.

"Go on upstairs." Sartain hardened his eyes and added even more firmly, with a single bob of his head. "Now."

She scowled at him, incredulous. "Well, you certainly are commanding, aren't you?"

"Yes. Now, please, go."

"I'm afraid I'll need a bath first. I've ridden a long ways, and . . ." She let her voice trail off as she glanced around as though looking for the *cantina*'s proprietor. Her gaze held on the men behind her, staring at her and Sartain. She turned back to the Revenger, leaned far forward, and whispered, "Who are those men, and why are they staring?"

She'd been so wrapped up in her own worries that she hadn't sensed the obvious threat.

The clock ticked on the wall near Sartain.

The two checker players had stopped sliding the painted bone checkers around on the board. They slid their uneasy glances between Sartain and the pretty blond woman and the five men pressing their backs against the counter.

Sartain's heart rarely raced, but it was picking up speed now. He did not want this bold beauty caught in the line of fire. On the other hand, he didn't want to make any sudden moves or raise his voice overloud and possibly hasten the imminent ruckus.

"We're old friends," said the man to the far left of the group. He was tall, dark, rat-faced, and harelipped, with long, stringy dark hair hanging down past his ears. His long nose was startlingly crooked. "Ain't we, *Sartain*?"

Sartain merely stared at him. The fires of hell couldn't have burned any hotter than the flames of fury burning behind his heart, threatening to turn that organ to ashes and melt his ribs.

Earlier, after the five riders had first walked into the *cantina*, he'd tried to pick Scrum Wallace, the one he was after, out of the pack. Now, he knew. Wallace had looked different back when Sartain had first known him—he'd aged a little and wore his hair longer and he'd grown a thin beard—but this man was Wallace, all right. He wore a gold spike in his right earlobe.

He was one of the men who'd been part of the pack of rabid, drunken cavalry soldiers who'd raped and murdered Sartain's woman and unborn child three years ago in the Arizona Territory. They'd killed young Jewel's grandfather, as well.

Sartain's eyes met the shit-brown gaze of Scrum Wallace. "Hello, Scrum."

Wallace curled the right side of his upper lip. "Been a while."

"Too long."

"I been wonderin' when you'd get around to it," Wallace said.

"Hey—wait a minute," said the man on the far right side of the bar. "Who's this Scrum person?"

Wallace curled his lip again. "I am."

The woman was looking around as though stricken. She turned back to Sartain, her eyes wide with fear. Slowly, she rose from her chair. "Mr. Sartain, I seem to have caught you at a bad time."

"Go on upstairs," Sartain said gently, smiling, though his heart wasn't in it, trying to keep her as calm as possible. "I'll be up in a bit."

"No, no," Scrum said, his lusty gaze returning to Maggie Chance. "*We'll* be up in a minute. Me an' the boys." He smiled and spat a long wad of chaw onto a table before him. It landed with a wet plop.

As though making her way through a field of coiled diamondbacks, Maggie Chance walked carefully across the room to the rear stairs. She glanced several times behind her and then slowly climbed the stairs, moving almost soundlessly, as though the slightest noise would detonate a bomb.

At the first landing, she paused, glanced behind her once more, then hurried over the landing and up the next flight to the second story.

Sartain kicked his chair back from the table and rose, flicking the keeper thong free from over the hammer of the big, silver-plated, pearl-gripped LeMat revolver housed in a soaped holster thonged low on his right thigh. The LeMat was outfitted with a twelve-shotgun barrel beneath the main, .44-caliber maw.

That was enough for the two checker players. They, too, kicked their chairs back. One of them held his hands out in supplication, and said, "Wait, *senores—por favor!*"

The Mexican closed up the checkerboard, quickly scooped the checkers into a leather pouch. He and his friend hurried past Sartain, tripping over chairs and table legs, and then ran out the front door and into the yard, scattering chickens.

"I don't get it," said the man standing to Scrum's right, looking at him. "I thought you was Chet. Chet Starr."

Sartain snorted. "Chet Starr. Yeah, that's what he changed his name to after he healed from the lead I filled him with . . . when I ran down him and the others in his pack of cowardly coyotes. He was *Sergeant* Scrum Wallace at the time him and four others—all federal cavalry—attacked an innocent young girl down in Arizona Territory. Attacked her and her prospector grandfather in their mining camp."

The Cajun paused, clenching his fists at his sides, feeling veins bulge in his forehead. "They raped the girl, who was with child. My child. Cut her throat. Shot the old man, shot their mule, and stole their gold."

The rider who had not yet spoken looked at Scrum and chuckled. "Well, sounds like you was havin' yourself a real good time, wasn't ya, *Scrum?*"

"Scrum's about to die," Sartain said with firm, quiet menace. "You boys want in or out, now that you know the lowly coward you've been ridin' with? You wanna die with a lowly scoundrel like this, so be it."

He raised his voice to a thunder pitch. "Don't just stand there—*draw* them hoglegs!"

CHAPTER TWO

"Ho, now!" said the second man from the door. He was the shortest of the group, with buckteeth.

He looked a little like William Bonney, or Billy the Kid, a young outlaw who was known to hole up with the *senoritas* in Fort Sumner from time to time. This young man even wore a squashed, ragged, black hat like the Kid's. "Just hold on, there, Mr. Revenger, sir!" He looked at Scrum. "You say Chet Starr here . . . or . . . *Scrum Wallace* mistreated a woman? A girl? One in the *family way*?"

His questions had all been directed at Scrum himself.

Scrum glared at Sartain.

"Tell him, Scrum," bit out the Revenger. "Tell your friends what you did."

Scrum shouted, "I reckon you done told 'em." He cut his eyes toward his pards. "That's what happened, boys. But I was egged on by the others. We'd all been drinkin' in Benson, see, and we was on our way back to the fort. We heard tell in Benson that our old pal, Sartain, was seen holed up with some old desert rat and his granddaughter."

He stepped forward and pointed an accusing finger at Sartain, narrowing one eye. "We thought Sartain was dead along with the rest of his patrol that was ambushed by Apaches. No one found his body, but plenty of them boys in the patrol had been cut up beyond recognition by the squaws. We figured that's what happened to the Johnny Reb here. Well, since we was just drunk enough, we thought we'd ride out and check if it really was him livin' out there. We thought we'd give him a hand back to Bowie, if he needed it." He added that last with sarcasm.

"Ain't that sweet?" Sartain said, giving an acid grin beneath his sand-colored Stetson's broad brim.

"When we got there, that old man and the girl clammed up when we asked about Sartain. We got the impression he'd been there, after all, but he maybe didn't want no one knowin' about it. Like maybe he'd fallen for that purty little blond-headed belle who filled out that tight blouse of hers right well and decided to desert."

In truth, Sartain had been intending to rejoin his regiment at Fort Bowie, but only after he'd repaid the old man and the girl for nursing him back to health. He'd been gone from the fort for three months. He hadn't thought an extra week or two would make any difference.

He'd had only eight months of service left before he'd have been a free man. He'd asked Jewel to marry him once he mustered out. He figured they could wait that long. Neither one had known she was pregnant.

Until then, he'd visit Jewel every furlough he was granted. Sartain had intended to help the old man out in his mine, once he and Jewel were married. A veteran of the War Between the States, he'd grown fond of the peace he'd found down there amongst those desert rocks and cactus, the shy, beautiful Jewel, and her strange but accommodating grandfather.

"Shit," Scrum said. "I'd have deserted for her, too. She sure could wear a shirt and a pair of jeans . . ."

Sartain said, "You and the rest of your blue-coated pards raped her, shot the old man in the belly, and ransacked their camp." He hadn't known that Jewel had been pregnant until he'd found her body lying with the child she'd miscarried when the brutes had so viciously savaged her.

She must have known, but she hadn't told Sartain. She'd probably been reluctant, wondering how he'd react to the news.

His head was fairly exploding as he stood here facing Jewel's last living rapist and killer.

"In or out, boys?" he bellowed. "You got two seconds to make up your minds before I draw and fire. I'll even tell you who I'm starting with." His eyes were boring holes into the rat-faced Scrum, who suddenly didn't look nearly as confident as he had only a few minutes ago. "I'm starting with your friend *Chet Starr.* And then it's you, you, you, and *you,* 'cause I'd bet the seed bull you're the slowest."

The four stared at him wide-eyed. They cut quick looks at each other.

Scrum glared back at him, saying, "We're all in this together, boys! Now, don't go gettin' nervy on me. This man put the word out he was huntin' me. We're just turnin' the tables, is all."

"Goddammit," said the kid, waving his hands dismissively before him. "I want no part of defendin' a killer of women and old men. Uh-uh. No, sir."

He swung around and headed for the door. "You fellas with me? Let that pervert shoot it out with the Revenger by himself."

"Goddammit, Kenny—get your ass back here!"

"No, sir!"

Kenny moved out onto the stoop.

The other three shared bolstering glances and then headed in the same direction as Kenny. "Forget it, Chet . . . er . . . *Scrum!*"

"You chicken-livered sonso'bitches!"

Scrum was crouched, hands dangling above his pistols. His eyes were so wide they appeared ready to pop out of his head. To Sartain, he said, "How in the hell did you find out I was alive, anyways?"

"I saw a 'Wanted' circular on you, Scrum. I'd recognize your ugly face anywhere. Of course the dodger only named your alias. Wanted for train and stagecoach robbery as well as cattle rustling and selling whiskey to the Apaches at San Carlos. My, you've been busy. Not sure how you managed to survive all the lead I pumped into you, but obviously you did. You must be part cat."

"Bisbee had a damn good doctor. A young fella from back east who enjoyed a challenge. He dug all the lead out of me and was pretty damn surprised that none of it had hit no parts I couldn't live without. I was laid up close to a year, but I'm just fine now. And you know what else, Sartain?"

"What's that, Scrum?"

"I had me a feelin' you'd come huntin' me again someday. So I got sharp with these here pistols. Shit, I practice my speed draw every chance I get." Scrum grinned shrewdly, shook his head slowly. "I don't need them yellow-livered pards of mine. I can take you *myself*!"

With that last word, he dropped both hands to his Colts.

He hadn't been whistling Dixie. He had become faster than Sartain remembered. Still, a rare hatred compelled Sartain to pull his big LeMat a tenth of a second faster.

Just as Scrum had gotten both his Colts out and up, Sartain's big popper roared.

Scrum triggered both his own guns wild and went howling back against the bar. Sartain fired again and meant to continue firing, but the woman screamed from the stairs, "Sartain—the door!"

He turned to see one of Scrum's partners standing on the stoop, aiming a pistol at him. Sartain wheeled just as the bushwhacker fired his Remington, the bullet burning a thin line across the Revenger's left cheek and thumping into the wall by the stairs.

Sartain fired twice and glimpsed the second shooter flying

backward off the stoop and into the yard.

Sensing trouble from behind, Sartain hurled himself over a table to his left. As he hit the floor, two more guns roared, and the kid, Kenny, shouted, "Whoopeee—burn him down, Ed. Burn him down! There's a bounty on that son of a bitch!"

The guns roared several more times as Sartain rolled, avoiding the bullets by inches before pulling a table down and using it for a shield. Another bullet plunked into it. It didn't go through, but the rounded tip of the bullet smiled through the splintered wood at Sartain.

The Cajun raised his head above the table. The kid and one of the others were thrusting their six-shooters through the open window to Sartain's left. Another was aiming through the window to his right. Sartain pulled his head down as the three guns flashed and roared once more. Two bullets hammered into the table without going through, the third one clipping an edge.

With an enraged roar, Sartain threw the table aside and rose, flinging a shot toward the man on the right, who gave a yowl and ducked down beneath the window. Sartain flicked the lever to engage the LeMat's shotgun barrel and hurled a fist-sized round of double-aught buck toward the window on his left.

The lead pellets peppered both faces, the kid's several inches lower than Ed's. The kid's right eye turned to jelly.

Both men stumbled backward, the kid screaming shrilly and falling. Ed dropped his gun and slapped his hands to his face as though he'd been attacked by angry hornets.

All three men had dropped out of sight, though Sartain could hear them stumbling around outside, cursing and howling.

The Revenger ran to the window on his left. Just beyond it, the kid was down on both knees, screaming, blood dripping from his ruined eye. Ed was stumbling around farther away from the window than Kenny. He was cussing, blood oozing from the many little holes in his face. He pulled the Schofield

.44 he wore in a holster over his belly.

Sartain shot him with the last .44 round in his LeMat, and then, holstering the LeMat and pulling the pearl-gripped, over-and-under derringer he wore in a small pocket inside his pinto vest, he ducked through the window and into the yard.

"You bastard!" Kenny screamed. "You ruined my eye! You ruined my eye!"

Sartain kicked the kid onto his back. "Why, you backshootin' little devil," Sartain said. "I'm gonna ruin more than that!"

He shot the kid through the middle of his forehead, instantly silencing the kid's infernal caterwauling.

Glancing to his right, he saw the third bushwhacker who'd been firing through the other window. He lay flat on his back, legs straight out, hands raised to his throat from which a small fountain of blood issued.

The fast-dying man quivered and jerked as though he'd been struck by lightning.

Sartain ran his right shirtsleeve across his forehead and looked into the saloon from the window the kid and Ed had been shooting through. He frowned, stepped closer, cast his gaze carefully around the room. He was looking for Scrum. The man's body was not lying where it should have been—in front of the bar.

Sartain stepped back through the window and strode toward the bar, continuing to swing his head from right to left and back again, looking around. A small pool of blood lay on the floor at the base of the bar. Part of it was smeared. The smear stretched, thinning at its far end, toward the door.

Sartain's belly soured when he saw a horse and rider galloping away from the *cantina,* framed by the empty doorframe. The rider rode low in the saddle as his dun horse with a white-tipped tail galloped off into the distance, a tan dust cloud rising behind them.

"Shit!"

Sartain ran through the door, across the stoop, and out into the yard. He squeezed the butt of his empty LeMat in its holster.

He needed his long gun!

He ran back into the *cantina* and swept his Henry repeater off the table he'd been sitting at. As he started to swing back around, something at the back of the room caught his eye.

The woman sat on the first step above the landing, leaning far back and sort of writhing, clamping her left hand to her side, just above her waist. She didn't say anything, but as she leaned forward over her knees, she squeezed her eyes closed as though in pain.

Her cheeks were mottled pale.

"Shit!" Sartain cursed again and ran to the back of the room and up the stairs.

He laid the Henry down on the first landing and dropped to a knee beside Maggie Chance. Blood trickled out between the fingers of her left hand pressed to that side of her body.

"Fool woman," Sartain said. "Why didn't you stay upstairs?"

"If I had," Maggie Chance said tightly, "you'd be dead as two fence posts, and I'd be on my back upstairs, with one of those low-down dirty ambushers pumping away between my legs in turn."

Sartain glanced anxiously over his shoulder and through the *cantina*'s door. The rider was gone. The man who'd fired through the door lay twisted in a bloody heap in the yard. Two magpies strutted around on the ground nearby, investigating a possible meal and clucking at one another with restrained enthusiasm.

Farther away, the chickens pecked the ground, oblivious to the recent ruckus.

Scrum would have to keep.

Sartain turned back to Maggie. "How bad is it?"

"I don't think it's all that bad," she said, wincing. "It just hurts."

Sartain slid her coat away from her side and lifted her shirt and camisole to reveal her flat, pale belly and the ragged hole. He inspected it closely. "Looks like it just clipped you. We'd best get you up—"

Someone moved behind him. He whipped his head around to see the *cantina* owner, a very short Mexican with thick salt-and-pepper hair swept back from his pronounced widow's peak, and a goatee of the same color, walk around from behind the bar and into the drinking hall, warily surveying the room.

He turned to stare up the stairs at Sartain and the woman.

"There a sawbones in town?" the Revenger asked.

The Mexican shook his head. "Not for several months." Lifting his extended thumb to his lips, he said, "He drank himself drunk. Drove his buggy over a cliff. He sings now with the saints." The man crossed himself and glanced toward the ceiling.

"Heat some water and bring me a few clean towels. I'm taking her up to my room!"

As the Mexican disappeared behind the bar, Sartain lifted the woman in his arms and carried her up the stairs. She wrapped her arms around his neck and stared up at him curiously. "I heard," she said. "I heard it all."

"What're you talking about?"

"Is that why you started hunting people for a living? Because of your girl?"

"You'd best hush. Save your strength."

He thought he caught a quirk of smile tugging at her broad, full mouth with a slightly, alluringly upturned upper lip. As he carried her down the hall, he felt her right breast press against his chest. It was full and firm. He turned his mind away from it.

He opened his door and carried her into his small room. He

155

laid her gently down on the bed, lifted her shirt and undershirt again, and more closely inspected the wound.

"It's not too bad," he said. "Looks like it went all the way through. I'll have it closed up in no time."

She stared obliquely up at him, not saying anything. Her lips were slightly parted.

"You rest easy."

"I am resting easy, Mr. Sartain. You have a way of making a woman feel . . . secure."

"How's that?"

"All those men you shot down there."

"Yeah, well—one of them got away."

"I'm sure you'll make short work of him." Maggie Chance smiled as Sartain ripped a strip from the sheet on the bed beneath her and then walked over to where his saddlebags hung from a ladder-back chair by the window. "I've read a lot about you."

"Oh?"

"Yes, the newspapers around here have covered you quite thoroughly. There are always supposed sightings, federal lawmen riding through the area, claiming they're on your trail and that you won't be mocking law and order for much longer."

"Yeah, well . . ." Sartain pulled his bottle of Sam Clay bourbon out of a saddlebag pouch and soaked the cloth with the whiskey. Returning to the bed, he sat down on the edge of it and went to work slowly, gently cleaning the blood away from the small, ragged hole.

"You cut a wide swath."

"I never intended to, Mrs. Chance. It's just how things worked out, I reckon."

She winced as the whiskey-soaked cloth touched an edge of the wound. "I'm sorry for your loss."

Sartain didn't know how to reply to that, so he didn't say

anything. When the Mexican had brought the towels and a pan of hot water and left, Sartain offered the Sam Clay to Maggie. "Better have you a swig. Then we'll get down to business."

She tipped the bottle back and made a face as the whiskey plunged down her throat. She took one more sip and then another, and then she returned the bottle to the Cajun.

He more aggressively cleaned the wound with the water and the whiskey, and then he laid a towel beneath her rump on the bed, to catch the blood, and threaded his sewing needle with the catgut he always kept on hand. The woman lay back on the bed and only groaned and sucked sharply through her teeth a couple of times, until Sartain had sewn the wound closed.

"There," he said, rinsing his needle with whiskey. "Only five stiches. Shouldn't even leave a mark."

"It doesn't matter," she said, staring at the ceiling. "Thank you, Mr. Sartain."

"Call me Mike."

"All right, Mike. I'm Maggie."

He returned his needle and thread to his saddlebags and set the pitcher of bloody water and the towels on the floor outside the door. He glanced out the room's single, curtained window. There was only a little saffron light shimmering in the east, beneath a dark-green sky.

It would be dark soon. Too late to start after Scrum.

That graveled the Revenger. The man had got away from him once, with a whole lot more lead than that rattling around in him now. But Sartain would catch up to him again. Sooner or later. It might do him some good to savor the experience of killing the last soldier who'd savaged and murdered Jewel.

He closed the door and turned to Maggie.

"Now, then," he said. "Should we discuss the urgent matter that brought you here?"

She didn't respond. Her eyes were closed. Her chest rose and fell deeply, evenly.

Apparently, the whiskey had knocked her out.

He stared down at the beautiful woman, her tangled, thick, blond hair fanned out on the pillow behind her. Beautiful and sad. The sadness had been like two deep wells behind her copper-brown eyes.

She looked as exhausted as she was tired from the wound and the whiskey.

Who was she?

Where was she from?

Who was it that she needed killed so urgently?

CHAPTER THREE

Sartain went downstairs and had a shot of tequila at the bar.

Then he went out to the stables on the far side of the yard and stabled Maggie's horse. He tended that mount as well as his own. When both mounts were fed and watered, Sartain headed back out into the yard.

It was dark now. The chickens had been secured in their coop for the evening. Thunder rumbled in the near distance. Lightning flashed in the southwest.

Sartain returned to the roadhouse, where the Mexican barman, whose name was Tio Rodriguez, served him a stew of beans, chicken, and onions. Rodriguez ate with Sartain, occasionally casting curious glances across the table at his guest. He hadn't asked any questions after returning from his private shack and finding his saloon shot up, four dead men in his yard, and a couple of puddles of blood on his floor.

In Lincoln County, New Mexico Territory, one learned at any early age not to ask many questions of anyone, for a good third of the population would shoot you for such impertinence.

When Sartain had finished his meal, he brought a bowl of the stew up to Maggie. He set it on the dresser where she'd find it if she awoke, though at the moment she still appeared deep asleep.

Back downstairs, he bought a bottle of Rodriguez's tequila. The barman announced he was turning in. His business this evening appeared to have been damaged by all the shooting earlier.

"Besides, with the rain . . ." The short Mexican shook his head and slapped his hands to his thighs. "You lock up?"

"Yeah, I'll lock up."

The barman left the room through a door behind the bar.

Sartain blew out the only two lamps that were lit. He wanted to sit in the darkness and watch the storm that was approaching like a bad-tempered giant from the southwest. He liked the cleansing of a good storm.

He sat at a table near one of the windows whose shutters remained open and poured himself a glass of tequila. Soon the storm was upon him, thunder peeling and shaking the floor beneath the Revenger's boots. The rain hammered past the window like slender javelins. It roared as it hit the dry ground, quickly forming puddles.

He sipped his tequila, his lips shaping a wry look of satisfaction.

It was nice to have the storm *outside* his head for a change. Sometimes, his fury over Jewel's and the old man's fate was as loud as this late-summer, high-desert squall blowing from the Sacramentos.

It also felt nice to have one more man to kill. The last man.

Scrum Wallace.

He sipped the tequila and set the glass on the table. The wind blew the rain at him. It was a tepid but refreshing spray. He closed his eyes to it. He jerked them open when a hand squeezed his shoulder. He reached for the LeMat on his thigh but left the gun in its holster.

Maggie Chance stood to his right, staring down at him. Her hair hung in thick curls past her shoulders. She wore only her shirt. It was halfway open, revealing the deep valley between her breasts. She was not wearing anything else. Her legs were bare.

160

As she stood before him, lit intermittently by the lightning flashes, the wind blew her hair sideways and sprayed her with the rain. The rain soon soaked her shirt, which clung to her like a second skin. Her pink nipples jutted against it from behind.

She stared at Sartain with a grave expression, her lips parted slightly. Sartain stared up at her. His heart pounded.

He felt the desire for this sad, beautiful woman deep in his loins.

He stood quickly, unbuckled his shell belt and coiled it around the holstered LeMat, and set it with his Bowie knife on the table. He fumbled his fly open, slid his denims and summer-weight underwear down to his ankles. He sat on the chair.

Maggie wasted no time in following him down, straddling his thighs. Sartain unbuttoned her shirt and slid the flaps back behind her nicely rounded breasts with jutting nipples.

She hoisted herself up slightly, grabbed his jutting member, positioned it carefully, and slid it inside her.

"Oh," she said as she wrapped her legs around him, sliding down on him. "Oh. Oh. That's . . . that's . . . *niiice*."

Sartain massaged her full breasts and nuzzled her neck. As they moved together slowly at first, he kissed her rich lips, her ears, her freckled shoulders. The storm had moved away now. Only a slight mist fluttered through the window. The room was silent save for the two moaning lovers and the creaking chair they were coupling in.

The moaning and the sighing grew louder, as did the creaking of the chair.

Maggie bucked against Sartain.

The Revenger lifted his hips to meet hers.

Suddenly, the chair seemed to disintegrate. Sartain flew backward. Maggie screamed and fell on top of him. They lay stunned on the floor for a few seconds. Then they laughed and finished.

She lay slumped on top of him, her open mouth pressed against his neck, warm breasts mashed against his chest. She was breathing hard, in time with the Cajun.

"Tell me, Maggie—what is it you came to see me about?"

She lifted her head and smiled strangely at him.

She lowered her lips to his, kissed him lightly, tenderly, then pulled away and stared at him again with that strange smile on her lips.

"I want you to kill my husband."

She didn't wait for a response. She rose, pulled her shirt over her breasts, and moved back to the stairs—a shadow in the night. Moonlight from a clearing sky reflected off the puddles beyond the window flashed in her hair and on her naked bottom. Then the room's deep shadows swallowed her, and she was gone, save for her light tread on the stairs.

Sartain lay on the floor, frowning at the ceiling.

Finally he rose, pulled himself together, and wrapped his gun and Bowie knife around his hips. He made sure the derringer was still snugged in the little pocket inside his vest. Then he grabbed his tequila bottle and shot glass and climbed the stairs.

He knocked once on his door and opened it.

She sat on the far side of the bed, her back to him, brushing her long hair. Lamplight reflected off the gold band on the dresser. He'd forgotten she was married.

She glanced over her shoulder at him as she continued to slowly brush her hair. As though she'd been reading his mind, she said, "By way of explanation of what just happened downstairs, I haven't enjoyed my marriage bed for a long time. And I thought prepayment couldn't hurt. For—you know—your killing him for me."

She rested the brush, which she must have found in one of the dresser drawers, on her thigh. The bandage shone on her lower left side, slightly bloodstained. Sartain went over and sat

162

beside her on the bed, brushing his finger against the bandage.

"We have to be more careful," he said. "Don't want to open up those stitches."

Maggie looked down at it. "It doesn't hurt much . . . thanks to your whiskey." She smiled. "And you, too, I reckon."

"Why do you want your husband killed, Maggie?"

"Because he's evil, Mike. Seven kinds of evil, each one worse than the one before it."

"In what way? Does he beat you?"

"Oh, no. That would be too obvious. He's never laid a hand on me. In fact, he's always been quite the gentleman. And he's been a good provider for me all the years we've been married."

Sartain studied her gaze. What was he seeing in those wide, soulful orbs?

Madness?

He reached up and slid her hair back from her cheek. "I'm not sure I understand. If he's never hit you and he's a good provider, what's . . . the problem?"

"He's killed all three of our sons. One after another. They're all buried in a little cemetery behind our place near Gold Dust."

"Killed your sons?"

"Yes. Of course, not in such a way that could prove he killed them, but each one of our boys was killed when they were with him. Alone. Each one, Marcus being the first, five years ago. He supposedly drowned. Daniel was supposedly kicked by a mule. I think Everett, my husband, beat him with a fence post. I found the fence post near where Everett said he found Daniel lying. Ephraim . . ."

Maggie let her voice trail off. A watery sheen had been growing steadily in her eyes, and now her upper lip quivered as she turned to look out the room's dark window over which the thin curtain danced. "Ephraim burned when the privy caught fire and the door stuck so he couldn't open it. Everett claimed he'd found the boy smoking in there once before and whipped him for it. My husband claims a cigarette had ignited a pile of newspapers and corn shucks. He speculated that Eph couldn't open the door because the floor was badly bowed, and he was probably choking on smoke after trying desperately to put the fire out, so he wouldn't get in trouble."

Her voice cracked. She sniffed, brushed a hand across her cheek.

"You don't believe him, I take it."

"I smelled kerosene in those flames. There was a large rock nearby. I believe that was what Everett had used to wedge the door closed."

Sartain thought about it. If she was touched, she had good reason. Three sons dead.

She stared expressionlessly out the window, tears rolling down her cheeks. The heartbreak in her had been obvious the first time he'd seen her. It had been in the too-firm set of her shoulders when she'd first ridden into the *cantina*'s yard, in her eyes when she'd stood in the *cantina*'s door.

Maybe that heartbreak, not unlike his own, was what had drawn him to her even before he'd seen how pretty she was.

"Why . . . why would Everett do such a horrible thing, Maggie?"

She turned slowly to him, blankly, as though she hadn't understood him. She scowled, impatient with the question. "Because he's evil. There's no other explanation. I've seen it in his eyes when he didn't think I was looking. I don't know how to describe it. It's a dark, vacant look. As though he's thinking about doing very bad things."

Sartain was having trouble comprehending what she was telling him. "There has to be something beyond evil that makes a man kill his own children. No man is that evil."

"Everett is."

"Maggie, do you think there's any chance he might have thought . . . ?" He didn't quite know how to finish the sentence.

"That the boys weren't his?" She'd obviously anticipated the question. "None. He had no reason to believe that. I've never given him any reason to believe that . . . until tonight." She lowered her eyes in faint chagrin. When she looked up at Sartain again, she turned her mouth corners down and shook her head slowly in frustration. "I know it's hard to believe. No one else I've ever told has believed me."

"Who else have you told?"

"My neighbor, Mrs. Douglas. And the minister who preaches at the church we go to—Everett and me."

"What did they say?"

"They said they thought I needed more rest. That I should come into town more, socialize with the other ladies. Maybe take part more in church activities—bake-offs, Bible studies, the Ladies of Gold Dust Sobriety League. They think the pain of having lost all of my children so tragically has addled me."

She shook her head. "That's not it, Mike. I assure you. Everett is evil. It's just a matter of time before he kills me . . . and others. His old father, Howard Chance, lives with us in a lean-to off the back of our cabin. I've caught Everett giving him that evil eye of his. Howard is senile. He'd be just as vulnerable as my sons were. In fact, I'm a little worried that . . . while I'm gone . . ."

"Where does Everett think you are?"

"He doesn't know I rode out. I left when he was running down some horses. I have no idea where he thinks I've gone. I'm going to have to come up with a story. One he'll believe. I am more worried about old Howard, though, than myself."

"How far away is Gold Dust?"

"Twelve miles, roughly."

"I'll get you back in the morning." Sartain looked at her

bandage. "If you think you can ride."

"I can ride. Not sure how I'm going to explain my absence overnight . . . or this."

"We'll say your horse ran off. You got caught in the storm, were wounded by a careless hunter's bullet. I found you and stitched you up, brought you home."

"Does that mean you'll kill him for me?"

The directness with which she'd asked the question was a little off-putting. Especially since it had been mouthed by such beautiful lips, by a brown-eyed woman who appeared as warm and tender as an early spring rain.

"It means I'll look into it."

"You're not convinced I'm telling the truth?"

"It's not that. It sounds to me like you believe you're telling the truth. But if I didn't look into the matter more closely, I'd be a fool—now, wouldn't I, Maggie?"

She gave a wan smile. "I reckon you would, Mike."

"And I should have told you this before. It was wrong of me not to, but I plum forgot after I saw you down there in the storm."

"What's that?"

"I don't take payment for what I do. If someone needs someone killed badly enough, for the right reasons, I kill them. No payment necessary."

Maggie frowned. "How do you earn a living then, Mike?"

"I take on jobs now and then, when I need a stake. Sometimes I'll hire on to a ranch for a roundup season. I've deputy sheriffed under made-up names, ridden shotgun for stage lines. Ridden guard on gold shipments . . ."

"That's all right."

"What is?"

"My prepayment." Maggie reached up and smoothed his thick, curly, dark-brown hair behind his ear. "I didn't make love with you for any reason other than you're a handsome, sexy man, a good man doing good for folks, and . . . because I wanted to so badly, I could feel the need for you all the way to my toes."

She placed her hand on his thigh.

"I'm feeling it again, Mike."

She shrugged out of her blouse and tossed it on the floor. Sartain leaned over and kissed her. He massaged her breasts while she did the same thing to his crotch. He nuzzled her neck. She groaned and massaged him with more vigor.

After a time they sank back on the bed together.

CHAPTER FOUR

Sartain woke up the next morning to find himself spooned against Maggie Chance. Fairly glued to her, in fact, by their mingled sweat and sundry other fluids. He was cupping her breast in his hand.

Slowly, so as not to wake her—she might as well sleep while he rigged their horses—he opened his hand and pulled away from her. Her pale breast, soft in her slumber, sloped down toward the other one buried in the sheets. He leaned down to inspect the bandage on her side. It didn't look like she'd bled anymore, despite the strenuousness of their couplings.

Maggie had made love with a desperation he'd rarely encountered. It was almost what the dime novels or Mr. Fennimore Cooper might call "ribald abandon," if the gentleman author had ever been given to write about such matters—or known about them. There had been a need in her that had not been sated for a very long time, and it had built to a torrid crescendo that had for a time caused Sartain to worry he might be paying the landlord for a new bed, though he was almost desperately low on greenbacks and coins.

As he quietly dressed, he scoffed at his chagrin.

While he did not make a habit of sleeping with married women, he'd done so last night, at least the second time, with full knowledge of what he was doing. Too late to feel guilty. His only defense was that she'd seemed so desperate for it, he hadn't had the heart to turn her down. Obviously, her own man hadn't been satisfying her needs, as natural to a woman as to a man.

He went out to the stable and rigged up Boss and Maggie's grullo. As he did, he wondered about this new job he'd been asked to take. Killing the woman's husband. He wanted to believe that Maggie was sane, because he didn't want to think he'd been lowdown enough to bed a vulnerable woman possibly suffering from some mental instability.

On the other hand, he found it hard to believe any man could be evil enough to kill his children without any motivation beyond the evilness itself.

Was anyone except Satan himself that malicious?

It was a cruel world. The frontier was one of the cruelest worlds on earth. Children died. Sartain had known entire families wiped out by typhoid or milk fevers. Drowning was one of the most common causes of death in the West, as was fire and getting kicked by horses, mules, or even calves during branding.

The possibility took firm root in the Revenger's mind that grief might have caused Maggie to stray from the path of sanity; that she now blamed her husband for what had happened to their children because she needed to hold someone responsible, and blaming Fate offered little satisfaction or consolation.

That scenario seemed the likeliest possibility. A sad one, but no more tragic than a man killing his kids because he was "evil."

Anyway, Sartain would take the woman home and see about her husband, Everett. Most likely he'd be back on Scrum's trail again soon . . .

Sartain led the fed, watered, and rested horses across the yard to the *cantina*. Boss was stepping high and switching his tail sharply, eager to hit the trail. The buckskin's mood seemed to infect Maggie's grullo gelding, who also danced a little and rippled its withers, so that it took some effort to get both mounts tied to the hitch rack.

The sun was just then poking above the eastern horizon, stretching long shadows as lemon light spread across the low, sandy hills tufted with prickly pear and bunch grass.

Sartain walked back into the *cantina*. Rodriguez was scrubbing one of the bloodstains near the bar. He gave Sartain a dubious look and then continued the chore as the Revenger climbed the stairs. He paused outside his second-floor room and raised his hand to tap on the door. He stopped, frowning, and tipped his head to the wood.

On the other side of the door, Maggie was crying. The sobs were muffled, likely by a pillow, but the pillow could not muffle the heartbreak inherent in the uncontrolled crying. The keen anguish was like a knife to the Revenger's heart. It awakened his own pain for his beloved Jewel.

He waited until the sobbing had dwindled to near silence, and then he tipped his head to the door panel and said softly, "The horses are ready. Take your time. I'll be downstairs."

He turned away from the door and walked back down the stairs.

The short Mexican was tossing a bucket of soapy, red water out into the yard as Sartain walked around behind the bar, helped himself to a bottle and a shot glass, and tossed a couple of his precious few remaining coins onto the counter. He took the bottle to a table, kicked out a chair, and slacked into it.

He poured out a shot of tequila and tossed it back.

Jewel . . .

He was glad Scrum had gotten away. The need to track the wounded man helped distract him from his heartbreak, which often, like now, felt as keen as it had when he'd first discovered the bodies of his lover, her grandfather, and the miscarried child.

He was sipping his second shot of tequila when he heard boots clomping on the stairs. He turned to see Maggie descend-

ing the staircase. She wore her hat and coat. She walked into
the drinking hall and crossed to Sartain's table.

"I'm ready."

"You sure?"

"I'm sure."

"All right." Sartain slid his shot glass toward her. "For the
road?"

"Why not?"

She threw back the rest of the tequila, wiped her mouth with
her hand, and set the glass back down on the table.

Sartain and Maggie Chance followed an ungraded stage road
straight south of Fort Sumner, in the direction of Gold Dust.

As they left the sleepy village of Sumner, following a nearly
dry tributary of the Pecos River, they passed the shabby fort of
a dozen or so tumbledown, adobe-brick hovels fronted by brush
galleries and flanked by a few brush huts and patches of torn
up desert that had once been corn fields. The slouching huts
were all that remained of the Bosque Redondo Reservation,
where about ten years ago the army tried unsuccessfully to turn
thousands of Mescalero Apaches and Navajos, traditional
enemies of each other, into farmers. The fort itself had been
abandoned in the late 1860s, and Sartain had heard the land
had been bought by a local cattle baron whose son was a friend
of young William Bonney.

The sheriff in these parts was an old acquaintance of Sartain's, Pat Garrett, whom Sartain had met in Texas gambling
dens in the years after the war and felt an affinity with. They
were of similar temperaments, at once sentimental, soft-spoken,
and hotheaded. Also, they'd both grown up in Louisiana, though
Garrett had come from a prosperous, land-owning family from
Alabama while Sartain had been a whore's homeless orphan,
growing up by his wits in the French Quarter of New Orleans

and taught to appreciate the finer things in life, including sex, by the *nymphs du pave* along Royal Street.

Sartain wasn't worried about Garrett. Of course, the sheriff of Lincoln County was aware of the federal paper on Sartain's head, but they'd run into each other before and had bucked the tiger and drunk tequila together in Los Alamos and Mesilla without either of them uttering one word about Sartain's bloody past in southern Arizona.

In fact, Sartain hoped he'd run into his old drinking buddy. Since Maggie's husband was a deputy sheriff of Lincoln County, he likely answered to Juan Largo, or Big Casino, as Pat was often known. Pat might be able to help Sartain clear up the matter of Everett Chance's culpability in the deaths of his and Maggie's three young boys.

As Sartain rode along beside Maggie, he scanned the relatively fresh tracks of a horse that had galloped up the trail ahead of them. Those had to be Scrum's tracks. He wanted to go after Jewel's killer in the worst way, but it seemed two assignments had overlapped. He'd give Maggie's problem priority and savor meeting up with Scrum again afterwards.

He hoped he didn't find the killer dead out on the desert somewhere, but, then again, dying slow and alone under the New Mexico sun might be just the sendoff Scrum deserved.

The Revenger and Maggie followed the stage road for about an hour through harsh, nearly treeless, sandy country pocked with buttes and crumbling escarpments, the cobalt sky arching broadly over them. After they'd crossed a dry wash white with alkali dust, they turned onto a barely marked trail that was merely a gap between mesquites and followed the old horse trail up a steep hill stippled with cedars and gnarled juniper.

Now they rode into even more forbidding terrain—badland country of steep hills creased by dry *arroyos*. It was a vast, harsh land. Sartain often wondered while traveling through such remote country what had possessed people to settle here.

He asked as much of Maggie.

"Everett's father, Howard, grew up in a small village in northern England. I guess once he got out here with his brother, looking for western gold, he thought it all seemed so inhospitable that one place looked as good as another. His brother died from a rattlesnake bite their second summer. That's when Howard decided to turn one of his mining claims into a homesteading claim. That's where Everett and I and old Howard live now."

"How did you and Everett meet, if you don't mind my asking?"

"My father and his own brother came out here from Tennessee to open a saloon in Gold Dust. The town was on a major stage road at the time, though travel has slacked off over the years. Both my father and uncle were killed during one of the many Apache uprisings in these parts, back when I was only fifteen. Everett's father was a friend of my father's, and he took me in. And that is how Everett and I became man and wife."

"I see," Sartain said, nodding as he turned to her, swinging easily with the sway of his sure-footed horse. "Tell me, something, Maggie—and please tell me if I'm prying too deep— did you ever love Everett?"

"No." She turned her frank, copper-brown gaze to Sartain once more. "But I never disliked him. I admired him. He was a hard worker, and when we couldn't make a living on the ranch, Sheriff Garrett made him a deputy, because the sheriff knew Everett to be an honest, upstanding man. And his easygoing, friendly nature made him good at collecting taxes. But he's also good with a carbine, and he can be uncompromising. We need good, uncompromising lawmen out here, where thieves and sometimes marauding Indians still run amok."

"That uncompromising personality probably kept him from being the ideal husband."

"Yes." Again, Maggie's gaze was frank. "Yes, it did."

That's all she said on the matter before adding nearly a minute later, "But that's not why he needs killing, Mike." Her grullo faltered as they climbed another steep hill. She took a firm, commanding hand on the reins, gritted her teeth slightly, and booted the mount on up to the crest of the rise.

Her raised voice quavered with the horse's pitch as she rode. "He needs killing because, as I've said, he's evil."

Sartain stopped as they rode around the shoulder of a steep bluff and looked into a slight clearing among prickly pear and scrub cedars and rocks. A rattlesnake slithered across the clearing and disappeared behind a human skeleton clad in tattered, dusty, sun-faded army blues. The skeleton leaned up against a gray boulder, slumped slightly to one side. Across his ankles—he still had his boots on—lay another skeleton. This one was clad in what remained of a red calico shirt and deerskin leggings. A few threads of a red bandanna clung to his skull that sported a hole a few inches up from and between the empty eye sockets.

The hole had probably been placed there by the rusty army revolver that lay near the dead cavalry soldier's skeletal left hand, to which strips of a gauntleted, leather glove still clung. An Apache war lance protruded from the skeleton-soldier's chest. It had little to support it anymore, however, so its end drooped in the dirt.

"Warrior Gulch," Maggie said. "Those two have been right there, like that, for many years. The Mexicans who live around here think the gulch is cursed, so no one has bothered with the remains. Not even after twenty years. There are more, many more, dead men up the draw a ways. Dead men as well as dead horses. Everett once scouted the entire canyon and said that, while some of the bones had been strewn by scavengers, many bodies had been left untouched, as though the carrion eaters, too, were frightened by the souls lingering here."

"A superstitious country, eh?"

"I guess you could call it that. Some say it's a haunted country."

Sartain lifted his canteen and pried the cork from the lip. "Is that what you think?"

"Yes," Maggie said flatly, booting her horse down the bluff, following the winding trail. "You have no idea how haunted, Mike."

Chapter Five

Maggie drew her grullo to a halt and sucked a sharp breath through her teeth.

Sartain drew rein beside her and followed her gaze down the slope and into the humble ranch yard along the northern bank of the Pecos. Like most, if not all, of the other ten-cow operations he had seen in this rough country, it wasn't much. Just a one-and-a-half-story, mud-brick cabin with a second half-story constructed of vertical, badly warped and weathered boards. It had a shake roof and a brush-roofed gallery, which was part and parcel of this hot, dry country. Stone pylons formed the gallery's front support posts, and the cabin's front wall was also partly stone.

To the left of the house lay the barn and three corrals and several other, smaller, outbuildings of stone and adobe. A well-worn path led into the yard from the Pecos, which was about ten feet wide as it curved through its low banks between mesquites.

Maggie wasn't staring into the yard but at a flat-topped slope on the other side of it, where a man was digging a hole in a fringe of scattered junipers. Several buzzards winged slow circles high above the slope as the man shoveled dirt from the knee-deep hole he stood in, near a trio of crude wooden crosses that probably marked the graves of the Chance boys.

Maggie glanced at Sartain. Horror flashed in her gaze.

She whipped the reins against her grullo's flanks, yelled,

"Hyahh, boy!" and galloped down the slope and across the yard and up the slope on the far side.

Sartain followed from several feet back. As he approached the crest, where Maggie was just then reining the grullo to a halt, Sartain saw the body lying in the back of the wagon parked near where the man was digging the hole. The body was covered with a black and yellow Navajo blanket. Mule-eared boots protruded out the near end of the blanket, and a fringe of thin, pewter gray hair showed where the blanket did not quite cover the man's head.

The man digging the hole had turned when he'd heard the horses galloping toward him. As was likely long-established habit in this country, he reached for a Spencer carbine leaning against a nearby mesquite but abandoned the movement when he saw that the rider approaching was his wife.

"Maggie!" he said. "Good Lord, woman—where have you been?"

Maggie swung down from her grullo's back and walked over to the back of the wagon. She stared down at the figure lumped beneath the blanket. She did not say anything. Her back was to Sartain as the Cajun rode up behind her and stopped Boss several yards away from her and the grave.

The beefy gent still standing in the grave cut his incredulous gaze to Sartain before turning back to Maggie. He stabbed his shovel down into the bottom of the grave.

"He's gone, Maggie," the man said, climbing out of the hole with effort. He stood beside the grave, opening and closing his gloved hands and shuttling his curious, wary gaze between his silent wife and the newcomer.

Finally, his gaze held on Sartain. "Who're you?"

"Mike Sartain. Mr. Chance, I take it?"

Chance turned back to Maggie. Slowly, he walked toward her. She turned to him, and her voice was crisp but quavering slightly as she asked, "How?"

Everett Chance rested an elbow on the side of the wagon. "Found him this morning. Down by the river. He went out first thing for water, like he usually does. Must have just started back with two buckets full and collapsed. His heart, most like."

Maggie turned and stared up at her husband. Her face was white. She glanced behind him at Sartain, who remained in his saddle, not knowing what to think, though he had to admit that the old man's death while Maggie was away certainly lent more credence to her story.

"I'm sorry, honey," Chance said. "But he was old. And, hell, most of the time he didn't even recognize us anymore. Where were you, anyway?" He turned to stare accusingly at Sartain. "You were gone all night. I was worried sick."

"Mrs. Chance went for a ride," Sartain said. "Storm came up, spooked her horse. Bought a graze from a stray bullet likely fired by a hunter. Fortunately, our paths crossed. I sewed her up. She'll be fine in no time."

Chance glanced at Maggie, who had turned back to the wagon. Then he studied Sartain again, skeptically. He was a big man, broad of shoulders, chest, and hips, with a firm, bulging paunch. He'd probably once been muscular, but now the muscle had turned to hard fat. Sartain guessed he was pushing fifty.

He wore a cap of thin, curly, gray-brown hair, thicker around the sides than on top, and long sideburns. He wore canvas work trousers and a dirty, sweat-soaked underwear top and suspenders. He was sweating and sunburned, his wedge of a nose pink and peeling.

He did not look evil. In fact, there was gentleness in the man's big, fleshy, roughhewn countenance. His eyes were large and blue, and the deep lines at their corners told Sartain he was a man of easy humor.

"Well, now," Everett Chance said, raking his thumb and index finger through the two-day growth of beard on his chin. "I reckon, then, I should be thanking you, Mr. Sartain." He didn't appear to have slept much recently. Had he been up all night, worried about his wife? Most men would have been.

"Not necessary, Mr. Chance."

"Sartain, huh? Sartain . . ." Chance's heavy brow furrowed as he pondered the name, as though he might have heard it a time or two in the past. He might have. Sartain hoped he didn't remember reading it on a "Wanted" dodger, because that could make matters even more complicated than they already were.

"I do appreciate your bringing her back to me, Sartain." Chance turned to his wife. "But I'm sorry you had to come back to this, Maggie. Truly, I am. But he was an old man, and he'd lived a good life. Leastways, as good a life as a man can live out here."

Maggie walked around to the far side of the wagon, placed a hand on the dead man's shoulder beneath the blanket, and said softly, "I'm sorry, Howard. Rest easy."

She gave her husband a cold glance, picked up her grullo's reins, and stepped into the saddle. To her husband, she said, "As a token of my appreciation for his kindness, I've invited Mr. Sartain to stay for a few days. He probably saved my life last night."

Her gaze flicked to Sartain, whose cheeks warmed slightly, before turning her bold, vaguely defiant eyes back to her husband. "He's been on the trail a while. Needs food and rest." She neck-reined the grullo around. "I'll start lunch."

She booted the horse into a gallop down the hill toward the barn.

Sartain watched her go. In light of what had happened between them last night, he felt awkward and ashamed in the presence of the woman's husband. He turned back to Everett Chance, who appeared to study him suspiciously.

The Revenger said, "I'd offer to help you dig, Mr. Chance, though I realize burying your own is a private matter."

Chance continued to study him for another few seconds, then stepped into the shallow grave and picked up his shovel. "I'd accept the help. Ain't as young as I used to be. Got another shovel in the wagon, under the seat."

Sartain swung down from Boss's back, loosened the horse's latigo strap, slipped his bit, and then, letting the big buckskin graze freely on whatever sparse grass he could find on the bluff, walked over and pulled the spade from beneath the wagon seat.

Chance watched him with that same slightly off-putting cast to his large, blue eyes. When Sartain dropped down into the grave, the men began digging in silence.

Stabbing through the rocky, sandy soil was tough work. The Cajun could scoop up only half a shovel load at a time. Soon he worked up a heavy sweat.

He paused to doff his hat and remove his shirt, wearing only his sweaty underwear shirt, the sleeves of which he rolled up his corded arms. As he worked on one end of the grave while Chance worked on the other, their shovels occasionally clattered together when they met in the middle, and he cast the man occasional, suspicious glances of his own.

Was this an evil man? Had Chance murdered his young sons and now, having taken advantage of his wife's absence, murdered his father? Sartain would like to get a look at Howard Chance's body, but he saw no way to do so without drawing even more of Everett Chance's suspicion upon himself.

It was one hell of a coincidence—Howard Chance turning up dead just after Sartain had learned of Maggie's fear of that very occurrence. Everett Chance did not look like a killer, but Sartain had known many killers who could have passed for parsons.

Just too damned much of a coincidence . . .

"Four feet's deep enough for these parts," Chance said when, a half hour later, both he and Sartain were standing that deep in the hole, which was roughly rectangular. The dirt piled to both sides was gray sand and red clay pocked with stones. "I'll cover it with rocks to keep the coyotes and mountain lions out. There's been a big female on the prowl around here of late."

Leaning on his shovel, he glanced at the other three graves lying about ten yards away amongst the cedars and junipers. Rocks had been piled over the mounded clay and sand. "Don't look like she's been at the boys' graves. Her main interest has been in my hosses and Maggie's chickens."

He grunted as he heaved himself heavily out of the hole. "Drink before we bury ole Howard?"

Chance propped his shovel against the same mesquite his Spencer leaned against. Crouching, he lifted a clear, unlabeled bottle and pried the cork from the lip. He took a pull, shoved the cork back into the bottle, and tossed the bottle to Sartain.

"Why not?"

As the Revenger took a pull, Chance sat on the ground and leaned back against the mesquite. Sartain took another slug of the whiskey, which was by no means from anyone's top shelf but more like panther juice distilled behind a Gold Dust saloon. Still, it took the edge off the heat and the Cajun's work-strained muscles.

When he lowered the bottle, Everett Chance was aiming his Spencer at him. He racked a round into the old carbine's chamber and gave a shrewd smile. "Sartain, huh? Also known as the Revenger—wanted by the U.S. marshals for gunning down cavalry soldiers in Arizona."

Sartain used the heel of his hand to hammer the cork back into the bottle's lip. "There you have it." He tossed the bottle back to Chance, who caught it one-handed. "You gonna arrest me?"

Chance studied Sartain amusedly over the barrel of his Spencer. He lowered the gun, depressing the heavy hammer with a ratcheting click. "Nah. Don't reckon. I heard Pat tell about you. Said if I was to see you in the county, to give you a wide berth . . . if I knew what was good for me."

He leaned the repeater back against the mesquite and dug a canvas makings sack out of a pocket of his shirt twisted on the ground beside him. "Besides, I do appreciate your bringin' Maggie back."

Sartain climbed up out of the grave and stretched from side to side, working the kinks out of his back. "No trouble, Mr. Chance."

"Everett."

"All right, Everett."

Sartain sat near Chance and leaned back against a rock. Chance took another pull from the bottle and offered it to Sartain, who took another sip.

"Sotol," Chance said. "I know some Mexicans who distill it down in Chihuahua and haul it up here to sell. All the saloons are stocked with it."

"Grows on ya." Sartain took another sip and handed the bottle back to Chance, who set it on the ground beside him and set to work building a smoke.

"I suppose you realize by now, Mike . . . well, that my wife, Maggie, is . . . uh . . . touched some. You know . . ." Chance tapped his left temple, then continued dribbling chopped tobacco onto the wheat paper troughed between the first two fingers of his left hand. "A little off her rocker."

"Oh?" Sartain hadn't come to a definite conclusion on the subject of the sanity of Chance's pretty wife. Apparently, Chance had.

"She rides off from time to time," said the rancher, staring down at the quirley in his thick fingers. "Gets some crazy idea in her head, saddles her grullo, and rides out. Unfortunately, she rode out yesterday when I wasn't home. I was off tryin' to run down some horses that the mountain lion had scared out of my corral the night before. By the time I got home and realized Maggie was gone, the storm was comin' on. I rode out a ways, tryin' to track her—she often gets lost out there, so toussled her thinkin' gets—but then the storm come up, and the rain wiped out her sign. I came back . . . had a worrisome night."

Chance offered Sartain his makings. The Revenger waved it off. He glanced at the three crude wooden crosses. Probingly, he said, "She told me about your sons, Everett. I hope you'll accept my condolences."

Chance poked the quirley in his mouth and rolled it, sealing it. He took it out and looked at Sartain. As he fired a match on his thumbnail, he said, "Did she also tell you she thinks I killed them?"

CHAPTER SIX

"Yes," Sartain said. "As a matter of fact, she did."

Chance touched the match to the end of his quirley and drew the smoke deep into his lungs. He blew it out and stared at the cabin for a time. Sartain wondered what the man was thinking. If he was thinking anything dark, it didn't show on his face. He merely looked sad.

"She started to lose her mind after the second boy was kicked by that mule. Became so protective of the third and last boy, Eph, I didn't think she was ever going to let him out of the house. One day, she took her eggs to town. I was working at my anvil, trying to get a rim on a wheel. I was distracted for hours. When Maggie returned, she screamed. Then I saw the smoke coming from the outhouse."

"She said there was a rock in front of the door."

"There was a rock near the door. Winter frost pushed it up out of the ground. But it wasn't within ten feet of the door. That door got stuck. Warped. Ephraim was a slight child. Apparently, he couldn't get it open before the smoke took him. He must've tapped his ashes on the dried up corn shucks we kept in a tin tub in there."

Everett's voice broke on that last. Sartain glanced over to see him brush a tear from his cheek as he looked over at the trio of crosses amongst the scrub cedars and junipers. Chance drew a ragged breath, shook his head, and looked down at the cabin.

"She blamed me. All three times I was the only one around. I

184

never gave that woman any reason to believe I'd ever do anything to harm my children." He turned to Sartain. A sheen of tears flashed in his eyes. "My *boys!* You understand, Sartain? What man would kill his *boys*—the fruit of my loins?"

He turned back to the cabin. Gray smoke was unfurling from one of the two brick chimneys. "I don't hold it against her. I did at first, but then I realized she needed someone to blame. I need someone to blame, too, so I suppose it might as well be me."

Chance took a deep drag on the quirley. "I love her, just the same. I remember how we used to be, Maggie and me an' the boys, and that's what keeps me from hating her for hating me . . . or for going out to the barn and blowing my head off. I love her. Always have . . . from the moment I first laid eyes on her. Hell, you've seen her. The prettiest woman in the county. But buryin' those three boys caused her to lose her mind."

He sighed again, loudly. It was partly a moan of deep, untouchable grief. "But so help me, I love her. I hope she stays, but now with old Howard gone—I think she loved him more than she loved me—she'll probably leave. She'll ride out again sometime when I'm out on the range, and she won't come back."

He shook his head.

There was a brief silence, and then Sartain said, "She was worried something would happen to Howard when she was gone."

"I don't doubt it a bit, Sartain. And now that old man's death, which had been comin' for a long time—he was senile and he'd suffered three heart strokes over the past two years—only confirms her suspicion that I'm some sorta devil." He took another drag from the quirley and flipped it onto the pile of dirt before him. "Oh, well. All I can do is love her as best I can and hope she comes around. That's all I can do."

He glanced at the Cajun, smiling, one eye narrowed wryly.

"What do you say, Sartain? One more drink and then help me lay old Howard to rest? I'll fetch Maggie, and she can say a few words over him."

"Ashes to ashes, dust to dust." Maggie tossed a handful of dirt onto the grave Sartain and Chance had filled in and covered with rocks. "Good-bye, Howard."

Maggie glanced at her husband standing beside her, holding his hat down in front of him. She looked at Sartain standing on the far side of the grave, also holding his hat. There seemed to be some unspoken communication in her look. Maybe a command for the Revenger to take his gun out and shoot her husband immediately. Also, there was a vague accusation in the gaze, as well, because she knew he was nowhere near ready to shoot a man he was far from convinced was a murderer.

Sartain switched his gaze from Maggie to Everett Chance and found the man staring at him with that same suspicious look as before. Did the rancher suspect that Sartain might be here to kill him?

"Lunch is served," Maggie said. "Cold sandwiches and coffee is all, I'm afraid."

She turned around and walked down the hill toward the shack. She hadn't taken her apron off for the funeral, far from a formal affair. The apron and her hair blew around in the hot, dry wind that had picked up now in the afternoon.

They ate a quiet lunch in the cabin. No one said anything of significance. The deaths that had occurred over the years and only a few hours ago hung like one thick, black cloud over the crude but tidy Chance cabin. When they'd finished the sandwiches and coffee, Maggie excused herself for a nap and climbed the stairs.

Before she'd disappeared, she cast Sartain one more conspiratorial, vaguely accusing glance.

Sartain spent the afternoon helping Everett Chance repair a corral that some of his broncs had broken down while fleeing the mountain lion. Chance had several other chores that had needed tending—some that had long gone undone because they required two able-bodied men, and Howard Chance hadn't been able-bodied in years. Chance's operation probably wasn't profitable enough for the rancher to afford a hired hand.

Sartain rolled up his shirtsleeves once more and set to work helping Chance move the privy to a new hole and resetting a ceiling beam in the barn. By the time they'd outfitted Chance's hay wagon with a new axle, another rain squall had come up, blocking out the light of the west-falling sun. The smell of roasting meat drifted to the men's noses on the wood smoke issuing from the cabin's chimney.

They put their tools away and stomped off toward the cabin, Sartain feeling that calm, soothing exhilaration that hard, homey work often visited on a man. He supposed it was especially keen for him, a man who spent most of his time in the saddle, hunting other men. But he sensed from Everett Chance's flushed cheeks and bright eyes and frequent quips and chuckles, that he felt it, too. He sensed that Chance didn't often have another man around the place, one close to his own age and capabilities, and that the rancher was enjoying Sartain's company.

The irony of the situation was not lost on the man who'd come here to possibly kill him.

On the gallery, they washed with fresh water, a fresh cake of potash soap, and clean towels recently placed out there by Maggie. As Sartain dried himself on a towel, he regarded Chance once more as the rancher scrubbed his face with his hands.

If Chance was an evil killer of children and his own father, he was one hell of a good actor, to boot. Sartain wasn't convinced the man was anything other than what he seemed—a hard-working, good-humored New Mexico rancher who'd been visited with one long run of bad luck, as had his pretty wife. The only difference was that Maggie Chance, sadly and understandably, had lost her mooring and was now wrongly convinced that her husband was Satan himself.

"Thanks for the help, Sartain," Chance said when he'd run a comb through his thin, curly hair and extended his open hand.

The Revenger shook it. "No trouble, Everett."

"You gonna stick around a few days?"

Sartain glanced around the yard. A light rain was falling from a sky the color of bruised plums, curling the hay- and straw-flecked dirt. Thunder belched and hiccupped. "No, I don't think so, Everett."

"You could cool your heels out here on the gallery and drink sotol," Chance said, encouragingly. "Hell, in four short hours we did everything that I needed two men for! We could even take a couple of cane poles and maybe see how the bluegills are biting on the Pecos."

Sartain's focus had now moved on to the hunt for Scrum.

"I appreciate the offer, but I'll pass. I'm not the sort to let the grass grow under my boo—"

The cabin's front door opened. Maggie stared out at the two men skeptically. She glanced at Sartain with that accusing expression again and then drew the door wider and turned back into the kitchen. "Supper's ready," she said coolly over her shoulder.

After supper, Sartain insisted on helping Maggie wash the dishes. He hauled water in from the river, and, while Everett sat on the front gallery watching the colors of sunset splash themselves across the western horizon as the rain tapered, Sartain and Maggie scrubbed the pots, pans, and dishes.

Sartain wanted to speak to her alone, but he saw no way to do it. Everett was within hearing out on the gallery. Maggie said nothing, either. She didn't even glance at him as they worked together.

That was all right. Sartain wasn't really sure what they'd talk about, anyway. He was in one hell of an awkward position. He'd slept with the wife of a man he'd sort of made friends with, the same man his wife wanted him to kill. And he had no intention of killing Everett Chance.

He guessed he was in a whipsaw of sorts. He'd be glad to ride on, which he intended to do first thing tomorrow. Scrum might have ridden to Gold Dust in search of medical help, so that's where Sartain would head, as well.

When the dark night had fallen, Maggie lit a couple of lamps. Everett came in from the gallery, grabbed her around the waist from behind, pecked her cheek, and said, "How 'bout I play some fiddle?"

Without waiting for an answer, the rancher grabbed his pipe and tobacco from one shelf, a scratched-up old fiddle from another shelf, and said, "Mike, I like to play the fiddle of a night when I'm not too tired. Always helped us sleep—Howard, Maggie, and me. Why don't you bring the sotol and three glasses and join us?"

Feeling about as awkward as he thought it was possible to feel, Sartain glanced at Maggie, who was sweeping the floor and keeping her attention on the broom. Then he grabbed the sotol and three glasses and walked over to the door they'd left propped open to the fresh night breeze touched with autumn's chill.

"Join us?" he said.

Maggie continued to sweep. She glanced up from her work with a strained smile and said, "I'll be out in a minute . . . Mr. Sartain . . ."

The formal way she'd addressed him spoke loads about the way she now felt about him.

The Revenger was going to be glad to ride away from the Chance place . . .

For the moment, however, he sat on the deacon's bench on the porch. As Everett packed his pipe, lit it, and then tuned his fiddle, Sartain splashed sotol into three glasses. He set one down beside Everett, who sat on the porch rail, and set the other two—one for him, one for Maggie—beside himself on the bench.

Chance started playing. Sartain sat back and enjoyed the strains of "My Old Kentucky Home." Sooner than expected, Maggie came out and sat down on the far end of the bench from him. Everett looked over his bow at Sartain and gave the Revenger a conspiratorial wink, pleased that his wife had joined them. Maggie had wrapped a knitted shawl about her shoulders, against the evening's damp chill. She sipped the sotol and sat back against the wall of the cabin, crossing her long left leg over the right one, closing her eyes.

Everett played a couple more bittersweet ballads and then he tried picking up the mood with "Little Brown Jug" and "Sweet Betsy From Pike."

"Why don't you two shuffle around a bit?" Everett said as he played.

"What's that?" Sartain said.

Everett jerked his head toward his wife. "Dance! Go on—the two of you!" He was tapping his foot and swaying from side to side as he played.

Sartain felt even more uncomfortable than before. "Oh, I don't think . . ."

Maggie scowled at her husband. "You buried your father this afternoon, Everett, in case you've forgotten."

"Ah, hell, you remember how Howard was. Before he went senile, he loved to dance and laugh. Hell, he used to paint the entire town of Gold Dust red of a Saturday night! He'd think it only fittin' we held our own private *baile* in honor of his saddlin' a cloud and sailing off to meet his maker! Come on, Maggie, get up and dance with the man! Howard's gone to his reward. We oughta celebrate!"

Sartain looked at Maggie. She looked back at him. Slowly, her features softened. A faint smile lifted her mouth corners. She slid her hand over to his on the edge of the bench. He'd hoped she'd refuse, but since she hadn't, he didn't see how he could.

He took her hand and rose and then clasped her other hand in his own other hand, and they shuffled around the gallery to the rollicking strains of her husband's fiddle. Maggie was a good dancer, better than Sartain, though the soiled doves had once taught him back in the Quarter. That was a long time ago, however. Maggie laughed when his boots brushed her feet. Sartain chuckled, his own mood lightening along with hers.

He liked the pliant warmth of her hands in his. He liked the smell of her on the damp breeze pushing in under the gallery's brush roof.

He looked at her pretty face, her pale ears, and long, fine neck against which the thick locks of her strawberry hair bounced. He glanced down into her open blouse to see the high plains of her breasts jostling as he and she shuffled in circles together.

He had a brief, remembered vision of her struggling beneath him the previous night on the lumpy bed of the *cantina* in Fort Sumner. Her naked breasts bouncing, her pale thighs lifting against him as she wrapped her legs around his back as he bucked against her, making her moan with desire in unison with the loud squawks of the bed legs grinding against the floor.

Desire was a warm liquor oozing through him.

He looked into her eyes. She was staring back at him, a know-

ing look in her gaze. Her cheeks were flushed, and he thought
he could see the glisten of perspiration on her brow.

CHAPTER SEVEN

"EEEEEEE-yi-howwwww!" Everett howled as he grated out the last notes of "Grandpap's Strawberry Wine." "Say, you two dance good together! If I didn't know any better, I'd say you been sneaking off together to practice them five-steppers!"

Everett laughed.

Maggie flushed. Sartain's ears warmed.

Maggie drew a deep breath and looked demurely up at the Revenger. "Thank you, Mr. Sartain. That was a much-needed distraction. Now, if you will forgive me, gentlemen, I believe I'll turn in."

She walked to the door, stopped, and looked at their guest. "Will Howard's room be all right, Mr. Sartain? You're not superstitious, are you?"

"I'm no more superstitious than your average Orleans Cajun, Mrs. Chance," Sartain said, drawing out his petal-soft accent so that "Orleans" came out "Oo-lenzz." "But the barn will be just fine. Boss and I are used to sharin' a pile of straw."

"No guest of ours will stay in the barn, Mr. Sartain."

She held him with a brief, commanding look, dipping her chin slightly, and then moved on into the cabin. Sartain heard her soft tread on the stairs.

"I think I'll turn in myself," Everett said, stretching and yawning. "Been a long day." He glanced toward where he'd buried old Howard. "Good night, Pop."

He nodded at Sartain and headed inside.

The Revenger sat on the gallery and sipped another drink before retrieving his saddlebags from the barn and checking on Boss, who was sprawled on his side in a pile of straw, half asleep. Sartain returned to the cabin, closing the front door and barring it, then heading off to old Howard's small bedroom at the back of the cabin.

He threw the shutter back from the room's lone window, letting in the cool night air, and crawled under a single, coarse cotton sheet. He lay there thinking for a long time, deeply troubled by the plight of both Maggie Chance and her husband.

From the ceiling above, voices rose softly. Everett was saying something, his deep voice making a low rumbling, the words obscure. Maggie said something in response, her voice softer, even more obscure, and then Everett said something else, and the ceiling creaked slightly.

Sartain frowned as he stared up at the ceiling beam from which an unlit lantern hung. The lantern began quivering, squawking faintly on the wire it hung from. A man grunted. The ceiling creaked. Maggie groaned and made what could only be a vaguely complaining sound.

Everett grunted again, louder, and the ceiling creaked louder, more regularly. Occasionally the legs of the Chances' bed leaped, hammered the floor.

Sartain felt a pang of jealousy.

Cursing under his breath, he rolled onto his belly and drew his pillow over his head, shutting out the sounds of the coupling.

When he opened his eyes, gray light was washing through the room's open window. He lay with his cheek pressed to the mattress. Sometime during the night, he'd shed the pillow. It lay on the floor. From downstairs came the sounds of footsteps, the squeak of a heavy iron stove door being opened, the thud of wood being shoved into the firebox, the squeak again of the door closing, and the faint clang of it being latched.

Sartain sat up and dropped his bare feet to the floor. He looked out the window. The large, orange-yellow sun was on the rise, the humidity from last night's rain ringing it with what looked like smoke. Sartain got up and checked his old Waterbury, which he carried in a vest pocket opposite the one that housed his derringer.

Almost six thirty. He'd slept longer than he'd intended.

Quickly, he dressed, washed at the basin resting on a wooden stand, ran his wet fingers through his thick, curly hair, and grabbed his hat, saddlebags, and rifle. He went downstairs to find Maggie scraping a flapjack from an iron skillet on the range onto a plate on the table. Beside that plate was another plate crowded with three sunny-side-up eggs, a steak, and a mound of fried potatoes. There were four more plates on the table, all containing the leavings of the Chances' breakfast.

"Holy smokes," Sartain said. "I slept in like a city-bred gentleman of leisure. You should have fired a shotgun outside my window."

"You were tired after all the work you and Everett did yesterday," Maggie said, filling the stone mug beside the plates that were obviously meant for Sartain. "Sit down and enjoy." She returned the coffee pot to the warming rack. "I understand you're leaving us today."

"This looks pure-dee wonderful," Sartain said, glancing at Maggie's buxom figure and trying not to remember the sounds of lovemaking he'd heard the night before. "I'm much obliged, but you shouldn't have." Sartain tossed his hat onto a peg by the door and sat down at the table. "And to answer your question—yes, I believe I'll be movin' on."

He looked at her. Standing with her back to the range, she crossed her arms on her breasts, gave a strained smile, pursed her lips, and nodded. She looked down at the floor. "Of course."

Sartain didn't know what else to say, so he didn't say anything. He slid his chair forward, took up his fork and knife, and set to work on the good food steaming before him. As he ate, Maggie refilled her own mug and sat at the end of the table to his right, opposite where Everett had apparently been sitting earlier.

"Everett went out early," she said. "That mountain lion has been up to her usual tricks. This time she struck our neighbor, Morgan Bentley. Killed one of his horses. Morgan came to fetch Everett, and they've gone out to track the critter before it gets any more of our livestock."

"That's too bad," Sartain said around a mouthful of food.

"I suppose if you'd been up, you would have joined them."

Sartain shrugged. "If I'd been invited."

"I'm sure you'd have been invited," Maggie said, smiling strangely over the smoking rim of her coffee cup. "Everett seems to have enjoyed your company yesterday."

There was an undeniable bite to her words, though she continued to smile at him over her coffee cup. Sartain felt guilty, though he knew he had no reason to. The way he saw it, he was caught in the middle between two ends at odds with each other, though really only one end was at odds.

What was he supposed to do—kill Everett Chance because his wife had gone off her rocker and now saw him as some sort of demon?

Sartain just didn't see it that way.

He finished his meal, slid his plates away, and wiped his mouth with his napkin. He looked at her still sitting at the end of the table to his right, staring at him now but not smiling. It was as though she were waiting for him to speak.

So, finally, he spoke.

"Maggie," he said, "everything's going to be all right."

"Is it?"

"It is. You just need to give it a little more time. Your wounds . . . they'll heal."

When she just continued to stare at him as though he'd been speaking in some foreign tongue, he continued with, "Everett . . . he's as broke up about your boys as you are. Just in a different way. Your believing he's some . . . I don't know . . . like he's some hoodoo conjure like we have down in the Bayou country . . . is just not right. I know that's what you believe, but you gotta see around it, somehow. Or maybe you gotta take a good, hard look and see *through* it."

Sartain slid his chair back from the table and rose.

He said, "You two are all each other has. You'd best hold onto each other."

He donned his hat and walked over to her. She was staring at the table now, dull-eyed, expressionless He squeezed her arm. It was a feeble attempt at reassuring the woman. He turned and walked to the door, opened it, and started out.

"He knows," Maggie said behind him.

Sartain turned back to her.

She looked up at him. "He knows why I brought you here."

"He does?"

Maggie nodded. "Oh, he didn't say as much. But I could tell by the way he stared down at me last night when he . . . when he was taking me. Those flat, cold eyes and that mocking grin . . . He knows." She paused, swallowed, a faint look of concern entering her brown eyes. "I'm sorry, Mike. I was a fool to bring you here. He's no ordinary man. I think he's going to be after you now. You watch your back and ride as far away from here as you can."

Sartain let Boss pick his way around the shoulder of a chalky bluff on which only prickly pear and a few tufts of Spanish bayonet grew.

He was following a horse trail he'd picked up just after riding out of the Chance ranch yard to the east and which, since it seemed to be heading both east and north, he assumed would meet up with the main trail, the old stage road, and take him into Gold Dust.

When Boss had followed the trail around to the far side of the bluff, Sartain checked him down. He stared out over the badlands through which the trail snaked, disappearing at times in dry washes and in the deep, narrow creases between bluffs and mesas, in small thickets of cedars and mesquites. Near Sartain lay the half-rotted carcass of a cow, some of the hide still attached to the flat rib bones.

Flies buzzed around the empty eye sockets and clung to the skeletal jaws. The stench was sour. It was made even more cloying by the burned-hair smell of sun-scorched needle grass.

It was a hard country the Cajun was riding through. Though the sun was high and bright and reflecting even brighter off the chalky terrain, death hung like a dark cloud over this stark, vast land burnished now with the hues of autumn.

Sartain glanced over his right shoulder and around the northeast shoulder of the bluff behind him. He was too far away from the Chance place to make out the buildings, but his attention was drawn in that direction, just the same. The last words Maggie Chance had said to him still echoed in his mind. The fear in her eyes had been so resolute, he'd felt a chill hand reach up beneath his sternum and clench his heart.

That fist still had a good hold on him.

Was Maggie even more insane than he'd sensed?

Or was her husband the crafty killer she'd tried to convince Sartain he was? A deeply evil man. If so, he was the most diabolical character the Revenger had yet crossed paths with.

Sartain ran his shirtsleeve across his forehead, jerked his hat brim low against the sun glare, and touched spurs to the buckskin's ribs. As the horse continued along the trail pocked with the marks of cloven hooves, cow pies, and deer droppings, he told himself that, against Maggie's warning, he'd remain here in this country. He'd hunt Scrum down and kill him and toss his carcass where the wildcats would have easy pickings, and then he'd ride back out here and check on the Chances again soon.

Maggie's parting words to him had been that strong. That gut-chillingly portentous.

A half hour later, Sartain and Boss were making their way through a deep canyon between steep, rocky slopes when Boss shied suddenly.

Sartain frowned down at the horse. "What the hell's the matter, old fel—"

Then he heard the rattle. The snake lay about six feet ahead, tightly coiled, button tail raised and quivering. Sartain jerked Boss to a hard stop and had just started reaching for his LeMat when something pinged into the slope on Sartain's left, pluming pale dust.

The flat crack of a rifle sounded from upslope on his right.

"*Hyahh, boy!*" the Cajun cried as he grabbed his Henry repeater with his right hand and threw himself hard left.

The horse whinnied and lunged forward. As Sartain dropped down his left stirrup fender, he watched in dread as the rattlesnake struck at Boss's scissoring legs. Because of the rising dust, he couldn't tell if the snake hit its mark to pump its poison into the Revenger's prize stallion.

Sartain hit the ground with a curse and rolled as another bullet ricocheted shrilly off a near boulder, the rifle's belching crack rolling out over the canyon a half a wink later. Sartain rolled behind the same boulder and racked a cartridge into his Henry's action. He glanced slightly ahead along the trail.

The snake lay smashed and bloody in Boss's still-sifting dust, the horse having pummeled it with his iron-shod hooves.

"Serves you right," Sartain growled, keeping his head down, jerking it even lower when another bullet screeched from the southeastern slope to hammer the incline behind him.

As the rifle's crack reached Sartain's ears once more, he jerked his head and Henry up. His trained eyes quickly picked out a plume of smoke from a nest of boulders capping the southeastern ridge.

Aiming just as quickly, he squeezed the Henry's trigger and felt the satisfying punch of the stock against his shoulder as the rifle's roar filled the chasm and the peppery powder smoke wafted back against the Revenger's face. He racked and fired, racked and fired until five brass cartridge casings lay on the ground behind him.

Holding fire, he heard the echoes of his thundering reports chasing themselves around between the ridges. Beneath the dwindling cacophony, he thought he heard a man cry out. A strangled cry, if a cry was what it was.

Sartain assumed it was.

He grabbed his hat and took off running toward the shooter's boulder nest.

CHAPTER EIGHT

Sartain held his rifle in both hands in front of him as he lunged up the steep slope. He kept his eyes on the boulder nest in case the ambusher was still in business.

It was a steep, seventy-yard climb. He slowed about three-quarters of the way up, and, breathing hard and keeping his gaze on the rocks at the ridge crest, he walked the rest of the way.

He stepped around a boulder and aimed his Henry into the gap behind it. All that was in the stone-floored gap behind a half-circle of boulders were a half-dozen brass cartridge casings. An old-model Remington pistol lay farther back behind the rocks, near where the backside of the slope dropped.

A couple of the cartridge casings were splashed with blood.

Sartain looked down the backside of the slope. It was a sharp drop for about fifty feet. A man lay at the bottom of the drop. He was moving a little, lips stretched back from his teeth. He groaned faintly. Sartain had halfways been expecting to see Everett Chance down there. Possibly Scrum.

The ambusher was neither man. Sartain couldn't see much of him from this distance, but he could tell who he wasn't.

Sartain looked around, saw a possible way to navigate the steep slope, and started the descent, holding onto rocks and a few cedar branches to break his pace. When he reached the bottom of the small canyon, he dropped to a knee beside the bushwhacker.

He was a middle-aged gent, small-boned, potbellied, and leathery, with a thin, gray beard and thin, gray hair edging his otherwise bald head. He wore old, worn buckskins, suspenders, and a shell belt with an empty holster. His rifle, an early-model Winchester, lay about seven feet away, near a canteen.

Sartain's bullets had taken him through his belly and his left shoulder. He lay on his back, one leg twisted oddly back at the knee, so that the heel of that boot was even with that hip. The man's face was mottled red. He squeezed his eyes shut and groaned softly, turning his head this way and that, writhing in deep pain.

"Well, it looks like I hurt you pretty bad, you son of a bitch," Sartain said, feeling no sympathy, looking around for more possible ambushers. "Who are you, and why were you shooting at me?"

Sartain couldn't tell if the man had heard him. He lay writhing and groaning, eyes squeezed shut, unable to lower his turned-under leg. Hoof thuds sounded. Sartain turned to see a horseback rider galloping toward him through a crease on his left. It was Everett Chance holding his old Spencer carbine across the pommel of his saddle.

He wore a funnel-brimmed Stetson, and a brown leather vest flapped as he urged the horse up the incline crease between bluffs.

Sartain stepped back, frowning suspiciously at the newcomer.

"What the hell happened?" Chance said. "I heard shooting!"

He stopped his piebald gelding and swung down from the saddle.

"This old fool took some shots at me from the ridge up yonder," the Revenger said. "Who is he?"

"Oh, no," Chance said, glowering as he dropped to a knee beside the wounded man. He touched the man's shoulder. His hand came away bloody. "Ah, shit, Morgan." He glanced up at

Sartain. "This is the man I was huntin' that wildcat with. Morgan Bentley."

"Why in the hell was he shooting at me?"

Chance slapped his hat against his thigh in frustration. "Ah, shit, I don't know. I doubt he even saw you. We'd seen that wildcat back a ways, and we split up to hunt her. Morgan was as nearsighted as a black-tailed deer without his glasses, which he broke pret' near two months ago. He must've spied movement along the trail and just started shootin'. That wildcat got two of his best horses last night—a mare and her foal."

Sartain studied Chance, suspicion still dragging cold fingers across the back of his neck. "What fool would shoot at something he can't see?"

"Apparently, that fool is Morgan Bentley," Chance said. "He was pretty broke up about his hosses. He lives alone out there on his little ranch, and all he's got is his hosses." He placed a hand on his friend's chest. "Morgan, can you hear me? Can you hear me, Morgan?"

Bentley only groaned, lips stretched back from his teeth. He looked about half unconscious.

"Ah, shit," Sartain said, dropping to a knee across from Chance. He inspected the wounds. "How far away is Gold Dust?"

"We're close. Only a mile or two. The wildcat was stickin' close to town for a time. Since spring, in fact. Folks been losin' chickens and pigs an' such. Apparently, it's widened its territory to include mine and Morgan's ranches, that caterwauling she-bitch!"

"There a sawbones in Gold Dust?"

"Yeah, a good one. Help me here, Mike. I think we best get his leg straightened out."

They lifted the right side of Bentley's body and gently slid his boot down. As they did, Bentley stiffened in misery. He gave a clipped scream and raised his head, eyes opening wide.

"Easy, Morgan, easy!" Chance said.

As they continued to straighten the leg, Bentley fainted, his head falling back against the ground, his eyes fluttering closed.

"Hip must be dislocated," Sartain said, suddenly feeling more guilty than angry, though he had no reason to. Whether he'd intended to or not, the old rancher had nearly killed him. It had been the snake that had saved Sartain. He just hoped Boss hadn't been bit.

"Poor old, stupid bastard," Chance complained. "Goddamnit, anyway, Morgan. I told you to leave the shooting to me!" Chance stood and looked around. "Let me see if I can find his horse, and we'll haul him out of here." He walked away and Sartain heard him mutter, "Simple fool!"

Sartain dragged the man into the shade of an escarpment. He removed his neckerchief, tore it in two, and stuffed both wadded up pieces into the man's wounds to stem the blood flow.

"Come on, you old varmint," Sartain urged the unconscious graybeard. "Hold on."

He climbed up and over the ridge Bentley had fired from. He descended the ridge, feeling owly and befuddled. He was also worried about Boss. When he found the horse grazing a couple hundred yards up trail from where they'd been fired on, he inspected the horse closely and was relieved to see no sign of snakebite.

Sartain straightened his saddle, tightened the latigo, and then rode back down the trail.

He was met by Everett Chance leading a dappled sorrel mustang. Bentley rode in the saddle, slumped forward, hands tied to his saddle horn. The sorrel was a handsome mount as well as a healthy, well-tended one. As Chance had said, Old Bentley obviously enjoyed his horses. Seeing the man's fine horse made the Cajun feel even lousier about having shot the man.

"I'd rig a travois for him," Chance said as he rode up to Sartain, "but we don't have far to go. I think it's best we get him to the doc as soon as possible. If anyone can save him, she can."

"She?"

"Yeah, Gold Dust got 'em a woman doc." Chance jerked the sorrel on up the trail. "A pretty one, too." He glanced back at his friend. "Hold on, Morgan. We'll have you in good hands soon."

Sartain fell in behind Chance, flanking him and Bentley to make sure the wounded man didn't slide out of his saddle. He thought they should rig a travois, but it was Chance's call. They rode slowly out of regard for the wounded rancher's condition, having to stop twice briefly so that Sartain could reposition Bentley on the saddle. Twenty minutes after they'd left the site of the ambush, Gold Dust began rising out of the rolling dun hills and spreading out before them.

As they neared the town, Sartain saw it was a humble little settlement sprawled across the hills and around a broad main street typically stretched between business buildings outfitted with garish false facades.

Sartain didn't think there were more than a dozen such business buildings, most comprised of gray adobe bricks and either front galleries or covered boardwalks. There were only a few horses on the brightly sunlit street. A couple of dogs were horsing around in the street between Johnson's Tonsorial Parlor and a large furniture store, growling and kicking up dust as they played.

One dog was old, the other young. The old one spied the newcomers first and stared with tail and ears raised. The young dog wanted to keep playing, which annoyed the older dog, so he gave the younger one an admonishing nip. The young dog leaped back with an indignant yowl, then followed the older dog's gaze. It raised its hackles and barked, glanced at its older friend conspiratorially, and then both dogs came running and barking.

"Scram, you cussed curs!" said Chance, gritting his teeth and jutting his chin at the pair, as though it were a club.

He'd admonished the dogs with a venom that Sartain found striking. So far, he hadn't heard the man utter a harsh word to anyone. The look on his face was dark and savagely, mindlessly malevolent.

Both dogs wheeled and ran around behind the furniture store.

Chance glanced back at Sartain, who was studying him skeptically. Chance grinned. "I was just funnin' with 'em." He laughed. "Did you see 'em run?"

Chance reined up in front of the furniture store. There was a sign on the side of the building announcing Clara La Corte Medical Services, with an arrow pointing toward a door atop the stairs that ran up the building's side. As Sartain put Boss up to the hitchrack and swung down from the saddle, the door at the top of the stairs opened, and a young woman came out. She was slender and pretty in a pale-yellow blouse with puffy sleeves and a dark-blue skirt with a wide, black, patent-leather belt strapped around her narrow waist.

She was a striking creature with curly, dark-brown hair spilling across her shoulders and serious, dark eyes set in a well-chiseled face that bespoke good Spanish breeding.

"Chance?" she called, shading her eyes from the sun. "What is it?"

"Bullet wound, Miss La Corte. Couple of 'em. It's old Morgan Bentley."

"Bring him up, bring him up!" The young woman, who'd spoken with a slight formal Spanish accent, strode back through the door.

Sartain and Chance eased Bentley down from his saddle, which was smeared from the blood that had leaked through Sartain's makeshift compresses.

They each took an arm and helped the man up the wooden staircase, Bentley groaning, his head wobbling heavily around on his shoulders. His eyes were still closed. Sartain thought he was unconscious but only calling out in his miserable sleep.

The woman was waiting for them inside what appeared to be a small waiting area of her office. There were four brocade-upholstered, straight-back chairs and a clock on one of the walls, which were tastefully papered in purple with butterflies printed in gold.

"Right in there, gentlemen," she said with what Sartain thought was a vague, faintly admonishing disdain. She probably saw a lot of gunshot wounds and the unsavory characters who inflicted them.

Sartain and Chance guided Bentley through an open door and into a bedroom-sized room with a leather examination table mounted upon a dais. Instrument-laden glass and wood cabinets lined the room, which was filled with the smell of camphor and other medicines. A large, clear-glass coal oil lamp hung over the dais on a pulley that raised and lowered it.

The curtains over the room's two windows were closed. The woman opened them, filling the room with sunlight as she said, "What happened? Who did this?"

"Took the words right out of my mouth," said a man's voice behind them.

Sartain turned to see a man with a hound-dog face standing behind them in the doorway, thumbs hooked behind his cartridge belt. He was probably about thirty, with a brown, soup-strainer mustache. He wore a badge on his pinstriped pullover shirt; a pair of gloves was hooked inside one suspender, just above the belt.

"I did," Sartain said. "I shot him."

The newcomer canted his head to see past Sartain and Chance. "Who is that there? Bentley?"

"That's right, Lyle," Chance said. "Sartain here shot him, but he didn't have no choice. It was an accident. Bentley's blind as a bat without his glasses, but we was huntin' that damn she-cat, and he got his neck in a hump and started shootin' at what he couldn't see for sure. Which happened to be Sartain here."

He looked at the Revenger, tossing his head toward the hound-dog-faced newcomer. "This here's the Gold Dust town marshal, Lyle Leach."

"Sartain?" said the local lawman.

"That's right," the Cajun said.

Leach studied him closely, brushing his hand over the hammer of the Colt resting in the holster on his right hip.

Chance said, "Lyle, let's go outside. I can vouch for Mike here. Purely, I can. It was an accident."

"Sartain," Leach said, keeping his gaze on the Revenger. "That's a name I know."

"How well do you know it, Leach?"

Leach brushed his thumb across the Colt once more. "Oh, I know it well enough."

CHAPTER NINE

"Come on, Lyle," Chance said, taking the man by a shoulder. "Let's go outside."

"Why don't *all* you gentlemen go outside," Miss La Corte suggested, pointedly looking at Sartain. "I need room to work."

As Chance got Marshal Leach turned around and headed through the outer office, Sartain doffed his hat and said to the pretty Mexican medico, "I'd like to stay and assist if you need it. I've sewn up plenty of wounds—mostly, my own, but I know how to do it."

She was crouched over Bentley, cutting off his shirt with a shears. "If you knew how to do it, Mr. Sartain, then why did you bring your handiwork to me?"

Her look was boldly reproving. There was no denying her disdain for him.

"I understand," he said. "I'll be across the street. I'd appreciate it if you sent word about his condition."

She merely shook her head in disgust as she continued cutting the old man's bloody shirt off his wounded shoulder. Sartain moved through the outer office and down the stairs.

When he hit the street, he saw Chance talking with Leach in front of the barbershop beside the furniture store. Chance was gesturing with his arms. Leach glanced at Sartain and started backing up the street, away from Sartain, saying snidely, "I know who you are, Sartain. I know who you are!"

Sartain just stared at him. Leach turned around and started

angling toward the Occidental Saloon.

Chance walked over to Sartain. "Don't worry about him. Wearin' the badge makes him feel like the bull of the barn. In all honesty, no one else wanted to be the town marshal of Gold Dust. The town don't look like much now, but at night things change around here. Punchers and no-accounts of every stripe in the county pour into the three saloons here. Lawmen have a tendency to die ugly. Lyle's had the job for nigh on a year now, and he ain't dead, so that's a big plus in his column."

"I hope he can stay upright," Sartain said, casting his slit-eyed gaze toward where Leach stood glaring at him from over an open batwing of the Occidental. Leach went inside and let the door swing shut behind him.

"Don't kill him, Mike. Please. If Gold Dust don't have a law-man, ole Pat makes me throw down a picket pin here till it gets another one." Chance shook his head as he untied his reins from the hitch rack fronting the furniture store. "Believe me—I don't want that job. Last time, they beat me so's I couldn't open my eyes for near on two weeks, and I still got some tender ribs."

"I'll do what I can," Sartain said. "Where are you going?"

Chance had untied his piebald as well as Bentley's sorrel. He turned out a stirrup. "I'm gettin' back after that cat. Then I'm gonna go out to Morgan's place and feed and water his stock. I'll take his sorrel. I got a feelin' he won't be needin' it any time soon. I'll be back tomorrow to check on him." He swung into the leather. "I sure hope the old boy makes it."

"So do I," Sartain said, feeling miserable. He'd killed a lot of men, but most had deserved killing. Old Bentley did not. He'd made an old man's mistake. The Revenger didn't want to be the one who made him pay the ultimate price for it.

"See ya later, Mike." Chance reined his piebald away from the hitchrack and spurred it west.

Sartain stood staring after Everett Chance. The man's dust sifted in the air over the broad main drag of Gold Dust, tinted orange by the sun.

The Revenger's scalp was beginning to crawl. He had a feeling it had more to do with Chance than his—Sartain's—shooting of old Bentley. There was something about Maggie's husband now that he didn't like. Or didn't trust. Wasn't sure of.

He wasn't sure why his perspective about the man had changed. It had something to do with Morgan Bentley.

Sartain turned his attention to the saloon on the opposite side of the street. The Whiskey Jim, built of adobe brick, was small and dark with a small boardwalk fronting it, behind a broad arbor stretching shade into the street. Sartain led Boss into the shade and tied him to one of the two hitchracks fronting the Whiskey Jim. One horse stood at the other rack—a tall, rangy, white-socked black with a speckled white snout.

Two old Mexicans sat on a deacon's bench under the brush arbor. One was asleep, head bowed over his folded arms. The other sat puffing a corncob pipe, one boot hiked on a patched, canvas-clad knee. Sartain unbuckled the latigo, slipped the horse's bit so he could drink from the stock trough behind the hitchrack, and headed on into the watering hole's cool shadows.

There were two men in the place. One was a long, tall *hombre* crouched over a beer and a whiskey shot at the bar, his back to Sartain. He wore a high-crowned tan Stetson shoved back off his forehead. He was so thin that his clothes sagged on him. He wore two cartridge belts. Sartain could see only one pistol, holstered high on his right hip.

A stocky, bald Mexican with a black handlebar mustache stood behind the bar, reading a newspaper and smoking a brown paper cigarette. A girl sat at a table near Sartain. Her occupation was obvious by her scanty attire—a pink and black corset and bustier—and the pink feathers in her hair. Her long legs were bare. She was resting her chin on the heel of her hand and absently curling a lock of hair around a finger.

She glanced sidelong at Sartain and grinned, showing a missing bottom tooth. She had a faint scar on her upper lip. Both flaws added a touch of child-like vulnerability to her woman's beauty.

Sartain pinched his hat brim to her and bellied up to the bar about four feet from the stringbean, who was just then taking a long, leisurely drag from his own brown paper quirley.

"Senor?" said the barman, blowing out a long plume of smoke.

"Give me a beer and a shot of tequila."

The stringbean turned his long, saturnine face toward the Cajun. "Well, I'll be goddamned. Look what the coon dogs just dragged out of the bayou."

"One of each for my friend here, too, will you, Apron?"

"Tryin' to get me drunk, Mike?" asked Pat Garrett, smiling beneath his brown, dragoon-style mustache. His steely-gray eyes were rheumy from drink.

"Looks like you're already headed that way, Pat."

Garrett smiled wider. "Been out shootin' Mescins. Cattle-rustlin' bean eaters hazin' our good Lincoln county beef down along the Pecos and across the border into Mexico. Shot the last one just this mornin'. I reckon you could say I'm celebratin' before I head on home to White Rocks and the missus."

"I understand." Sartain raised his shot glass. "Cheers."

He downed half the shot.

Pat threw back the whiskey he'd been drinking and picked up his beer. He belched. "What brings you to this boil on the devil's ass?"

"I shot a friend of your Deputy Chance's."

"Anyone I know?"

"Old Morgan Bentley."

"Now what did ole Morgan Bentley do to climb the hump of a man like you, Mike?"

"Took pot shots at me. Thought I was a mountain lion, according to Chance."

"Oh, shit. How bad?"

Sartain turned his head toward the far side of the street. "That purty sawbones is tendin' him. I hope he makes it. I don't like shooting old men. Even old men who were shooting at me. Old men, women, and children."

"If anyone can pull him through, *Senorita* La Corte can. She ain't much on personality, but she learned from the best—her pa, Ramon. He was university educated in Mexico City."

Sartain glanced around. The barman stood on the far side of the bar, smoking leisurely and staring across the narrow room and out a front window with a philosophical air. The whore was filing a nail.

Sartain turned to Garrett. "Let's get us a table, Pat. I'd like a private palaver."

"Oh, shit," Garrett said, feigning a gravely serious air. "Well, then, I reckon you'd best give us a bottle, Hector. How 'bout some of that pulque you're so almighty famous for?"

"Okay, but please, Sheriff," Hector said, setting a clear bottle containing a milky substance onto the bar, "only one, huh? I don't want you getting drunk on the pulque and shooting the good men of Gold Dust and stealing their women. It is unseemly for a man of your stature—and I am not talking merely height, *senor!*"

Hector blew smoke out his nostrils, chuckling. He was missing two front teeth.

Sartain knew Garrett's reputation for having shot several men over women, though that had been some years ago, before

213

he'd become sheriff of Lincoln County. Pat was still the rowdy sort, however, and his flinty eyes still sparked with a coltish gleam that Sartain remembered from their spirited Texas days.

"Ah, shit, Hec," Garrett said, now feigning injury as he wrapped a long-fingered hand around the neck of the bottle and began staggering toward a table. "You always take the fun out of things." He glanced at the whore and stopped. "Oh, there you are, Magdalena. I was wondering where you were."

She smiled coquettishly. "I've been down here waiting for you to notice me, Juan Largo. You know I am a shy *puta.*"

Garrett said, "Maggie this is a friend of mine, Mike Sartain. Mike, Maggie. Maggie, dear, show Mike your pretty tits. I don't think I've ever seen a prettier set of tits than them of Miss Maggie's, Mike."

Maggie chuckled and pulled down her corset until her pert, pale breasts bobbled free. Broad areolas ensconced budlike pink nipples.

"My, my," Sartain said and whistled. "You weren't exaggeratin', Pat!"

Garrett clucked. "Shit, now I'm probably gonna have to have me a poke before I ride out of here, and that's gonna get me back to the ranch late, and I'm gonna be sleepin' on the parlor floor."

"Ah, but a small price to pay for such a tumble!" Hector said from behind the bar and chuckled again.

Chapter Ten

"All right—what's so powerful important, Mike?" Garrett said when they'd both slacked into chairs around a small, square table at the other end of the room from the whore and the barman. There were only six tables. The head of a large mule deer buck stared down at the men from a beam over the bar.

Sartain splashed pulque into his shot glass and swirled it. "What can you tell me about your deputy, Chance?"

"What can I tell you? Well, he's got a right pretty wife." Garrett grinned.

"He does at that." Sartain glanced away as he sipped his pulque.

It tasted a little like very thin grapefruit and coconut laced with sour mash. It went instantly to his head, filing down several of the day's edges at once, though he wasn't sure that was such a good thing. He wasn't in the celebratory mood Garrett was.

"Do you think he's a killer, Pat?" he continued. "I mean—do you think he has it in him to kill in cold blood?"

Garrett frowned. "Now, Mike—you're gonna have to chew that up a little finer for me and spit it out slow. The man's a deputy sheriff of mine. Why would I pin a badge on a killer's vest?" He paused. "Come on, Mike. If you've met the man, you know him. That's the way Chance is. What you see is who he is, and you see it all in your first five minutes with the man. Now, look; I've heard the rumors goin' around about his wife thinkin' he maybe killed his boys. But, Mike, you gotta understand. The woman's—well, her boys are all dead. One after another in terrible accidents. She's come unhinged, poor woman."

Garrett glowered and sat back in his chair. His heavy, dark-brown brows were beetled over his steely gaze. "Ah, shit. Is that why you're here? Did Maggie Chance call for you?"

"All right—enough about Chance," Sartain said, wanting to change the subject and taking another sip of the Taos Lightning. "You know a rat-faced harelip named Scrum Wallace?"

Garrett's eyes brightened. "Yeah."

Sartain waited, staring flatly, expectantly at his old friend. It was obvious that Pat had something on his mind about Scrum Wallace.

"He's over at the Occidental," Garrett said, jerking his head toward the saloon of topic. "Holed up with a bullet wound. Or did Lyle say *wounds* . . . ?"

Sartain arched a skeptical brow. "Lyle?"

"The town marshal here in Gold Dust. Lyle Leach. Scrum's an old friend of Lyle's, see, and when Scrum rode into town bleeding like a side of fresh beef, Lyle tucked him into the back room of the Occidental. That's a little outlaw hole in the wall here in Gold Dust."

Garrett was grinning, and he kept grinning across the table at Sartain as he took a drag from his quirley and blew it over the Revenger's head. "I got that secondhand from a liveryman, you understand, so I can't personally vouch for its veracity, but the liveryman's been a good pair of eyes and ears for me in this neck of the county, and I trust him a whole lot more than I do Lyle."

"Shit."

"It's your lead rattling around in Scrum, I assume?"

"Pat, you're taking far too much delight in my travails."

"An old habit. Hearin' about other folks' burdens makes mine seem lighter somehow."

"What burdens are currently bowin' those wide shoulders of yours, Big Casino?"

"Lincoln's a big damn county, and I'm currently on the trail of three different groups of owlhoots, one lead by Little Casino himself, and I am way under-manned as well as pressured both ways by the rich cattleman who are done tired of havin' their cattle sold across the border in Mexico, and the Mexicans in these here parts who think that bucktoothed tyke is the second comin' of *Jesucristo* his ownself. Don't let's even start with ole Governor Wallace."

"So Billy Bonney's nippin' at your short hairs?"

"Yup. Keeps me on my toes, I'll give the Kid that. When he ain't screwin' *senoritas,* he's rustling cattle and shootin' folks. Busted out of jail up in Sumner couple weeks back, and I'm tryin' to break his trail and run a ranch over at White Rocks at the same time."

"When you're not sparkin' the ladies here in Gold Dust." It was Sartain's turn to grin. He glanced at the whore, who was leaning forward to pick at a toenail, her comely wares threatening to spill out of their scant confines.

"Relieves stress." Frowning, Garrett looked at Sartain askance. "What's Scrum Wallace done to climb the notorious Revenger's hump?"

"He was one o' them soldiers that killed Jewel and her grandpap. Somehow, I didn't kill him. Thought I did, but when I ran across his likeness on a "Wanted" dodger in Mesilla, it got clear as April rain he was still kickin'. Shot him again up in Sumner day before last. Wouldn't you know the bastard got away again?"

"The truly bad are hard to kill. Take Billy Bonney, for instance." Garrett gave Sartain a devilish look. "What're you gonna do about Scrum?"

Sartain hiked a shoulder, as though it were a foolish question. "Finish him."

"Well, good luck," the Lincoln County sheriff said, skidding his chair away from the table and tossing back the last of the pulque. "He's got Lyle Leach sidin' him."

Sartain was incredulous. "The town marshal's sidin' Scrum Wallace?"

"I think they're cousins. Scrum's got quite a few kin around here, not to mention owlhoot friends. Lyle's as rotten as the rest, lookin' the other way when sundry nefarious deeds are done around Gold Dust. Go ahead. Kill him for me. He's been a thorn in my side ever since I was elected sheriff. Every time I come to town I feel like the *loco* bastard's drawin' a bead between my shoulder blades."

"In that case, I look forward to doing your dirty work for you, Pat."

"Tread lightly, Mike. Scrum's got more than just Lyle sidin' him. I wouldn't doubt it if, knowin' you're in town, he doesn't have half a dozen or more cold-steel artists over there right now, filin' down their firing pins."

Sartain studied Garrett dubiously. "I'll be hanged, Pat, if you're not just thrilled over this."

"It's always fun to see you shoot, Mike. I've seen it once or twice, and it's a picture. You got killin' down to a fine art. I'd just as soon you did it here as anywhere. Cull the bad herd that's been grazin' in my fair county. I got enough on my plate with Billy Bonney and friends."

Garrett set his hat carefully on his head and ran the first two fingers of both hands around the brim, adjusting the angle. "I hope we meet up again in more peaceful times for a night of buckin' the tiger. But if it's your grave adorning our humble Boot Hill, I'll lay some wild daisies on ya."

"Why, thank you, Sheriff."

"What are friends for, Mike?" Garrett winked, then strode over to the doxie. He tipped her chin up and kissed her on the lips. He slid his hand up her naked thigh, waggled his fingers. "I'll see ya again, Maggie."

"You don't want to make love this afternoon, Pat?"

"What I want and what I got time for is two different things, darlin'."

He kissed her once more, straightened, and regarded Sartain again, this time skeptically. "You can shoot Lyle and Scrum Wallace and their friends all you want, Mike. But you leave my deputy alone, hear?" His eyes twinkled as he quirked a grin. "He's the best tax collector on my payroll."

Garrett waved, ducked out through the batwings, mounted his horse, and galloped away.

A minute later, the beautiful sawbones, *Senorita* La Corte, strode into the saloon, looking dark.

CHAPTER ELEVEN

Sartain said the words before she had a chance to.

"He's dead."

"Yes," the pretty medico said tonelessly as she stood by his table. "He'd lost a lot of blood. Several organs were irreparably damaged. There was nothing I could do."

She was pressing the tips of three fingers onto the table as she stood scowling at him like a disapproving schoolmistress.

Sartain looked at his empty glass, refilled it from the bottle. He didn't say anything. His throat was dry. He felt heavy inside. He felt the vague, nibbling anger that comes when you're not sure who you're angry at.

He threw back half the shot and looked up at Clara La Corte. She still scowled at him, her ivory cheeks mottled red, her dark-brown eyes hard and angry. But now they were narrowing slightly at the corners as she studied him.

Sartain held her gaze until she backed off a step and folded her arms on her chest. She jerked her chin to indicate behind him, east along the main street. "I'm tending more of your handiwork over at the Occidental."

"There's no point tending a dead man," Sartain said. "The old man was a mistake. That one over at the Occidental was not."

"What'd he do to you?"

"Enough." The Revenger felt his eyes burn from that deep, well-tended rage smoldering inside him, fueled by sorrow. He felt, in a way, that every bad man he killed tempered it a little. Just a little. Scrum Wallace would temper it a lot, maybe, though the Revenger knew he could never stop doing what he did. He would die killing for others those who needed killing.

He leaned back in his chair to dig some coins out of his jeans pocket. He tossed five silver dollars on the table. "That should bury him."

"Burial is only three dollars."

"Death is cheap in these parts."

"Cheap and easy, yes." She pocketed the coins. "We have two undertakers competing for business, so they keep their prices down."

"Consider the rest for his tending."

She pocketed the other two coins and started to turn away.

Sartain, who was getting pleasantly drunk, said, "Drink?" He was intrigued by the regal Spanish beauty, who seemed tightly ensconced in an air of prideful independence. To distract himself from the pain of having killed the old man, he wondered what she would look like without her clothes on.

She stopped and looked at him over her shoulder, catching his eyes raking the generous mounds of her breasts. She stared at him as though flabbergasted by the question, as well as repelled by his gaze.

"No," she said on the heels of a caustic chuckle and strode out of the saloon and across the street to her office.

He'd also wanted to probe her about Scrum Wallace—his condition, how many men were guarding him at the Occidental. It didn't look like he'd get any information about anything from the beautiful medico.

He waved a fly away from his shot glass and turned his attention to a near, street-facing window. Two horses stood tied before the Occidental—a shabby, two-story wood and adobe watering hole with a brush-roofed front gallery. No one stood on the gallery. In fact, there didn't appear to be anyone on the main street of this bedraggled little town.

Word had probably spread quickly that Scrum Wallace was here, wounded. That the man who'd wounded him was here, as well. The townsfolk of Gold Dust, likely accustomed to trouble, probably didn't want to risk catching a stray bullet or a ricochet.

Sartain hoped they kept their heads down. He didn't want more innocents getting beefed.

Just Scrum and anyone foolish enough to stand between the Revenger and his prey.

Movement across the street caught Sartain's eye. A lean man wearing a red shirt and black leather chaps stepped out of the shade of an alley mouth and onto the raised boardwalk fronting Parnham's Drug Store. He turned toward Sartain and leaned against an awning support post, flanked by a CLOSED sign hanging in a window.

He used the barrel of the carbine he was holding to nudge his hat brim up off his forehead. He was too far away for Sartain to see him clearly, but the man appeared to smile.

The batwings behind Sartain creaked.

The whore screamed.

The Revenger bolted from his chair, crouching, twisting, and clawing the LeMat from its holster. Flames lapped from the barrel of the gun poking between the batwings.

The bullet shattered Sartain's shot glass. The shooter screamed and lurched into the saloon, aiming again at Sartain, who squeezed the trigger of the big LeMat. The shooter fired his pistol wide, screaming and stumbling hastily back against the batwings.

The Cajun fired again.

The man standing suspended between the batwings lurched backward once more, the doors swinging into place before him. The Cajun fired a final shot, drilling a round through the right door and into the hip of the man who'd just then turned full around and was staggering, screaming, out into the street. He triggered his pistol into the ground near his right boot and then dropped to his knees.

"*Bastard!*" he bellowed before pitching forward and sliding his knees up beneath his belly, quivering.

On the far side of the street, a rifle cracked.

Having expected it, Sartain was already on the floor, rolling toward the window. The rifle spoke again. Another one thundered, as well, both slugs ripping into the table at which the Cajun and Garrett had sat.

"No!" the whore screamed. "Stop shooting!"

"Stay down, darlin'!" Sartain shouted, having glanced over to see that she was cowering beneath her table, poking her fingers in her ears.

Two more bullets came hurtling through the window over his head. As they slammed into the table, he ran to the window on his right, snaked his LeMat over the sill, drew a quick bead on the gent firing from one knee in front of the drug store, and sent him triggering his carbine into the air before flying backwards, limbs windmilling, through the window bearing the CLOSED sign in a screech of shattering glass.

The man shooting farther to Sartain's left sent a bullet slamming into the window frame, just left of the Revenger's cheek. Sartain aimed at the second man, who was firing from over a rain barrel in an alley mouth between the furniture store and the barbershop. As Sartain planted a bead on him and started to take up the slack in his trigger finger, the man lurched back into the alley, out of sight.

"Coward," the Revenger raked out through gritted teeth.

CHAPTER TWELVE

The Revenger looked around. There appeared to be no more shooters.

He kept searching anyway, with one eye on the batwings. A man stepped out of the Occidental Saloon across the street a block and a half away on Sartain's right. The Revenger aimed his LeMat, knowing it wouldn't do him much good from this distance. But he didn't have his Henry, so he aimed it, anyway.

The man standing there spread his arms away from his sides, as though to show his guns were still in their holsters. A silver badge glinted on his striped shirt.

Leach.

The town marshal's bowler hat shaded the upper half of his face, which he turned to his right as a man appeared out of the alley and stepped up onto the boardwalk beside him.

It was the man who'd been shooting at Sartain from over the rain barrel.

Both men stood facing the Cajun. The sole surviving member of the trio of ambushers was shorter than Leach. He wore a sun-coppered bowler hat similar to Leach's and a bright green neckerchief. When he'd been closer, Sartain had seen that he had a playing card wedged behind the band ringing the bowler's rounded crown.

His and Leach's mouths appeared to move as they conversed. Then they glanced once more at Sartain and walked into the Occidental, the batwings flapping into place behind them.

Sartain looked around.

Save for the two horses standing in front of the Occidental, the street was abandoned. The only movement was the dust being lifted and swirled by the hot, early-autumn breeze. An old newspaper was picked up by one of the gusts. It blew up against the front of the drugstore and then seemed to be sucked through the window broken by one of the two bushwhackers Sartain had shot.

As for the bushwhacker himself, Sartain could see only the gray soles of the man's boots, which had got hung up in the broken glass.

The door to the town medico's office opened. *Senorita* La Corte stepped tentatively out onto the second-floor landing, looking around, her hair blowing in the breeze. She held a brown medical kit low by her side. A broad-brimmed straw hat shaded her face.

Her skirts swirled out from her long legs as she descended the steps, holding the hem of her dress up above her black, high-heeled, gold-button shoes. She glanced toward Sartain with a sour, reproving expression. Then she strode resolutely to the drugstore, casting the Revenger several more disgusted glances, and looked through the broken window.

She glanced once more at Sartain, then continued walking east along the side of the street, dust billowing around her, the breeze by turns basting her skirt against her legs and lifting it above her ankles.

Sartain glanced at the Whiskey Jim's bar behind him. The barman was gone. The whore peered at him from beneath her table. Sartain went over and gave her his hand. When she stood before him, she pushed up her breasts and threw back her hair with a sigh.

"A friend of Juan Largo's, eh?" she said, looking him up and down.

"Yep."

"It figures." She glanced out the window. "Will there be more shooting?"

"Yes. I'm sorry, darlin'. You'd best go on upstairs and stay there. Keep your head down."

"What's it all about?" she wanted to know.

"Revenge," Sartain said matter-of-factly.

"Ah." The girl nodded her South-of-the-Border understanding of the concept, pushed up her splendid breasts once more, retrieved a bottle and a glass from behind the bar, and climbed the stairs to the second story.

Sartain walked outside. Boss must have ripped his reins free of the hitch rack when the shooting had erupted. The horse now stood at the west end of town, staring back at its rider, reins dangling. To the east, *Senorita* La Corte was just then pushing through the batwings of the Occidental Saloon.

Sartain studied the street carefully. Deeming it as deserted as it appeared, he walked over to Boss, swung up into the saddle, and rode through town to the east. As he did, he slid his Henry from its boot, pumped a cartridge into the chamber, set the hammer to half cock, and rested the barrel across the pommel of his saddle. He kept the barrel aimed in the general direction of the Occidental.

He studied the shabby building as he passed, the west-angling sun turning its adobe and weathered wood front to copper. The large window to the right of the batwings was too dusty and dark to be seen through. The sun glinted off the smeared dust.

No sounds issued from inside.

Sartain heard the scratchy strains of a fiddle from farther up the street. They seemed to be coming from the Lincoln County Inn sitting another block to the east on its own sage- and rock-stippled lot. It was the last building on that side of town, just beyond a low, flat-roofed stone structure that a wooden sign, which stretched a few feet into the street on ironwood posts, identified simply as GOLD DUST JAIL.

The two buildings were separated by a good twenty feet and flanked by shacks, small farmsteads, windmills, and stock pens that comprised the rest of the town. They stretched across the low, sage- and yucca-tufted hills, as did the occasional goat and cow. Chickens clucked from somewhere unseen.

The scratching of the fiddle grew louder as Sartain approached the hotel, which was a two-story, barrack-like affair with a rough wooden gallery on both its first and second floors. Its brown adobe bricks were as bulging, cracked, and pitted as an old man's spine. Its large sign was stretched across the top of the second story, the black-painted letters badly faded against the moldering gray wood.

The fiddling—if you could call it fiddling and not merely the raucous plucking of fiddle strings—didn't seem to be coming from inside the place, but from outside. And so was the deep, mournful howling of a dog as though in tune—if anything could be in tune with something so *out of tune*—with the fiddle.

Sartain reined Boss around to the building's far front corner. Along its east side, a canvas awning had been erected on spindly poles. A large iron range abutted the side wall of the Inn. Gray smoke issued from its chimney pipe and from the spout of the fire-blackened coffee pot residing on one of its iron lids.

An old man with a long, tangled, gray beard sat several feet away from the range, on a ladder-back chair, scratching away on the fiddle while a beefy, dark-yellow hound gave its back to him, staring off toward the ragged southern reaches of Gold Dust, lifting its snout and mournfully howling every ten or twelve seconds—either in time with the old man's "music" or in protest of it; it was hard to tell which.

A couple of aged horses stood switching their tails in a lean-to shelter behind the inn.

"Holy shit in the Catholic boneyard!" the old man bellowed when he saw Sartain, dropping his fiddle and springing out of his seat to turn toward the stranger, his leathery cheeks above his thick, gray beard flushing sunset red.

He reached for the '51-Model Colt revolver he had wedged behind a belt holding his patched canvas trousers up on his bony hips.

"Hold on, oldster," Sartain said, aiming the Henry negligently at the old man. "Keep that old hogleg behind your belt and live to scratch another tune."

The old dog had sprung to life, as well, facing Sartain and barking angrily, hackles raised. It was an old critter—probably as old in dog years as the old man—with a grizzled snout and a tumor as large as a man's balled fist bulging just behind its right front leg.

The old man froze with the big horse pistol only half up from behind the belt. He narrowed his watery blue eyes as the dog continued barking loudly. He looked at the Revenger's rifle and removed his hand from the hogleg's worn walnut grips.

Shuffling back on his skinny legs, he said, "You one o' them?"

"One o' who?"

"One o' them's been shootin' up the town?"

"I reckon so," Sartain said. "But you got nothin' to fear from me unless you're in with Lyle Leach and Scrum Wallace."

"Leach? Hah!" The old man spat distastefully. "I wouldn't have nothin' to do with them curly wolves. I'm a law-abidin' man. Why, I run this here hotel, don't ya know. I'm a respectable citizen of Gold Dust." He canted his head toward a shoulder, squinting at his tall, broad-shouldered visitor. "Who're you?"

"Tell that long-toothed mutt of yours to pipe down," Sartain said, holding Boss's reins taut in his left hand. "Me an' this buckskin didn't wander over here to be barked at." He glanced at the big pistol behind the old man's belt. "Or shot at, for that matter."

The old man turned to the dog. "Pipe down, Spider!"

Immediately, the dog stopped barking. It gave a little mewl, turned a complete circle, and sank to its belly, still regarding the stranger suspiciously.

"If you didn't come to be barked or shot at, what did you come over here for, mister?" the old man asked with a wry twinkle in his eye. "I was enjoyin' myself just fine."

"Anyone else enjoy that fiddle?"

"Spider does." The old man grinned, slitting his long eyes.

The dog gave another quiet mewl and then rested his snout between his paws.

"Why the name Spider?"

" 'Cause he was bit by a spider when he was just a pup. Head swelled up like a wheel hub. Still deathly afraid of the dastardly things. Scouts a room thoroughly before he lays down in it. Say, what's your name, anyways?"

"Mike Sartain."

"Hmmm."

"You got one?"

"Jordan Pepper. Folks around here call me Pops."

"To answer your first question, Pops," Sartain said, "I'd like a room. But only if Spider checks it out first." He glanced at the large, humble building towering over them. "If you have any rooms to spare, that is."

"Don't get smart with me, sonny. I get right busy on weekends and over the Fourth of July." Pops stepped out away from the building to see down the main street before looking suspiciously back at Sartain. "You won't make trouble, will you?"

"*I* won't make any—no."

The old man frowned, not sure what to make of the answer.

229

"Well, all right," he said. "Take any room you want. You can stable your horse out back."

As Sartain rode Boss around the side of the building, heading for the stable, Pops said, "What's your business with Leach's bunch?"

Sartain glanced over his shoulder. "You know Scrum?"

"Scrum Wallace? Yes, I do," the old man said, making a sour expression.

Sartain turned his head forward and continued heading for the stable. "I'm gonna kill him."

CHAPTER THIRTEEN

Sartain took a room on the hotel's second story and far to the east, from which he had a good view to the west of the Occidental Saloon.

He hauled all of his gear, including his Henry repeater, into the room and took a sponge bath in tepid water while staring out into the street through his double windows, neither of which had glass in it. There was a shutter for each, but Sartain had thrown them open to the cooling afternoon air.

Refreshed by the bath as well as the autumn air sifting into the room, he sat in front of the window, his rifle leaning against the wall before him. He nibbled jerky from his saddlebags and sipped lightning from the bottle he'd taken from the Whiskey Jim. So as not to get pie-eyed, he occasionally cut it with water.

He also paced himself.

The giant, orange ball of the sun sank slowly. The western horizon was a painter's palette of bright colors that dulled slowly until only a salmon streak remained. The salmon streak narrowed, then disappeared, and the stars kindled in the darkening sky.

The town was as quiet as a held breath. It was as if everyone in the surrounding countryside knew about the trouble and steered clear. There were a few riders, but very few, at that: a couple heading for the Whiskey Jim, a couple of others heading for the Occidental—mostly Mexicans but a couple of Anglos, as well. Two of the Mexicans stayed most of the night at the Occidental. There'd been no noise anywhere around the town except for the occasional dog barking, until the Mexicans left the Occidental, both singing softly as their horses clomped slowly back toward the west and likely to the ranchos they worked for.

Just after dark, a slender figure moved toward the Occidental from the west. Sartain couldn't tell for sure, but it appeared to be a female figure. The pretty sawbones left the watering hole about a half hour later, heading back in the direction from which she'd come.

If it was her. Sartain thought it was—thought he'd seen long hair and a billowing, Spanish-style skirt in the dim lamplight pushing through the Occidental's front window.

Clara had been checking on Scrum.

Sartain found himself hoping the killer hadn't yet died. He wanted him to linger a good long time. He hoped he was in a lot of pain. The Cajun would stay here until Scrum gave up the ghost or until Sartain got the opportunity to drill another round into him.

Scrum would not leave Gold Dust alive.

After midnight, Sartain sank back into his chair, took another sip from his bottle, and contemplated catching forty winks. Could he afford to? There was a good chance Leach would try to hit him again. He'd have to sleep sometime, though. He was accustomed to staying awake for days at a time, but the longer he didn't take at least a catnap, the less sharp his senses became.

Just thinking about sleeping made him yawn.

Then he turned his thoughts to Maggie Chance, and that braced him.

He wondered what was happening out there on the Chances' ranch. He'd never had two jobs overlap, but it was happening now, and he felt torn. He'd kill Scrum soon, and then he'd look into the Chance situation. Something about that old man's death didn't feel right, and it wasn't just the fact that Sartain had killed him.

There was something else nibbling at the edges of his consciousness.

He stripped down to his summer-weight underwear, which were merely balbriggans with the arms and legs cut off, took a long drink of tepid water, and crawled on top of the bed's single sheet. He must have dozed, because he had the sense that some time had passed, before he heard a soft tread in the hall outside his room.

He reached for the LeMat and clicked back the hammer.

The footsteps grew louder until they stopped outside his door.

Two soft taps. A woman's voice said, "Mr. Sartain?"

Sartain stared at the door, which was a black rectangle in the slightly less black wall. "Who is it?"

"Clara La Corte."

Sartain's heart thumped at the image of the pretty young woman in his mind.

Still holding the LeMat, he walked to the door, turned the key in the lock, and opened it. The hall was dark. She was a shadowy female figure against it. He could smell the female scent of her. It tickled his loins.

Always cautious, he looked both ways down the hall. No shadows moved.

"Well, *senorita*," the Cajun said in his bayou-languid drawl, "what brings you out so late? Change your mind about that drink?"

"As a matter of fact, I did." She held up a bottle by its neck. She held up a paper bag in her other hand. "And I thought you might be hungry. We have a café in town, but it's out by Sandy Wash, and I doubt you would have found it."

Just the mention of food made Sartain realize the jerky he'd washed down with tequila had been like throwing a few pebbles into a deep well. It hadn't come close to filling him up.

"Come in."

He stepped back, poked the LeMat into the holster hanging off a bedpost, and lit a lamp. The watery light spread across the floor to her standing by the door, which she closed. She wore a white blouse and a spruce-green skirt with black boots.

The blouse was low cut. A gold chain with a small crucifix hung across the high plains of her breasts, which jutted sharply against the blouse, each pointing slightly away from the other.

Her recently brushed hair glittered in the lamplight, as did her dark eyes.

Sartain swallowed. She glanced away.

"Forgive me for staring," Sartain said. "But it's not every night a man gets a visit from a woman so beautiful as you, *Senorita* La Corte."

"Are you trying to seduce me, Mr. Sartain?"

"I was raised in the French Quarter of New Orleans," the Cajun said. "I was taught the art of seduction by the very best pleasure girls north of the border. So, in a word, yes. But remember—you came to me."

It seemed to be the woman's turn to swallow nervously as her eyes flicked across his broad chest, the hair of which poked out through the gaping V of his wash-worn red undershirt. She looked away again, awkwardly this time, as though not sure where to fix her gaze.

Then she shook her hair back anxiously and thrust the bag and the bottle toward him.

"Why don't you eat, Mr. Sartain? That should sate your hunger."

Sartain took the bag and the bottle from her. It was very much a desirable young woman who'd come to visit him this night, not the rigid and formal Spanish queen he'd met earlier.

Why exactly she was here so late, however, he had yet to find out.

He couldn't have been more intrigued.

He offered her a chair. He sat on the other side of the small half-table from her and ate the bean burrito she'd brought him. It was the best burrito he'd ever eaten—still hot and liberally seasoned with roasted lamb, chili peppers, and onions. Maybe not *the* best, but it tasted like the best tonight.

He thanked her as he ate hungrily. She chuckled at the fervor with which he tore into the food and opened the bottle of good Spanish brandy, filling two water glasses.

She sat and sipped her brandy and watched him eat, smiling delightedly, her perfect, white teeth gleaming in the light of the guttering lamp.

"You always visit men's rooms so late?" he asked her when he'd taken the final bite of the delicious food and brushed his leavings off the table with the end of his fist.

Clara La Corte laughed softly. "This is the first time, in fact."

"To what do I owe the pleasure?"

She sipped from her glass and then held it against the V between her breasts, regarding him pensively. She took another sip of the brandy and then slowly lowered the glass to the table. "I was hoping I could convince you to leave tonight, Mr. Sartain."

"No. I'm sorry, Miss La Corte. You can't."

Staring at him, she pulled the corners of her mouth down.

"Why do you ask?"

"Why do I ask?" She paused, incredulous. "Why do I ask?" she said again, quietly berating him with her words. "Because this is my town, and I don't want to see it all shot to hell. I don't want to see anyone else killed. Especially innocent old men like Morgan Bentley."

Sartain glanced away from her, tugging on his earlobe in

frustration. There it was again. Bentley. The old man he'd killed, though he wasn't sure why.

"A killer with a heart," Clara said softly, speculatively. "How odd."

"I'm not a cold-blooded killer, Miss La Corte. I kill for a reason."

"I know who you are, Mr. Sartain. Word is going around. You're the one they call the Revenger. Wanted in nearly every territory on the frontier. You killed many soldiers because they killed your woman and unborn child, and now you kill for others who cannot kill for themselves. How odd that after all your killing you still have a heart."

Sartain only shrugged.

"Or maybe you really don't. Maybe you only wish to believe you do, because you don't wish to believe you're as bad as the men you kill. You somehow hold yourself above reproach because you have a conscience. You believe you're somehow better than the men you hunt."

Clara shook her head slowly, holding his gaze with a hard one of her own. "But you aren't. You can't be. Otherwise you would hang up that big pistol of yours. What's more, you would ride out of here because a woman asked you to, because she doesn't want any more of the innocent citizens of her town killed by you or by the men you are here to kill."

Sartain picked up his glass. His hand shook. Brandy sloshed over the rim and onto the table.

He threw back the rest of the liquor and then, feeling as though his heart were fairly exploding with rage and frustration, he flung the glass against the door. It thudded with the sound of a pistol shot and shattered.

Clara gave a clipped yell and lowered her head, raising her hands to her ears. She swept her hair back from her eyes and stared up at him. Trembling, Sartain stood and walked around the table to her. He drew her up by her shoulders.

Beneath his rage, passion thundered. It pierced his loins like the blade of a dull bayonet.

She stared at him fearfully in the lamplight. Her ripe upper lip trembled slightly. He placed his hands on her cheeks. She shook her head violently. *"No!"*

Sartain released her. She stumbled back against the wall, kicking her chair. She leaned there, half falling against the wall, hands splayed against it on either side of her, staring at him like a deer knowing that a hunter's sights were lined up on her.

She glanced down at his crotch. Her eyes widened. Her tongue flicked against her upper lip. A sheen of sweat glistened on her forehead.

"Oh, god," she whispered. "Oh, god, forgive me!"

She pushed herself off the wall and into his arms.

He closed his mouth over hers. Her breasts heaved against him. He shoved her back suddenly and, with blind passion, ripped her blouse from her shoulders. That stunned her. Shocked, she gaped at her exposed breasts, her hair hanging around her cheeks.

He'd ripped off her camisole as well as her blouse. Both torn garments hung off her shoulders. He himself was stunned by the sudden violence of his passion. He half-expected her to flee.

Instead, she looked up at him, her lips parted. She stepped to him and placed his hands on her heaving bosoms.

"Take me," she whispered.

He swept her up in his arms and threw her onto the bed.

CHAPTER FOURTEEN

Later, the Spanish beauty snuggled against him, the two of them naked on the bed, not even covered by the sheet. The air blowing through the window was fresh and a little cool, but they were still sweating from the passion of their coupling.

The Revenger had taken her twice in a half hour. She'd not only been receptive but demanding, desperate, as though she hadn't had a man in a long, long time, and her body was fairly exploding with natural desire. That part had reminded him of Maggie Chance. But while Clara had responded to his every touch and had demonstrated her ability at curling a man's toes, something told him she, unlike Maggie, was relatively inexperienced.

"That was . . . rather impetuous," she said softly, raking her fingers through the thick hair curling on the broad, bulging slabs of his chest.

"Regrets?"

Clara glanced up him, one eye partly covered by a mussed lock of her hair. She nodded. "How could a woman regret anything so . . . satisfying? I only wonder . . . what is in me that a man like you could arouse such passion?"

"You mean because I'm a killer?"

"Of course."

"Maybe it wasn't the killer you were making love with."

She smiled pensively as she continued to rake her fingers across his chest. "Who, then? Just a handsome, blue-eyed Cajun from the bayous?"

Sartain's left arm was wrapped around her, his hand cupping the side of her left breast, his thumb slowly sliding across her petal-soft nipple. He shrugged. "Whatever you prefer."

"Okay," she said, groaning a little at his ministrations and planting her lips against his chest. Her lips were almost hot as she kissed him, her saliva warm as butter melting on a skillet.

He felt the tug of arousal once more. She seemed to sense it and slid her hand down his belly.

He groaned.

"Hold on," he said, ten minutes later.

Her hand stopped moving on him. "What is it?"

Sartain pushed up onto his elbows. He stared at the door. The lamp had almost gone out, casting a flickering, red-brown light across the mostly dark room.

She turned to the door as well.

Faintly, a floorboard creaked in the hall. When she jerked her head back to him, he placed a finger against his lips. He pushed her down onto the bed beside him, reached out, and slowly slid his LeMat from its holster hanging from the bedpost on his right.

"Stay very quiet," he whispered.

A floorboard in the hall creaked again, a little more loudly than the first one. Sartain looked at the floor in front of the door. The boards there bowed slightly downward. Sartain raised the LeMat and quietly flicked the lever to engage the twelve-gauge shotgun shell in the stout tube beneath the main barrel.

He waited, ears pricked, listening intently.

Just outside the door there was the soft click of a gun hammer being cocked.

Sartain aimed the LeMat at the door. He was in an awkward position, but he managed to steady the gun. He could take no chances on Clara being hurt by an ambusher's blast.

He squeezed the LeMat's trigger.

The heavy pistol flashed and roared.

Clara jerked with a start and a clipped, involuntary scream. In the hall, a man yelped. Boots thudded as the would-be attacker stumbled away from the door. There was another thud as the attacker struck the wall on the far side of the hall, yet another when he hit the floor, groaning.

Downstairs, Pops's dog began barking angrily.

"I'll be goddamned!" yelled another man in the hall.

Boots thudded loudly. Sartain felt the floor reverberating beneath the bed.

"Let's get the fuck out of here, Frank!" came another man's voice in the hall, above the groaning of the man who'd taken at least part of Sartain's blast.

The Revenger had leaped out of bed. Two long strides took him to the door, which he threw open, extending the cocked LeMat into the hall. As he'd thought, one man was down. He lay at the base of the wall on the other side of the corridor, holding a hand to the side of his chest.

Two more men disappeared around the hall's far right corner. Their boots echoed loudly on the stairs.

"What the hell is goin' on in here?" yelled Pops Pepper from below, the old man's scratchy voice nearly drowned out by Spider's wild barking and the thudding of the two fleeing bushwhackers.

Sartain looked down at the man on the floor. It was Lyle Leach. He gritted his teeth as he writhed, holding his right hand to his bloody chest.

Blood oozed from between his fingers and dribbled onto the floor. He slid his left hand out from under him and stretched it toward the cocked carbine lying about three feet away from him.

"Leach, you stupid son of a bitch," Sartain said, planting a bare foot on the Winchester and sliding it off down the hall. He reached down and pulled Leach's pistol from its holster and sent that skidding down the hall, as well.

"Oh, my god," Clara said behind Sartain. He turned to see her peering over his shoulder, holding a sheet across her breasts.

"Nah, it's just the Gold Dust town marshal." Sartain depressed the LeMat's hammer and extended it to Clara. "Here—hold that for me, will ya, darlin'?"

The Cajun pulled the wailing, grimacing Leach to his feet. The man stood, leaning against the wall, holding both hands to his bloody chest now and cursing. Sartain grabbed the man's Winchester and held it on him, waving the barrel toward the stairs.

"Get movin', you stupid bastard." Fury was a hot iron inside him. "One wrong move and I'll drill you again—this time for keeps!"

"Fuck you, you crazy son of a bitch!" bellowed Leach. "I'm the marshal here! You shot me through a door! Through a *door!*"

"I'm sorry I didn't wait for you to shoot first, *Marshal.* Now, get down the stairs or I'll push you down 'em."

At the top of the stairs, Leach stopped and turned toward Sartain. "Now, you just hold on!"

His eyes widened and his mouth opened even wider as Sartain rammed the butt of the man's own gun against Leach's chest, throwing him down the stairs. Leach struck the steps about four steps from the top and tumbled unceremoniously, screaming all the way to the bottom.

Pops Pepper, clad in a sleeping gown and nightcap, held a lamp high in his right hand. The light fluttered over Leach writhing at the bottom of the stairs, wailing.

Spider had been barking, but when the dog saw Leach rolling violently toward him, the dog had wheeled and run out the front door and into the night, yipping.

Sartain moved down the stairs.

"You boys are a mite loud this evenin'," Pops said, gumming the words. He hadn't put his teeth in. "Me—I keep strict rules. No rifle fire after midnight."

"I shot him with a pistol, Pops," Sartain said, prodding Leach with the Winchester's barrel.

Pops shook his head as he stared down at Leach. "You opened a mighty big hole in him—I'll give you that."

"Get the hell up, Leach," Sartain ordered.

Leach cursed. He was almost sobbing.

When Sartain finally got the shot-up marshal on his feet, he hazed him out of the hotel and prodded him down the street toward the town marshal's office. Leach held both arms across his chest, his head down. He was dragging one foot slightly. "I think you busted my ankle on top of everything else, you crazy bastard!"

Sartain stared toward the Occidental. The building was eerily dark and silent. He looked around, ready for another onslaught from the other two men who'd been with Leach.

"Who was sidin' ya?" Sartain asked the marshal as they approached the stone jailhouse. "If you could call that sidin'." He chucked caustically.

Leach only cursed him again.

Sartain prodded the marshal up the steps to his own office. The front door, constructed of bowed, unpainted vertical planks, was unlocked. A lamp glowed on a roll-top desk to the left. Four cells were lined up along the back wall. Sartain used the Winchester barrel to shove Leach across the earthen-floored room, which was as cool and dank as a root cellar, and into the cell farthest right.

"You can't arrest me," Leach snarled, glaring at the Cajun, and pressed a bloody finger to his bloody badge. "I'm the marshal. That's my job!"

"You're not the marshal any longer, Leach." Sartain plucked the badge from the man's bloody shirt and tossed it against the front wall. "This citizen has done fired your worthless, bushwhacking ass."

"You ain't even a citizen of Gold Dust!"

Sartain slammed the cell door closed and was about to respond to Leach when soft footsteps rose behind him. He wheeled, leveling the Winchester.

"It's me, it's me!" Clara stepped slowly into the room, holding her left hand up, palm out. Her hair was still a mess. She'd donned her skirt and Sartain's shirt in lieu of the blouse and camisole the Cajun had ripped from her body.

She must have retrieved her medical kit from her office, because she held it in her right hand.

"What kind of a lady are you, Doc?" Leach said, sagging onto the edge of the cot. "Cavortin' with killers . . ."

Ignoring the bushwhacker, Clara looked Sartain up and down, then arched a brow. "Uh . . . Mike, you're not wearing any clothes."

Sartain looked down at himself. It was like having a pail of cold water thrown on him. He'd been vaguely aware of his bare feet as he'd prodded Leach over here from the hotel, but his heart had been racing so quickly, he'd somehow shut out the fact that he was as naked as he'd been when he and Clara had tussled.

"So I'm not," the Cajun said, holding the stock of his rifle over his crotch and backing slowly toward the door. Pops Pepper stood there, holding his lantern in one hand, his old Colt in his other hand. "Pops, would you make sure your former marshal doesn't go anywhere, and that no one breaks him out of that cell? I'll be back after I've donned my duds."

"Sure, sure," Pepper said, raising his pistol and stepping into the jailhouse as Sartain moved out of it. "Be glad to." He held an arthritic hand to the side of his mouth and yelled to the retreating Sartain in a hoarse whisper, "Say, your dick's still wet!"

He cackled.

CHAPTER FIFTEEN

The false dawn was a pale wash in the east when Clara finally finished plucking the twenty-odd pellets out of Leach's upper right chest and sewing him up. His ankle was only sprained, but she wrapped a taut bandage around it and then left the outlaw marshal, groaning and moaning on the cell cot, as she stepped out of the cell and closed the door.

She'd fed her patient half a bottle of whiskey in an attempt to quell the pain, so Leach was as drunk as an Irish gandy-dancer on Saturday night in Abilene. But, while drunk, he was obviously still in pain. That was all right with Sartain. If Leach had had his way, he likely would have drilled both him and Clara through that hotel room door.

"I'll give you your shirt back tomorrow," Clara told the Revenger, who sat in Leach's swivel chair, facing his prisoner with his Henry rifle resting across his thighs. "Thanks for . . . an eventful night." She gave a wry smile.

"Any time, darlin'," said the Cajun, returning her smile with a wink. She looked beautiful standing there before him, her hair still mussed from their lovemaking, one side hooked behind her ear.

She looked at the badge he'd pinned to his pinto vest.

"You've promoted yourself."

"Yeah, I'm movin' up in the world."

She arched a skeptical brow.

"Just until my work here is finished, anyway," he said, hiking a shoulder.

"I'm sure that won't take too long." Holding her medical kit in both hands before her, she glanced into Leach's cell. "You clean up right well, Mike."

"Thank you, honey. I'll take that as a compliment."

She turned to the door but he stopped her with: "Been meanin' to ask you—how's Scrum Wallace?"

"Miraculously, on the mend."

"How long before he's on his feet?"

"A few days, maybe."

Sartain pursed his lips, nodding.

Clara opened the door, went out, and closed the door behind her.

Sartain went outside and sat on a bench to the right of the door. He rolled a cigarette and smoked it, his rifle resting across his thighs.

He watched the dawn wash over the town, lifting shadows. The Occidental Saloon seemed to be drawn gradually by a deft painter's brush down the street to his left. When the rising sun had burnished the shabby watering hole burnt copper and he could see shadows moving around behind the windows, he rose from the bench and shouldered the Henry.

He dropped down into the street and started walking toward the saloon where Scrum was recuperating. He kept a close eye on the Occidental's dirty windows as he mounted the small front gallery. His boots clomped loudly on the gallery's rough wooden boards. He pushed through the batwings, stepped to the left, so he wouldn't be outlined against the bright morning light, and loudly racked a shell into the rifle's breech.

There were eight or nine men in the dingy place, most sitting at tables playing cards. Two were standing at the bar to Sartain's right and down the room a ways. One had just been biting into a thick ham, egg, and cheese sandwich when Sartain had cocked the rifle, and now, turning to see the Revenger standing with his back to the front wall, the man convulsed violently, blowing the food onto the bar before him.

Part of the mouthful ended up in his beer, where it foamed.

The man beside him, who'd also turned toward the new-comer, jerked with a start. "Holy shit!" He reached for the carbine on the bar beside him but stayed his movement, knowing that if he did not, he'd likely receive a .44 caliber chunk of lead for his indiscretion.

Several of the others had started to rise from their chairs, but now they were easing back down, faces flushed. One man dropped his cigarette in his lap and yowled, brushing the coals away. The door at the back of the room opened, and a plump, round-faced, young Mexican woman in a sleeveless blouse and ruffled, blue skirt with ornate red stitching came into the main room.

When her eyes found the Revenger, she stopped in her tracks. She was barefoot. Her long, straight, dark-brown hair hung down past her exposed shoulders. She held a porcelain wash pan in her hands, mounded with bloody bandages.

A fat man with long, gray hair and thick, gray muttonchops and wearing an apron stood behind the bar, tending a range on which coffee boiled and bacon fried. He turned away from the bacon and regarded Sartain with mean, angry eyes, pointing his spatula, from which hot grease dribbled. "What the hell are you doing here? You get out! Get out of my place!" He spoke with a slight Irish accent.

"Shut up," Sartain said with a weary air. "Anyone makes any sudden moves gets drilled. Shit, I could drill all of ya before a single one of you fools could clear leather." He chuckled at the men's carelessness. They hadn't been expecting a visit from the man they'd been gunning for.

A man sitting at a table near the bar with three other men, playing poker, had lowered his hand beneath the table while sitting stiffly in his chair and keeping his gaze on Sartain. He wore a buckskin shirt and an ancient, battered Union army hat bearing the flying eagle insignia of Berdan's Sharpshooters.

Sartain blew a round into the table fronting the man, scattering coins and playing cards.

"Get your hand back up on the table, bluebelly," Sartain raked out as he pumped a fresh round into his Henry's breech. "I would hate to have to shoot one of Berdan's Confederate-killin' finest when so few of you made it out of the war upright."

The veteran sharpshooter swallowed and set his hand back up on the table, near the other one.

"Good Christ," muttered the man sitting beside him, looking down at the bullet hole in the table with a sour expression, as though it were a snake coiled to strike.

"Yes, sir," Sartain said, aiming the smoking Henry from his right hip. "If that hit anything important, it would have stung like hell. Don't worry, though—I got fifteen more in this sixteen-shooter. Enough to shoot all of you fellas once and some of you twice, if I'd need to, which I wouldn't."

The barman looked at the hole in the card player's table. Then he glowered at Sartain. "Why don't you just turn Leach loose and ride on out of here—eh, bucko? Then the trouble would be over. Scrum's got two of your bullets in him. That's bloody well enough of this nonsense!"

"He's not dead," Sartain said. "So it's not enough."

"Scrum's related to everyone in this room except Salma there," said the man wearing the federal hat, jerking his chin to indicate the scantily clad girl still standing at the back of the room, her brown eyes wide and shiny with nerves. "And we ain't gonna let you kill him."

"You got no choice," Sartain said, curling his upper lip with a devilish grin. "If my heart weren't so goddamn big, all you dumbasses would be dead by now or close enough to it that the undertaker would be dancin' a jig. Scrum Wallace would be dead, too."

"Well, what the hell is this all about, then, for cryin' in the preacher's ale?" the barman wanted to know, hammering his spatula angrily on the bar top. "You gonna kill us all, you big-talkin' Johnny Reb, or you gonna just stand there, makin' threats?"

Sartain said, "I'd just as soon not have to kill you. That's not why I'm here. I came over here to talk some sense into your fool heads. If you turn Scrum Wallace over to me at the jail, as I'm the law here in town now until further notice"—he tapped a finger against the badge on his vest—"I'll turn Leach back over to you . . . with this badge here returned to him. And then, after Scrum Wallace finally pays for his sins, I'll ride on out of here. If you boys behave yourselves, you'll never have to look at my handsome Cajun mug ever again."

The men in the room all glanced at each other. A few wore ever-so-vaguely sheepish expressions, as though they might be thinking about the proposal.

The barman just kept glaring at Sartain, his lower jaw jutting. The Revenger had sized the man up as an uncle to Scrum. He probably needed killing as much as Scrum did, but the Cajun was willing to let the man live as long as he turned his nephew in to receive his just deserts.

"You don't have to answer now," Sartain said. "Take some time to think it over. I'll give you twenty-four hours. However, if any of you tinhorns tries bushwhacking me again, like you did last night, this truce will be over. I'll kill every one of you, and then I'll kill Scrum, like I'm gonna do anyway."

Sartain grinned and pinched his hat brim to the room. "Good day, fellas. Think it over. I got a feelin' you'll come to the right decision."

CHAPTER SIXTEEN

Keeping the Henry trained on the room, the Cajun backed through the batwings and into the street.

As he did, horse hooves clomped to his left. He glanced over to see two horseback riders moving toward him from the west edge of town. The shapes looked familiar. One was a man's, the other a woman's. The man rode ahead of the woman, leading her grullo by a lead line attached to a hackamore.

The woman had red-blond hair. She was dressed in a worn, brown and cream gingham dress. Black shoes showed beneath the hem. Maggie Chance rode with her back straight, her hands behind her back. Everett rode with his old Spencer carbine resting across the pommel of his saddle.

Sartain glanced once more at the saloon behind him, making sure none of its occupants was poking a rifle over the batwings at him. He walked out into the street to meet the Chances.

"What the hell's going on here, Everett?" he asked as Chance kept riding, passing him, heading east along the street.

Maggie followed him on the grullo, regarding Sartain almost wistfully.

"Maggie?" Sartain said. "What the hell's . . . ?"

As she rode silently past him, he saw that her hands had been handcuffed behind her.

Sartain poked his hat brim off his forehead as he strode after them. Chance pulled his piebald up to the town marshal's office. Sartain caught up to him just as he was swinging heavily down from his saddle. Chance looked tired, worried, his fleshy features drawn. The sun had blistered his broad, pudgy nose.

The rancher tied the two horses to the hitch rack. He looked at the badge on Sartain's chest, and he gave a half-hearted smile. "We got us a new marshal in Gold Dust, I see. How'd that happen, Mike?"

Sartain gazed up at Maggie, who stared stiffly ahead at the stone building before her, though she didn't appear to be seeing much of anything. She wore a very faint smile on her rich, dark-red lips. The upper lip wore a small gash, and it was swollen. Her left eye was slightly discolored. Her hair was piled loosely and pinned atop her head, several stray strands caressing her cheeks in the warm morning breeze.

"Leach had a little accident," the Cajun said absently, sliding his questioning gaze back to Everett. "You better have one hell of a good reason for this, mister."

Chance sighed and shook his head. "She tried to kill me last night. Sliced into my back, and then, when I turned around in bed, she tried to cut my throat. I woke at the last second and grabbed her wrist, or I'd have bled out by now. I thrashed at her—didn't mean to hit her—but have you ever had a knife this close to your throat, Mike?"

He held his thumb and index finger a quarter of an inch apart.

He sighed again, shrugged, and looked sadly at his wife. "I didn't know what else to do, Mike. I can't go on livin' like this, not knowin' when she's gonna make another try for me. I thought I'd bring her into town, lock her up for a time. Maybe get Clara La Corte to take a look at her, though there ain't nothin' wrong with her physically. It's all in her head. Maybe the preacher . . ."

Sartain stepped up close to Maggie and placed his hand on the saddle horn. "Is this all true?"

"Yes," the woman said blandly.

"I've got a cut back to prove it," Chance added, wincing as canted his head toward his left shoulder. "I'm gonna need a stitch or two, I'm afraid."

Sartain said, "Why don't you go on over to the doc's office, Everett? I'll see to Maggie."

Chance looked at her again sadly, speculatively. "What's got into you, honey? Why'd you do me like that? You can't really think I killed our boys? Do you? Do you *really*?" His voice cracked on the last word, and a sheen of tears shone in his eyes.

Maggie stared at him blankly, her mouth corners raised ever so slightly, in a vague, far-away smile.

Chance stared back at her as if awaiting a response. When he did not get one, he shook his head, gave the handcuff key to Sartain, shouldered his Spencer, and began walking back in the direction of Clara La Corte's office. Several of the men from the Occidental had come out to stand on the gallery, looking around speculatively.

The beefy gent in the barman's apron said, "Finally gonna lock up that demon woman of yours, eh, Chance?"

Chance muttered something in response that Sartain couldn't hear. It didn't sound friendly.

The Cajun gazed up at Maggie, who said with flat, menacing certainty, "Don't trust him, Mike. Don't trust him as far as you can throw him."

Sartain reached up and unlocked her handcuffs. When her arms were free, he pulled her out of the saddle and set her on the ground before him.

"Did you stab him?"

"Yes. Are you going to lock me up?"

Sartain sighed. "What else can I do?"

Maggie nodded. Sartain gestured at the jailhouse's front door, and Maggie walked to it. Sartain stepped around her and threw the door open. He grabbed the keys off a spike that had been driven into a stout ceiling support post and led the woman to the far left cell, two cells away from where Leach slumbered on a cot, one boot on the floor, one arm thrown over his forehead.

"What happened to him?" Maggie asked as she stepped into her cell.

"I shot him."

"Any particular reason?"

"He was going to shoot me. Apparently, he took it personally, my wanting to kill Scrum Wallace."

"Ah," Maggie said when Sartain had closed and locked the door. "You have a lot on your plate, Mike."

"Maggie, tell me what happened."

"Just what Everett said. I tried to kill him. I had every intention of doing so. I decided to do it after you left, because I knew you didn't believe me. That you believed Everett. I knew then that it was up to me, and that if I didn't do it, more people would die."

Maggie wrapped her hands around the bars of her cell door. "More people will die, Mike. I guarantee it. Now that he's through hurting everyone out on the ranch, he will bring his madness to town. He's kill-crazy."

"If you're so sure he's gone mad, Maggie, what do you think caused it?"

She glanced down and tucked her bottom lip beneath her upper lip, thinking. "Do you remember Warrior Gulch, Mike?"

"The wash we crossed on the way to your ranch? Yeah, I remember it. Who could forget those two skeletons lying there together?"

"Then you might also remember that I told you that many of the local Mexicans believe the gulch is cursed. That's why most of the bodies were never bothered by scavengers, carrion-eaters, or by most folks from the area. The Mexican folks as well as the animals knew to stay away. Some think that the battle that was fought there unleashed the demon spirit of one of the Apaches who was killed there—a shaman warrior named Or-ay-li-no-nooo. In the Lipan Apache language it means 'black spirit' or 'black god.' "

"All right, I'm with you so far," Sartain said. "Local superstition. I could tell you some hoo-doo stories from my neck of the bayou country. What's that have to do with Everett?"

"Many of the Mexicans around here, whose families have been here for generations and who have lived amongst the Apaches for as many generations and know the Apache language and folklore, believe the shaman's spirit will haunt the gulch until it can find a home in another man or beast. Anyone—man or animal—who visits that area will be infected with the dark, malicious spirit of Or-ay-li-no-nooo."

Sartain stared at her skeptically through the bars, waiting. He knew what she was going to say before she said it, but he let her say it anyway.

"Everett is the only man I know who has visited the gulch. He looted the bodies of the dead soldiers and the Apaches a few years after the battle occurred. He and another young man from a neighboring ranch got drunk on sour mash and dared themselves to venture into the wash and take what valuables they could find—mostly coins, guns, ammunition, and knives. Mostly, they did it for the thrill."

She waited, staring through the bars at Sartain as though to stamp the words into him with her copper-eyed gaze.

"Okay . . ." said the Cajun.

"Everett confessed this to me a couple of years after we were married. He started to believe that he might have been infected by the black god's spirit. He told me he was having abnormal thoughts. Dark thoughts. Evil thoughts about doing horrible things for no apparent reason, but because he just felt compelled by something inside him, something he'd never known before he and Wendell Aimes wandered into the gulch.

"He started to believe this after Wendell came to Gold Dust one night, murdered several of the sporting girls in a whorehouse, and burned the place to the ground with several more girls locked inside. A posse caught Wendell and hanged him. And after that, Everett started to believe they'd both become infected by the evil shaman's dark spirit.

"I didn't believe it at first. I tried to assure him it wasn't true. He was a good, kind man. But then, after he told me about his own suspicions about himself, I saw changes in him. They were very subtle and gradual. It was like a dark cloud hovered over him. He grew angry more easily, and I'd see a strange light in his eyes at times."

Maggie paused. Her eyes became wet as she stared at Sartain. "And then . . . the boys started to die in tragic ways. I continued to see that strange, unsettling light in Everett's eyes. One night, after Ephraim burned in the privy, I awakened to hear my husband speaking—no, *chanting*—some strange tongue, likely Apache, in his sleep."

"Why didn't you leave?" Sartain asked her.

"Because by then we were caring for old Howard, whose mind was quickly leaving him. I couldn't abandon Howard to his son, who I knew by then to have been infected by the spirit of the evil shaman. Instead, I plotted ways to kill Everett. I was biding my time, gathering my courage, weighing my options." Maggie opened and closed her hands around the bars. "Then I read a newspaper article about a man known as the Revenger. A man who helped in such matters as killing for folks who couldn't do the killing themselves . . ."

Sartain stared back at Maggie, pondering what he'd just heard. It was too much to take in all at once. She'd seemed so sane, telling it. Yet didn't most insane people—if they were really all-the-way *loco*—didn't they all believe what their insane minds were telling them and seem sane when telling about it?

Sartain didn't know. He'd only brushed elbows with a few truly insane people in New Orleans—street people, mostly. Drunks living in alleys or abandoned warehouses. Whores or jakes whose brains had been eaten out by syphilis—or Cupid's itch, as it was often called. But most of them had *seemed* insane, speaking gibberish. Here was a woman who, by looking at her and talking with her, you'd think as sane as the sanest person on earth.

Until you heard her tell her story . . .

"Let's say I believe you, Maggie," Sartain said, hearing the bewilderment in his own voice. "What do you propose I do about it? Just go out there and shoot him down in the street?"

"You'd better," Maggie said. "You'd better do just that before he starts killing people here in town, Mike."

As if to punctuate the woman's warning, a shrill, horrified scream rose from outside the jailhouse.

Everett was with Clara . . .

Sartain wheeled and ran to the door.

CHAPTER SEVENTEEN

Sartain ran into the street and angled east toward Clara's office. As he ran, the scream came again.

Several men came out of the Occidental, some wielding carbines. Sartain palmed his LeMat and aimed it at the four men on the Occidental's front gallery. They got the message and lowered their weapons.

"Go on back inside!" Sartain shouted.

He ran past the Occidental and was nearly to the pretty young medico's office when another scream came vaulting out of the gap between the furniture store and the barbershop beside it. The shrill cry lifted the hair on the back of Sartain's neck.

As he dashed past the drug store, he saw Everett Chance bound out of the doctor's office and onto the landing atop the stairs.

"Put the gun down, Chance!" Sartain shouted.

He frowned when Clara came out behind Chance, both of them staring into the alley between the furniture store and the barbershop. The Cajun followed their gazes.

The Mexican whore whom Sartain had seen step out of the room in which Scrum Wallace was mending in the Occidental now stood in the alley, lurching back as though something had hold of her ankle. White bandages were scattered on the ground around her. She held her hands to the side of her head as she continued to leap and jerk, struggling with something Sartain couldn't see, and finally screamed once more.

"Hold on, honey!" Chance shouted, aiming his Remington over the side of the stair rail.

The man's pistol roared twice. He raised the smoking barrel. "Got him!" he said.

The girl stepped back, tripped, and fell on her rump in the dirt.

Frowning incredulously, glancing warily up at Chance grinning down at him, Sartain walked into the gap between the buildings. He was very much aware that Chance still had his pistol out.

Then he saw the large rattler lying in a bloody pile a few feet away from the groaning whore.

"Shit!" Sartain holstered his LeMat and ran over to the girl, dropping to a knee beside her. "You bit, sweetheart?"

She had her blue skirt raised above her knees, and that seemed to be what she was inspecting herself for now. She ran her hands down her plump, brown legs and shook her head. "I don't think . . ."

Clara and Chance walked up behind him. Chance was holstering his Remington. "She bit?"

Sartain closely scrutinized both the girl's legs. Clara did, as well.

"I don't see any bite marks," the medico said, running her hand down the whore's right shin. "Do you feel any pain, Esmeralda?"

The whore shook her head.

"He must have struck but only caught her dress," Chance said. "When I first seen it, I thought for sure it'd bit her."

Sartain lifted the hem of the girl's torn skirt. "It must have gotten its fangs caught in the fabric." He smiled at the whore. "Close one."

"*Si*," the girl said with a relieved sigh. "Cristo—I was very frightened."

"She'd just left my office with more bandages for Wallace," Clara said as she helped Esmeralda pick up the bandages scattered around them.

When Clara took Esmeralda back up her office for a fresh batch of clean bandages, Chance followed Sartain out of the alley. He said, "Say, Mike, what was all that about . . . you tellin' me to drop my gun?"

Sartain's ears warmed a little with chagrin. "Just force of habit, I reckon," he said with what he intended to be a reassuring grin, feeling a little silly for having halfway believed Maggie's story. "When I see a man with his gun out, I reckon I just naturally think it's intended for me."

"I suppose that goes with the line of work you're in." Chance studied Sartain with a wry half smile, then cocked his head slightly to one side. "Unless you was a little unnerved about . . . well, about somethin' else. Like what Maggie might have told you over at the marshal's office?"

Sartain shrugged and kicked a dirt clod. "I don't know . . . I suppose that might have been part of it."

"That's all right, Mike." Everett patted the Cajun's shoulder. "She does make it all sound so reasonable. Credible. I suppose she told you about her theory that I been cursed by that spirit she and the Mexicans believe is roaming around Warrior Gulch . . ."

Sartain hitched his gun belt higher on his hips as he stared back at the marshal's office. "She did, yes." Hearing it put that succinctly made Maggie's assertion sound all the more ridiculous. Again, the Revenger's ear tips warmed. "It's just so damned hard to believe she's mad, Everett. Insane."

"Don't I know," Chance said with a ragged sigh, running a hand across the back of his neck. "Don't I know . . ." He wagged his head. "Me? I'm gonna go over and get me a drink at the Whiskey Jim. You want one? I'll buy."

"No, thanks, Everett." Sartain glanced east along the main street toward the Occidental, where five or six of Wallace's cronies were milling, staring at him. "I reckon I'd better go check on my prisoners."

"What're you gonna do about Leach?"

"That's up to him." Sartain started walking back toward the jailhouse.

"I'll see you later, Mike," Everett said. "Tell Maggie I'll be over in a bit to check on her. I've asked Miss Clara to look in on her, too; maybe help us figure out what we can do for her."

"That sounds about right," Sartain said, graveled by the problem. What did you do about a woman who thought her husband was haunted by a demented ghost and tried to stick a knife in his back? It wasn't really his problem.

Yes, it was.

He'd spent a beguiling night with the pretty woman, and he felt a deep tenderness for her. He didn't want to see her locked up in a prison or an insane asylum. He kicked another dirt clod in frustration and looked back at the Occidental once more, at the men gathered there, staring at him with menace.

"I thought I told you tinhorns to get back inside!" the Revenger shouted.

They cursed him, laughing.

He muttered a few oaths of his own and pushed into the jailhouse to see about his prisoners.

CHAPTER EIGHTEEN

An hour later, Sartain was kicked back in a chair on the jailhouse's front stoop, his Henry across his thighs. He was staring at the Occidental. A half-dozen sat on the gallery over there, returning the Revenger's gaze. They all held carbines across their thighs. A couple, like Sartain, had their boots crossed on the rail before them.

One man was busily cleaning his pistols, dribbling oil over the parts and rubbing them down with a white cloth. The men talked amongst themselves, occasionally chuckling. At one point, they all broke out in raucous laughter as they cast their sneering gazes toward Sartain.

"Yeah, well, we'll see who laughs last," the Cajun muttered to himself.

The latch clicked behind him. The door opened. He turned to see Clara walk out of the jailhouse. She was carrying her brown medical bag. She'd come over nearly an hour ago to take a look at Leach's wounds and to talk to Maggie.

Now she closed the door and stood atop the porch steps, staring at the Occidental.

"Well, what do you think?" the Cajun asked her.

"She seems sane to me. At least, as sane as you or I." Clara looked at Sartain, frowning. "But I don't know any more about the mind than you do, Mike. My father taught me nearly everything he knew about healing the body." She shook her head. "We never talked once about doctoring minds."

Sartain sighed and recrossed his boots atop the rail. "Yeah, that's sort of what I thought."

"What are you going to do?"

"I got no idea."

She still stared at the Occidental. "You have your hands full."

"Yup."

"What're you going to do about them?" She meant the men on the Occidental's gallery.

"That's up to them."

"What about Leach?"

"He's up to them, too. How's he feeling?"

"Sore." Clara glanced at him with a dry smile. "And angry."

"I bet he . . ."

Sartain let his voice trail off. There was movement down at the Whiskey Jim, across the street from the furniture store and Clara's office. The bald, stocky Mexican who ran the little *cantina* stumbled out of the shade of the brush arbor fronting the place. Sartain's heart skipped a beat. The man carried a body in his arms.

A woman's naked body lay slack across his forearms. The woman's—or girl's—head hung slack, as did her arms and her bare legs. Her long hair hung to the ground.

"Good lord," said Clara through a breath.

"What the hell . . . ?" Sartain dropped his boots to the porch floor and followed Clara into the street, both angling toward where the Mexican barman was moving toward them.

"*Senorita!*" he called, his voice hoarse with emotion, stretching his lips back from his teeth. He was running awkwardly with the girl in his arms. "*Senorita* La Corte! It is Magdalena! Can you help?"

Clara ran to meet the man. He was breathing hard, sweat dribbling through his several days' worth of brown beard stubble and his handlebar mustache. When he moved to ease the girl to the ground, his legs buckled. He fell to his knees with a groan, and the girl tumbled into the street.

"Oh, my god!" Clara cried.

Sartain saw the blood then, too, which had been obscured by her hair. It was issuing from a long, thick gash across the girl's throat, stretching from the lobe of one ear to the other. The dark-red blood glistened in the afternoon sunshine.

"She's had her throat cut!" Clara exclaimed.

"*Si!*" the barman cried. "I know. I heard her cry out, and then . . . and then there was a gurgling sound! Is there anything, *senorita*? Is there anything you can do to help her?"

Clara smoothed the girl's hair away from her bloody throat, and shook her head. "No. There's nothing I can do, Hector. She's gone."

She looked at Sartain, who said, "Who in the hell did this?"

Somehow, he knew the answer to the question even before Miguel, staring at him in exasperation and disbelief, said, "*Senor* Chance! He was with her . . . in her room! When I heard her cry out, I ran upstairs. *Senor* Chance was running down the hall, heading for the back door!"

Clara jerked a startled look at Sartain.

"Where is he now?"

"I don't know, *senor*," Miguel said. "He ran out the back. That is all I know! I wanted"—he lowered his sad eyes to the dead whore—"I wanted to try and help Magdalena . . . !"

Sartain took his Henry in both hands and ran down the street and behind the Whiskey Jim. Hooves thudded loudly from behind a stand of scraggly, dusty mesquites. As Sartain turned toward the trees, a horse and rider exploded out of the brush.

It was a wild-eyed Everett Chance astride an equally wild-eyed brown-and-white pinto. Sartain started to bring the Henry up, but he was too late. Chance turned the pinto toward him, and the last thing Sartain saw before he was hammered to the ground was the pinto's bright, fear-glazed eyes.

When he finished rolling, aching in his hips and shoulders, a sleeve of his shirt hanging torn and frayed, he saw Chance galloping off through another stand of mesquites.

"My horse!" someone cried in Spanish. "My horse! My horse! That *bastardo* stole my horse!"

The boy came running through the brush—a tall, skinny Mexican lad with short, dark-brown hair. He was clad in Mexican pajamas and rope-soled sandals. A straw *sombrero* dangled down his back, held by its horsehair thong.

The boy ran past Sartain and screamed, "Come back here, you common thief! Come back!"

He swung toward Sartain. "He came out of nowhere, pulled me off my horse, and—"

"I'll get him, son," Sartain said in his rudimentary Spanish, limping off to the livery barn. "Don't worry. I'll get him . . ."

CHAPTER NINETEEN

Sartain limped back to the Lincoln County Inn and clomped wearily up the stairs. His joints ached. He especially ached in his right hip and shoulder, both of which had taken the brunt of the pinto's hammering charge. The other shoulder and hip ached, as well, for he'd landed on those, too, but it was his right side that was causing him to see red and wonder if he could ride.

"What the hell happened to you?" asked Pops Pepper, walking through the front door as Sartain continued to climb the stairs. "You look like you been hung on a line and beaten with a broom."

The old man's old dog barked once as though to punctuate his owner's comment.

Sartain stopped. "Saddle my stallion, will you, Pops? I gotta go see about killin' a demon."

"A *demon?* Why, you're *drunk!*"

"Wish I was," Sartain grunted as he reached the hotel's second floor.

Fifteen minutes later, he rode Boss out of town to the south and then circled west, so the men in the Occidental wouldn't see him leave. He didn't want them trying to bust Leach out of jail, though they probably would anyway, when they didn't see Sartain around for a while.

Likely, they'd leave Maggie alone. They had no reason to hurt her.

266

If they busted Leach out, Sartain would see to them sooner than expected, that's all . . .

He picked up Chance's fresh tracks at the west edge of Gold Dust and followed them along the main trail. The man was galloping hell for leather—it was obvious by the length of his stolen horse's stride. Sartain held Boss to a canter, avoiding an all-out run and possibly riding into a bushwhack. He rode with his Henry resting on his saddle pommel, raking his gaze carefully across the country around him—all rolling, sage- and creosote-stippled hills and buttes with crumbling orange dykes cropping up here and there.

A couple of miles out of town, Chance had swung off the main trail and headed cross-country to the north.

Where in hell was he going?

Sartain followed the man's spotty trail with a perplexed feeling weighing heavily on his shoulders. Was he really tracking a demon—some ancient, black-spirited Apache god?

He'd never been a religious man. Or rarely given much consideration to anything he couldn't understand through his senses. He couldn't wrap his mind around Maggie's story.

The country started chopping up into washes and shallow canyons. Chalky buttes rose to either side of the faint horse trail Sartain was following. About twenty minutes after he'd left the main trail, he found himself in a badlands of sorts—a deep canyon whose floor had been carved up by an ancient river. Giant haystack bluffs rose all around these dry watercourses that were white with alkali and showed the serpentine tracks of rattlesnakes and the prints of coyotes and wildcats. They were edged with rocks and patches of prickly pear and Spanish bayonet.

Sartain came upon several cow skulls and even a skull that appeared human—probably the bone of some ancient settler, maybe an old prospector—that had been washed up by recent rains.

The sun hammered out of a clear, brassy sky.

Sweat trickled down Sartain's back, tickling him. It rolled down his forehead and stung his eyes. Several times he dabbed at his eye corners with the ends of his neckerchief.

As he rode, closely following the recent horse tracks, his perplexity over the state of the man he was tracking gave way to a sense of menace that gradually ratcheted his nerves, until he could feel an almost painful tension in his back. The feeling told him Chance was trying to lead him into an ambush.

It made sense. For what other reason would the man have ridden into this devil's playground?

Sartain checked Boss down and was about to swing from his saddle when he spied movement ahead of him. The blurred shape of a man was running up the shelving slope of a high bluff. Chance had his rifle in one hand, and he dropped forward, grappling with brush and rocks as he climbed the butte, dust rising behind his hammering feet. He was moving quickly, casting quick glances toward his back trail, obviously trying to stay out of sight.

Sartain swung down from Boss's back and led the horse into a ragged patch of shade.

"You stay, boy," he said, patting the buckskin's neck.

Boss rippled his withers and shook his head uneasily, rattling the bit in his teeth. He'd been in enough tight spots with the Cajun to know they were in another one here.

Sartain moved to the east, following a gravelly wash between high banks tufted with wiry brush and prickly pear. There were several intersecting washes. He took one to the north, which is where he'd seen Chance running up the side of the bluff. He moved slowly, cautiously, blocks of water-scored earth rising and falling around him.

Something hammered the shoulder of a butte in front of him and to his left.

He pulled his head down as the rifle's crack flatted out over the canyon.

Hearing the distant but clear rasp of another cartridge being racked into the rifle's breech, Sartain took off running straight ahead along the wash.

Another bullet plumed dirt and gravel to his left, and it was followed a quarter-second later by the rifle's echoing report.

Sartain threw his left shoulder against the side of the bluff, pulling his head low as yet another bullet clipped the bluff just above him, spraying his hat with small rocks and dirt clods.

"I got you, Mike!" Chance shouted. "You shouldn't have followed me in here!"

Sartain doffed his hat and edged a look over the brow of the bluff. He saw Chance sprawled atop a bluff about a hundred yards away. Smoke puffed from the man's rifle barrel. Sartain pulled his head down as the bullet slammed savagely into the butte about a foot above his head.

"Your game is over, Chance!" the Cajun shouted. "You've exposed yourself to the whole town!"

"Nah, I don't think so, Mike." Chance spaced his shouted words a half second apart so they were nearly obscured by the echoes. The amphitheater of the canyon, as well as the dry air, brought them cleanly to Sartain's ears. "I'm a great liar, Mike! This county trusts me! Hector saw me running away! All I need to do is grin and smile and tell everybody I was chasing the *real* killer, and they'll be back thinkin' I'm the ace of hearts!"

"You and I know better, though—don't we, Chance?"

"That's right, Mike! You and I know better!" Chance laughed raucously, demonically.

Sartain bounded off his heels and scrambled up and over the shoulder of the bluff. He threw himself down the other side as another bullet tore into the bluff just behind his boots. He hit the ground on the other side of the bluff, for the moment out of Chance's line of fire.

The last report echoed shrilly, dwindling gradually.

Sartain ran along the base of a low, shelving butte, stopped suddenly, raised his Henry, and fired three quick rounds toward where Chance was sprawled over his Winchester. The Cajun's bullets blew up dirt in front of the killer, causing him to crab back behind the lip of the ridge he lay on.

Chance laughed raucously, crazily.

Sartain bounded up and over the shelving ridge. He saw Chance lift his head and rifle. The Cajun dove behind a boulder as two more bullets sliced the air around him, spanging loudly off rocks.

"No one suspects a thing, Mike!" the shooter bellowed. "No one but Maggie. All these years!"

"No one suspects what, Chance? That you're infected by some Apache demon?"

"That's right! Maggie knows! You know! I know! No one else." Chance fired two more rounds. "As soon as you're dead, I'm gonna go to work on Gold Dust in earnest!"

"Why didn't you kill Maggie?" Sartain wanted to know. "You just wanted to toy with her all those years?"

Chance laughed maniacally. "Sure—why not? It amused me, Mike!"

He fired another round. It blew up dust from the small shelf of sandstone Sartain crouched behind.

The Cajun shouted, "You know what I think, Chance?"

Then he fired three rounds at his quarry, though Chance had seen them coming and drew his head down. Sartain began running up the slope atop which Chance hunkered. The Cajun traced a circuitous path between boulders and scrub pines. When he saw the killer's rifle aimed at him once more, tracking him, he dove behind a boulder.

A bullet crashed into the rock with a thundering concussion, spraying shards in all directions.

"What's that, Mike?"

Sartain ran out from behind the boulder and dove behind another one just beyond it as Chance's next shot sliced across the side of his left boot. "I don't think you have any demon in you at all!" the Cajun shouted as the shot's echo dwindled. "I think you just *think* you do. By thinking you do, you woke up some very *human* evil that was sleeping inside you!"

He fired up the hill. When Chance pulled his head back down behind the lip of the ridge, Sartain ran hard. He dove behind a clump of cactus as Chance fired again, the bullet blowing up the ears of a prickly pear and flinging them onto the Cajun's back.

"That's a nice theory, Sartain! Too bad it's not true. The demon's in me, all right. He's sittin' right here on my shoulder!"

He fired two more shots.

"Know how I got old Morgan to fire on you?" Chance laughed again, loudly. "I told him you was an owlhoot with a big reward on your head. I told him I was gonna move around and catch you in a crossfire! I told Morgan to shoot at the first thing he sees moving in that canyon, and I'd back him up from the other side!"

More wild laughter.

Sartain cursed as he ran. He dove, pressing his face against the desert as two more slugs hammered the ground around him.

"That's right convenient, Everett—blamin' your wickedness on some Apache medicine man!" Sartain edged a look around the stout cactus clump to see Chance toss his empty Winchester aside and raise his pistol. "I don't believe it."

"What man in his right mind would kill his kids, Sartain? His *boys?*"

Chance fired his pistol into the cactus clump. Sartain rose and ran.

Chance fired twice more.

Sartain hunkered down beneath a shelving lip of rock protruding from the bluff, about ten feet below Chance.

The Revenger shouted, "One that's tired of feeding three young, hungry mouths when he doesn't have a pot to piss in. Maybe tired of the responsibility of fending for a family including his decrepit old man. Very easy for that man to kill them— even enjoy killing them and taunting his wife with their deaths— and blame it on a demon. Oh, it wasn't good ole Everett Chance who did it. It was the laughing demon inside him!"

Sartain gave a sardonic laugh. "Bullshit! I've seen enough of human doin's, Everett. I know it don't take no *Apache demon* to turn even so-called *good* men into demons of their very own making!"

"You go to hell, Mr. Revenger, sir!" Chance fired three more rounds at Sartain. Two bullets screeched into the rock shelf. Another flew over it to plunk into the ground just downslope from the Cajun.

That was six shots. If he only had one pistol and one rifle, both guns were empty.

Sartain leaped out from beneath the rock shelf and dashed up the slope, grinding his boot heels into the chalky earth and gravel. Chance no longer showed himself atop the bluff. As Sartain gained the crest, breathing hard, sweat trickling down the sides of his face and burning in his eyes, he looked around.

Chance was gone.

There were only his empty cartridge casings littering the bullet-shaped crest of the butte. A few lay a few feet down the other side, amongst tufts of sage, Spanish bayonet, and cedars.

The slope dropped gradually away toward a sharp drop-off. Beneath the drop-off ran a twisting dry watercourse paved with sun-bleached gravel.

Holding his Henry straight out in front of him, heart thudding heavily, Sartain looked around for Chance.

As he turned to his right, he spied movement from the corner of his left eye. He wheeled but didn't get turned full around before Chance, having bounded up from behind a flat-topped boulder, leaped up onto the rock. He launched himself off the rock with an enraged scream and, with a Bowie knife in his right fist, dove toward Sartain, driving the blade of the knife at the Cajun's neck.

Sartain dropped the Henry and reached up to grab the killer's wrist and to stop the knife's plunge toward his jugular. Chance's considerable weight drove the Cajun backward. He was punched back hard against the ground, the air hammered from his lungs in a bellowing grunt.

Chance dropped the knife. His face was a foot from Sartain's; for all the fury showing in the eyes, in the bulging veins and crimson cheeks, it was a man's face. Not the face of some spectral beast.

Chance hammered the Revenger's jaw with his fist. Sartain returned the gesture with a stiff right jab to the man's own lower jaw.

Chance jumped off of Sartain and rolled several yards down the hill, quickly gaining his feet in a thick cloud of wafting dust. Before he could get his feet set beneath him, Sartain dived from the upslope. He slammed his head and shoulders into the big, fleshy man, violently bulling him over backward.

Chance screamed as he hit the ground, Sartain on top of him.

The Cajun hammered the man's face with his right fist. He was about to ram the fist once more against the man's heavy jaw, when Chance arched his back, gave a bellowing roar, and, gritting his teeth, slammed his forehead against Sartain's mouth.

The Revenger hadn't been prepared for the move, or the fierceness with which Chance pushed him off of him. Brains momentarily scrambled, Sartain felt warm blood trickling from the gash in his lower lip.

The Cajun rolled down the steep hill, piling up within a few feet of the drop-off. He set his feet and raised his fists. He had his LeMat, but the fury in him wouldn't settle for merely punching a .44 round or a twelve-gauge wad of buckshot through the man's heart.

He'd hammer him into submission with his fists, then toss him into the cell his tortured wife currently occupied.

Chance gave another, lion-like roar, lowered his head, opened his arms, and threw himself at Sartain.

The Cajun stepped aside and flung a haymaker up from his heels. It connected so soundly against Chance's mouth, with a sharp smacking sound, that Sartain could feel the jarring ache of the blow up into his shoulder. He felt the warm blood from the man's exploding lips as the shards of Chance's broken teeth tore into his knuckles.

Chance stopped dead in his tracks, his head whipping up. His eyes acquired a startled, dazed expression. Blood oozed from his ruined mouth and dribbled down his chin and his stout neck. He lowered his arms as he staggered around, turning, and fell backward over the edge of the drop-off behind Sartain.

The Revenger turned to watch the man fall. Chance waved his arms and kicked his legs as though he were trying to fly. His round eyes stared up at Sartain in desperation. His thick body grew smaller.

"H-help meeeee!"

The cry dwindled as the man fell farther and farther away

from Sartain before the ground appeared to rise up to stop his descent with a solid, crunching thud.

Chance lay on the dry watercourse, on a bed of sun-bleached gravel, arms spread out away from his shoulders, one leg curled precariously beneath him.

"See there, Chance?" Sartain yelled, staring over the drop-off. "You might have thought you were an Apache spirit, but you died just like a man!"

CHAPTER TWENTY

Sartain whistled for Boss and tracked down Chance's stolen horse. He led both horses into the dry wash in which Chance lay staring at the sky as though aghast at what had become of him.

Twin streams of blood had trickled from his nose to dry on his lips.

The Revenger hoisted his dead quarry over the man's saddle and tied him with rope from Chance's saddlebags. He swung up onto Boss's back and, trailing the pinto, retraced his and Chance's route from town, reaching the ragged outskirts late in the afternoon—around four, four thirty, judging by the shadows.

It had been a long day. The Revenger was hungry and dry. First, a couple shots of bourbon or whatever passed for bourbon in Gold Dust, and then a meal.

He halted his horse where the town proper began, staring down the broad main street limned in smoky, dark-green shadows. There was no one, nothing, on the street. Not a horse or a dog. There hadn't been much movement in Gold Dust since Sartain had first ridden into the town on the heels of Scrum Wallace. Now, not even the tumbleweeds were tumbling.

An ominous stillness and deathly quiet hunkered down over the gaudy, sun-faded false facades on both sides of the street.

The Revenger lifted his right leg over the saddle horn and dropped straight down to the dirt. A cottonwood stood to the right of the trail, off the corner of a dilapidated stable. Sartain tied the pinto to the tree. He swung back up onto Boss's back and rode on down the street, holding the barrel of his Henry on his right shoulder. The rifle was cocked and ready to go.

He stared at the Occidental. There was no more movement there than anywhere else. He looked beyond and to the opposite side of the street at the jailhouse, which was around a slight bend and sitting slightly back from the buildings on either side of it. Jerking Boss to a sudden halt, the Cajun lowered the rifle from his shoulder, taking the long gun in both his gloved hands.

A man sat in the chair on the jailhouse's front stoop. He wore pants and a very white shirt, his suspenders hanging down off his arms. He was bareheaded.

No, he wasn't wearing a shirt, after all. Those were white bandages crisscrossed on his chest.

Leach.

Boots thumped inside the Occidental. A man's tan, unshaven face beneath a dark-brown hat appeared over the batwings and turned toward Sartain. He set both hands atop the doors. He smiled at the Revenger astride Boss in the street, about a half a block away from the Occidental. The man pushed through the doors and sauntered across the gallery and down into the street.

More boots clomped behind him as several other men tramped out of the Occidental, each one catching the doors on their backswing and pushing through them. They followed the first man into the street to form a line in front of Sartain, facing him, each one holding a carbine.

There were seven of them. The same seven who had been in the Occidental earlier that morning when the Cajun had issued his ultimatum. Most were attired in the colorful garb of the country—bright shirts, billowy neckerchiefs, and Sonora-style hats.

They all smiled.

Sartain gave a deep, inward sigh. He had a feeling his drink and his meal were going to have to wait a bit.

Despite the sourness of his mood, he returned the smiles of the unshaven, armed men facing him and said, "You fellas look like you've come to a decision."

Movement in the corner of Sartain's left eye. He jerked his head in that direction, but it was only Clara La Corte moving slowly down the outside stairs of her office. She was ghostly pale and stiff as she descended the stairs, taking one step at a time, sliding her anxious gaze from Sartain to the men confronting him and back again.

High-pitched laughter rose from behind the Occidental's batwings. More boots clomped. Another figure pushed out through the doors, and Sartain's heart skipped a beat as it burned like molten lava in his chest.

Scrum Wallace.

The last living killer of Sartain's beloved Jewel was clad in only threadbare balbriggans and his scruffy slouch hat. He wore his pistols in holsters around his waist. He was gaunt and unshaven, but his eyes flashed merrily.

He used a crooked ironwood stick for a cane. He leaned into it hard as he sat in a Windsor chair on the saloon's gallery and, leaning forward against the stick, stared at Sartain and snickered.

"They done thought about it, all right, Sartain," Wallace said. "Oh, yes, sir, they done thought about it real good."

Beyond the men lined up before Sartain, he could see the white line of Leach's teeth as the former Gold Dust town marshal also laughed his delight at the situation.

The Revenger had just started to wonder about Maggie Chance when the batwings were flung open once more. The barman tramped out onto the gallery, holding Maggie before him, a knife to her throat. The fat man was nuzzling the woman's neck and grinning at Sartain. As he did, he placed his left, pudgy hand over Maggie's left breast, drawing her taut against him.

"Lookee here, Sartain. Look what we boys found over at the jail of the new town marshal! A Gold Dust woman—a real pretty one locked up with Leach over there. We decided to take our chances and hope she wasn't nearly as bloody crazy as what everyone's been sayin'." The Irish barman sniffed her left ear and mashed his hand against her breast. "Sure smells nice!"

He laughed.

Maggie groaned and struggled against the fat barman, glancing from the knife held to her throat to Sartain.

"You know what I'd do if I was you?" asked the man standing farthest right of Sartain, ten feet away. He was the one with the badly faded, Union-blue hat trimmed with the insignia of Berdan's Sharpshooters. "If you don't want that purty woman pestered and killed, you'd best throw your guns down here in the street."

"She's got no part in this," Sartain said, his calm voice belying his anxiety.

"Well, now," said the ex-sharpshooter, "any damn fool can see that she does."

The barman yelled, "Drop the weapons, Sartain, or I'll cut her throat! You just watch—in five seconds this gallery's gonna be painted blood-red!"

Sartain looked at Maggie leaning back against the barman, his hand squeezing her breast. He looked at the men sneering or chuckling before him. He looked at Clara, who stood staring at him in silent horror. It almost appeared as though she were trying to communicate with him.

Sartain glanced once more at Maggie, who said tightly, "Don't . . . do it . . . Mike!"

"Do it, and she'll live!" the barman shouted. "Don't do it, and my gallery's gonna get a fresh coat of badly needed paint!"

Sartain looked at the leader of the seven men before him. "You'll turn her loose."

"You have my word as a gentleman," the ex-sharpshooter said.

Sartain scowled. "You'd better do it."

The former soldier smiled. "I'll do it."

"Mike . . . don't . . . !" Maggie said.

Sartain glanced once more at Clara. She continued to stare at him as though she were silently conferring with him.

The Revenger licked his lips, spat to one side. "All right." He uncocked his rifle and tossed it into the dust at the bluebelly's feet.

"Now, the big popper," the man ordered.

"Now, the big popper," Sartain drawled.

He wasn't a religious man, but he'd held out hope that when he gave up the ghost and crossed over to the Big Bayou in the sky, he'd run into Jewel again. He didn't give a shit about seeing anyone else. Just Jewel. He had a feeling he was less than a minute from finding out if he'd hoped in vain . . .

He unsnapped the keeper thong from over the LeMat's hammer and slowly lifted it from the holster with two fingers. He looked at the pretty, pearl-gripped, silver-framed popper and regretfully tossed it into the dirt beside his Henry.

"Whoever gets those guns—you keep 'em clean, or I'll drop down out of the golden clouds and skewer you up the ass with 'em," he raked out.

Several men chuckled.

"Don't you talk tough?" said the man to Sartain's far left, wrinkling his nose. "For an unarmed man?"

Maggie squealed. The barman dropped his knife on the gallery floor and, laughing loudly, grabbed Maggie's blouse in both hands and gave it a savage tear. The blouse came away to reveal her bulging camisole. The barman ripped the camisole down the middle, and Maggie's creamy breasts bobbed free. The barman grabbed the twin mounds savagely and pulled the woman back through the batwings and into the saloon.

The bluebelly scoundrel glanced toward the Occidental and laughed.

"Let her go, goddammit!" Sartain barked, leaning forward in his saddle, fury nearly causing his heart to explode. "Let her go *now!*"

The men laughed at him.

From the Occidental came the sound of a bottle breaking.

A mewling scream vaulted over the batwings.

Sartain jerked his head in that direction, frowning, puzzled. The scream hadn't been Maggie's voice. That had been a man's voice.

The scream came again, shriller this time. "Ohhh, gawd! Ohhhhhh, GAWD! Hel—. . . help me . . . help me, boys! Oh, GAWDDD—look what she *done* to me! Why . . . why . . . she cut it *offfff!*"

"What the fuck?" said one of the men before Sartain. They were all staring at the saloon.

Clara said in a loud whisper, "Mike!"

Sartain turned to her. She tossed a revolver toward him. It turned end over end in the air. Sartain grabbed it, clicked the hammer back, and swung it toward the men standing before him.

The former sharpshooter had seen the toss and jerked to life, raising his Winchester.

Sartain palmed the ivory-gripped Smith & Wesson .44, extended it over Boss's head, and fired. The sharpshooter screamed and fired his Winchester wide as he staggered backwards, glancing down at the hole pumping blood from the center of his chest.

Holding Boss's reins taut in his left hand, Sartain emptied

the rest of the Smithy's wheel into the men standing before him, curveting Boss as he fired the sixth round and then hurling himself out of the saddle. He hit the street with a grunt, aggravating the sundry other aches and pains he'd incurred over the past couple of days.

Men were screaming and writhing, some were shooting, the bullets pluming dust around Sartain, who reached for his LeMat, palming it as a bullet fired by the last man standing in the street creased his right thigh, just above the kneecap. The man, whom Sartain had heard called "Critter," ran toward Sartain, screaming and shooting. Another bullet sliced a cold line across the side of Sartain's neck.

The Cajun rolled, avoiding one more bullet before rolling up on a shoulder, raising the LeMat. He held fire.

Critter staggered forward, lowering his old New Model Remington conversion revolver while raising a hand as though to stop the blood from spurting from the hole in his chest, about three inches below his throat. Behind him, Scrum Wallace stood on the porch, staggering forward on his cane and triggering one of his pistols into the street toward Sartain.

Critter had obviously blocked a shot.

Wallace squealed, "No! No! No!" as he fired yet another wild round into Critter, blowing Critter's hat and the top of his head off.

Sartain slid the LeMat away from Critter, lined up the sites on Wallace, clicked the twelve gauge wad into play, and flung the nasty, fist-sized swarm of lead pellets into the dead center of Scrum Wallace's dirty underwear shirt. They ripped little holes in the shirt and in the pale, exposed flesh revealed by the unbuttoned V in the neck.

The rat-faced killer gave a yowl and flew backwards against the Occidental's front wall. As he did, he flung his own pistol up beneath his chin and inadvertently fired it, turning the tips of both his chin and his nose to red jelly. Bone chips and blood sprayed toward the gallery's rafters, painting the clay *olla* pot hanging from the ceiling.

He opened his mouth, but a full five seconds elapsed before he screamed.

Sartain pulled the LeMat down and looked around. Critter was the only one writhing before him now, lying belly down in the street and rolling his shoulders from side to side as though he were trying to carve out a grave for himself. The other six lay like brightly colored birds that had dropped out of the sky.

The late, saffron light caressed them almost tenderly as the sun dropped behind the man who had punched their tickets. A couple of neckerchief ends lifted in the slight breeze.

Sartain climbed heavily, creakily to his feet and stared at the marshal's office. Leach was on his feet, holding onto a roof support post, staring toward Sartain. He was too far away to be seen clearly, but Sartain thought he could make out a look of extreme frustration on the former town marshal's hound-dog-ugly face.

"Ah, shit!" Leach shouted, punching the support post.

"Shit!" he said again as he swung around and walked into the jailhouse. A few seconds later, Sartain heard the clang of a cell door closing as Leach locked himself inside.

Sartain turned to see Clara rising from behind a stack of crates, where she'd crouched on the periphery of the lead storm. Now she stood where she'd been standing before, on the boardwalk at the base of the stairs rising to her office. She looked shocked as she slid her gaze from Sartain to the dead men, to the howling Scrum Wallace atop the Occidental's gallery.

She returned her stricken eyes to Sartain. "Are you all right?"

Sartain nodded. "You?"

She nodded, slid a lock of hair back from her cheek and

turned back to the howling Wallace.

Sartain remembered Maggie and started jogging around dead men toward the Occidental. He stopped when Maggie moved out through the batwings.

She looked as though she were sleep-walking. Her blouse hung in tatters. Her camisole barely covered her breasts. She was spattered with blood. There was more blood on her right hand, which hung low against her skirt. She was holding a broken bottle in her fist, also blood-covered.

Blood strung down from the broken shards.

Maggie glanced at Scrum Wallace lying to her left. She looked at Sartain, the men lying dead around him. She dropped the bottle and walked down the gallery steps and into the street.

Sartain noted that the bar tender's agonized screams were no longer careening out from behind the batwings.

The Cajun wrapped his arms around Maggie, drew her tightly toward him, rocked her gently. She wrapped her arms around him but said nothing until she lifted her chin and asked, "Everett . . . ?"

"Dead." Sartain glanced back to where he'd left Chance's body tied over the man's stolen pinto. "I'd best fetch him."

He glanced at Clara, who was already walking toward Maggie. The young medico nodded. As Sartain moved away from the two women, he heard Clara say, "Come on, Mrs. Chance. Let's get you up to my office and clean you up."

"You have any tequila up there?" Maggie asked in a quiet, raspy voice.

"Tequila? Oh, *si*."

"Might as well call me Maggie, then, I reckon."

As the two women climbed the stairs, Sartain swung up onto Boss's back. He galloped westward, to where he'd left Chance. He hadn't galloped far before he slowed Boss to a walk, then to a halt. He stared at the cottonwood to which he'd tied the pinto.

The horse and Everett Chance were no longer there.

There were no tracks leaving the tree. Only the shod hoof prints the horse had stamped into the finely churned dirt when it had been standing there.

Sartain stared dubiously at the trail.

No tracks . . . ?

The Cajun poked his hat brim off his forehead and looked around, tendrils of dark foreboding wrapping around him as the light continued to fade and a chill breeze rose.

ABOUT THE AUTHOR

Western novelist **Peter Brandvold** was born and raised in North Dakota. He has penned over 90 fast-action westerns under his own name and several pennames, including **Frank Leslie.** He wrote 30 books in the popular, long-running *Longarm* series for Berkley. He is the author of the ever-popular .45-Caliber books featuring Cuno Massey as well as the Lou Prophet and Yakima Henry novels. The Ben Stillman books are a long-running series with previous volumes available as ebooks. Head honcho at "Mean Pete Publishing," publisher of lightning-fast western ebooks, he has lived all over the American west but currently lives in western Minnesota with his dog. Visit his website at www.peterbrandvold.com. Follow his blog at www.peterbrandvold.blogspot.com.

The employees of Five Star Publishing hope you have enjoyed this book.

Our Five Star novels explore little-known chapters from America's history, stories told from unique perspectives that will entertain a broad range of readers.

Other Five Star books are available at your local library, bookstore, all major book distributors, and directly from Five Star/Gale.

Connect with Five Star Publishing

Visit us on Facebook:
  https://www.facebook.com/FiveStarCengage

Email:
  FiveStar@cengage.com

For information about titles and placing orders:
  (800) 223-1244
  gale.orders@cengage.com

To share your comments, write to us:
  Five Star Publishing
  Attn: Publisher
  10 Water St., Suite 310
  Waterville, ME 04901